A Heart Purloined

Lisa M. Lane

Also by Lisa M. Lane

The Tommy Jones Mysteries
Murder at Old St. Thomas's
Murder at an Exhibition
Murder on the Pneumatic Railway

Literary Fiction
Before the Time Machine

Academic Non-Fiction
H. G. Wells on Science Teaching, 1886-1897

A Heart Purloined

Lisa M. Lane

Published by Grousable Books
Encinitas, California
979-8-9869845-1-3 paperback
979-8-9869845-2-0 e-book
LCC: 2023900948

1 - The Darkened Study

25 October 1880

The old man upstairs was dead, and the servants had all been sent away, so there was no reason to be quiet. But Jack was conscious of the fact that he really didn't belong there at Naedre Manor, and he went quietly downstairs to the study to commence his search. The papers must be there. They had to be.

He began at the desk, which was piled with contracts, books, and maps. The items on top were covered with fine dust, testifying to the fact that George Soffitt had been unwell for some time, and unable to enjoy his usual hobbies. Jack cautiously blew off the top layer of dust, which formed a cloud in the murky air. The windows can't have been opened in here for months. Since the servants were all from an agency, rather than attached to the house or its owner, it was obvious no one had been assigned to tend to the study.

Lighting the lamp carefully so as not to cause a conflagration with the papers, Jack decided to be methodical. The top drawer was locked. He'd get to that in a minute. The deep side drawer was piled to the top. Obviously, whatever filing system Soffitt had used was either extremely esoteric, stashed in his brain, or non-existent. Jack pulled over a chair, pulled the stack out of the drawer, and placed it carefully on the desk. He began thumbing through the top pages.

The grandfather clock out in the hall struck two. There were still at least six hours before the undertaker came, so no reason to rush. The first stack and the top of the desk took about half an hour. He set those papers aside. Time to see about that lock.

It was a rather ordinary lock, but the drawer was solid. He used the penknife that was lying on the desk next to some unopened letters, and started to pick the lock.

Then he heard a scratching near the window. Quickly extinguishing the lamp, he peered toward the drapes, heavy damask curtains running from floor to ceiling. There was no movement yet, but he heard the creak of hinges and dived under the desk.

He listened to the intruder climb over the sill to enter the room, then a bump followed by a distinctly female voice saying, "Bloody hell!" Then there was a noise that sounded like a boot on one foot, hopping across the room toward the desk. He stilled his breathing as much as he could. There was a flap, flap sound on top of the desk. The intruder must be looking for matches.

With the lamp lit, Jack was able to look up toward the mirror on the wall behind the desk. It was a large, extravagant mirror with a carved gilt frame. It must have been intended to intimidate whoever was sitting in front of the desk to do business. They would feel exposed seeing themselves in a mirror, groveling for money or a better deal or whatever Soffitt's victims did when they came to call.

The figure he saw in the mirror wore a long cloak and hood, but no gloves. Her hands shone white in the light of the lamp. What was a woman doing here? Could Soffitt have had a paramour? It seemed unlikely. He'd been ninety-two.

The intruder moved toward one of the cabinets in which Soffitt liked to display his collections, holding the lamp over each glass case and leaning over to peer in. This was no paramour, and no ordinary burglar, either. She was looking for something in particular, and the lack of gloves meant that when she found it she'd leave fingermarks everywhere. An amateur. A female amateur who swore like a hostler. Intriguing.

Having perused the cabinets, she came around the desk and put the lamp down on its surface. He saw her boots, sturdy boots of nice leather. Not expensive, but not cheap either. The hem of the gown, which looked to be a light gray, was soiled with mud.

"Ah!" she mumbled to herself, and he saw her hand reach for the drawer. Well, it couldn't be helped.

"It's locked," he said.

She gasped and jumped back suddenly, almost falling against the bookshelf. He took that moment to exit quickly and gracefully from under the desk.

She stared at him, her hand at her throat and her feet apart to balance herself.

He was about to say something about how it was good she had put down the lamp, but for a moment he couldn't speak. Her expression was shocked rather than afraid, but underneath he saw a curiosity. One dark eyebrow was raised, and her brown eyes were open wide, magnified by the spectacles she wore. And somehow she looked, no, she seemed, familiar.

"Do I know you?" he said.

"Goodness, I hope not," she said, her eyebrow lowering. "I am not in the habit of keeping company with burglars."

She stood up a little prouder and he couldn't help it. He started to laugh.

"Hush!" she said, looking around. "You'll wake the whole damn house."

He considered for a moment.

"Quite right," he whispered. "I am sorry."

She listened intently, but heard no suspicious sounds.

"Now," she said quietly, taking a deep breath. "Who are you, and what are you doing here?"

This is preposterous, he thought.

"Jack Strawman," he answered with a bow. "Burglar and general miscreant. And which fellow burglar do I have the pleasure of addressing?"

She frowned. "I am not a burglar, Mr. Strawman."

"And yet you are burgling, madam."

"And I am not a madam." She pulled back her hood, showing brown curls pulled back from her face and falling past her shoulders.

"Forgive me, miss," he whispered gallantly. "In this light, you looked older than a maid."

"How dare you?" she hissed. Then she peered at him. "I am twenty-seven. Not, I see now, as old as you."

"Not nearly." Her face, he had to admit, was plain, but her hair was glorious. Not thinking, he reached out to touch it. She stepped back and raised her hood.

"Forgive me, Miss . . . ?"

"Goodwin. Amanda Goodwin."

"And what are you doing here, Miss Goodwin? I am clearly robbing the house. Is that your intention also?" He had trouble keeping the amusement out of his voice.

"Not at all," she said. "I am retrieving something that belongs to me."

"What might that be? Perhaps I have stolen it already and could return it to you."

She answered immediately. "It's a miniature of a woman with chestnut hair and a blue gown. She's my grandmother. Have you seen it?"

He shook his head. "I am sorry to say I have not. I assume that, since you believe it to be here, the owner of the house must have taken it from you?"

"He took it from my grandfather in payment for a debt. But the debt was a lie. It was a swindle, sir, a calculated swindle, and I intend to have my property back."

Jack knew well about Soffit's swindles, particularly the one that caused outrage in the Bank of England. It had even gone to Parliament for angry and recriminatory discussion. Surely that couldn't be the same swindle?

"Was it in 1856?" he asked. "The Lesgus Scheme?"

She nodded firmly.

Lesgus had been the South American country that Soffitt had invented out of whole cloth. He'd attracted investors to a place that didn't exist, inventing trade relations, a national constitution, and reports of minerals waiting to be exploited. Some upstart composer had even written Lesgusian traditional music. But it had all been a ruse, and many had lost their fortunes. It made Jack angry just thinking about it.

But he had work to do before dawn. He jumped and looked toward the study door as if he'd heard a sound.

"Did you find the miniature?" he hissed.

Amanda shook her head.

"No," she said, glancing toward the door, "but we should get out of here."

He blew out the lamp and escorted her to the window where she had entered. He climbed out first, regretting that he was in house shoes as his feet squelched into the lawn. He turned back to hold out a hand to assist, but she shook her head and used the window frame, then sprung ahead of him down to the road.

Jack caught up with her. "Miss Goodwin, if I can be of any assistance in the future, I rob houses, clean stables, and do a passable job of reading aloud. I am also an excellent lover."

She spun toward him and he caught her arms. Without thinking, he kissed her mouth. A second later, he felt his body pushed upward and his left leg kicked out from under him. He was lying on his back on the wet ground, looking up at the sky.

He heard himself cry out. The world was spinning. Amanda looked down at him.

"Goodnight, Mr. Strawman. We will not see each other again." She turned and disappeared into the bushes that lined the road.

Jack rose slowly and limped back to the house. His feet were wet and his back cold and filthy. He recalled that the front door was unlocked, but instead went back through the window into the study.

"I doubt that, Miss Goodwin," he said to himself. "I doubt that very much."

2 - The Miniature

Amanda found Vesta, the mare she was allowed to ride whenever she wished, tethered to the tree where she'd left her. She stroked her muzzle.

"My apologies, Vesta. I know it's cold. And I'm afraid I have failed."

She swung up into the saddle and headed across the fields for Heddington Hall, the home of her employer Lady Constance Brandon. Although cloudy earlier, the sky was now clear and the half moon helped light her way.

Lady Brandon had no idea she was out at this hour, of course. She'd be very unhappy if she knew. But she had shared gossip with Amanda that George Soffitt was very ill, that a doctor had been summoned and then a priest. Once he died, everything he owned would surely be divided up. Relatives would make their claims, and items would be sold. The miniature would become impossible to find.

Amanda had made it her business for years to know what Soffitt was doing, even though she knew this just fed her hatred. Her grandfather had urged her to ignore him, had told her over and over that nothing could be done about what happened.

"You must be your own woman," he had encouraged her many times. "It is no use carrying bitterness through your life. I have done so, and have been a poor example to you, my dear."

But now he was ill too, and on her last visit he had talked to her again about the miniature. These days he had only been happy talking about her grandmother Emily, the woman of his life.

He had recalled more of their adventures as he'd gotten older, and when Amanda visited him now, their evenings were often spent in reminiscences. She loved listening to him talk about their younger years, how they had travelled to Egypt for their honeymoon, against everyone's advice, and had returned with the desire to travel even more. Lufstow Farm had earned enough that they could do so even once they had a child, Amanda's father, Edmund. Then when the crisis had happened, when they'd lost everything they'd invested, it was Emily Goodwin who found them caretaking jobs nearby so they could feed the family. And they'd been so proud of Edmund, who had become a botanist and taught at a grammar school. It was Emily who'd encouraged him to follow his passion.

"If I could just see her, one more time," Grandfather would say to Amanda. He had carried that miniature with him for years, so pleased that he could see Emily's face whenever he wanted. But then it had gone, sold in a packet of valuables to repay the investment debt to George Soffitt. At the time, Emily had just died, and he was tearfully ridding his house of everything that reminded him of her, trying to make his own way. But as he aged, he missed her so, and wanted the miniature so he could see her again.

Amanda had said nothing to him, but had vowed to herself to get it back.

She gazed up at the sky. It must be past three, she thought. She would be tired tomorrow, but luckily Lady Brandon had no plans. It should be a quiet day at the manor. Perhaps they would do some embroidery together, then Amanda would read to her when her eyes tired. The role of a companion was complex, Amanda had learned, but Lady Brandon was kind and paid her well.

She had failed tonight at Naedre Manor, she berated herself. Surely her failure was because of that man. Who was he? Jack Strawman, he'd said. Amanda scoffed to herself. A straw man? Very likely. And a burglar. A burglar in house shoes. She must remember that if she ever needed to sneak around a house at night—it seemed quite practical, at least once inside the house. He'd looked rather daring with his cravat almost undone and that perfect mustache next to the imperfect scar down his cheek. In fact, she had to admit, he had been quite attractive. The lamplight had made his eyes look green, and the lines near his mouth showed a willingness to laugh. And he'd certainly been nimble enough when he'd burst out from under the desk, and again when he kissed her. She felt bad about taking him down with a leg sweep, but it had been a case of pure instinct.

Goodness, she was thinking like a green girl, she thought. Her childhood was sheltered, growing up in Haslemere, living with her parents and visiting her grandfather at Lufstow Farm, her grandmother having died when she was three. But when Amanda was nineteen, her parents had died in a boating accident while visiting a cousin in Scotland. She decided to visit an aunt in London to learn about city life. Her grandfather assured her he could tend the farm himself.

Aunt Sophronia had been eccentric and not well-equipped to chaperone a young woman. She was bohemian in her tastes and thought that youth should be given free rein. She had friends among the well-connected gentleman and ladies, which Amanda thought would be educational. In the evenings, however, Sophronia's Camden Town house would be open for social occasions, parties where young men might bring the latest gins or light rums and upstairs rooms would sometimes be found unlocked.

One horrible night, Amanda had been accosted in her own bedchamber by a drunken guest, a man she had liked and trusted. By the time her aunt died from a fatty liver, Amanda was no longer naïve, and had happily returned to Lufstow Farm.

She'd met men like Jack Strawman, she thought, and their attractiveness could be a lure. Even the most pleasant of them could become bestial, the veneer of civilization dropping at the first temptation.

"That way madness lies," Amanda murmured to Vesta as they approached the stable. She put away the tack and saddle, brushed Vesta down, put the blanket on her, and kissed her muzzle.

"Thank you, Vesta. I will put you out to fresh grass tomorrow."

Yawning her way to the house, she carefully brushed her boots outside and went quietly up the stairs. It wouldn't do to have anyone see her, especially Timothy.

The groom had gotten bolder with her as he'd gotten older, and she didn't fancy encountering him alone at this hour. It was far too late to pour a bath, and the new boiler would wake Lady Brandon, whose rooms were down the hall. Amanda contented herself with washing her feet in cold water, braiding her brown tresses, and folding the trousers she had worn so she could secure them at the bottom of her trunk. They'd been a gift from her grandfather on her 16th birthday, given with a wink and a smile out of sight of the rest of the family. They would shock anyone here at Heddington Hall.

Amanda's mind was still spinning as she fell into bed, where Maxie the orange cat had been for hours, curled up on her pillow. How could she obtain the miniature? And who was Jack Strawman, really? She closed her eyes and could see him reaching out to touch her hair, and instead of taking him down, she was stepping forward—

Suddenly she sat upright, causing Maxie to meow and jump off the bed. That man had thought she was a burglar. She had stupidly given him her name, and told him why she was there. Why couldn't she keep things secret? He'd asked and she told him, as she would with anyone. But he had never said why he was at the house or what he was looking for, and she sincerely doubted that Strawman was his real name. Would he betray her? Tell the police she was there? Laugh about her with his robber friends? There must be a way to find him, to beg him not to tell anyone. She stared at the circle of plaster roses on the ceiling, and worried until dawn.

3 - An Uninvited Guest

"I want Louis' birthday party to be the event of the season," said Lady Brandon, "even if the real season happens in London."

"I'm sure it will be, Lady Brandon," said Amanda. "Shall we look at the menu from Lafitte's?"

Lady Brandon's nephew had spent years in France, and he'd named his son Louis, so Lady Brandon wanted French food. She looked at the list.

"I think escargot may be a bit esoteric for those who are coming," said Lady Brandon with a frown. At sixty-eight, she was still a lovely woman, with a round bright face and eyes that missed little.

"And the birthday boy won't touch it," added Amanda. Little Louis was only four.

"We'll need a different menu for the children. How many are coming?"

"Six, I think," said Amanda. "Perhaps Cook can manage dinner just for the little ones?"

"Yes, please ask her. Where should we set up the band? Last time we did a party it was summer. A brass band is a little loud for inside the hall."

"If we put them in the corner of the ballroom, perhaps the opposite wall might attenuate the sound?"

Lady Brandon smiled. "Amanda, you always have the best ideas." She reached out toward her cane, which was leaning on the table, and wiggled her fingers. Amanda handed it to her.

"Penelope will take care of the guest list and replies to the invitations," said Lady Brandon. "She'll also make sure rooms are ready for my friend Marjorie, who will be staying till Monday. Would you help me up to my room, please?"

Amanda took Lady Brandon by the arm and helped her up the stairs, step by step. She had no nursing duties to speak of. Lady Brandon was in excellent health, except for tiredness and a touch of arthritis. Her mind was quick and she was always better after a rest. Amanda helped her to the chaise, took off her shoes, and put the woolen blanket over her.

"Shall I close the drapes?" she asked.

"No, thank you," said Lady Brandon, shifting herself further up on the pillow. "I do not want to sleep all day. Please awaken me at one, if you would. We should be at Emma's by two."

Amanda promised and went down the hall to her own room. Maxie was in the window, chattering at doves sitting in the tree outside. Amanda sat down at her writing desk to finish the letter she'd begun to her grandfather. She couldn't tell him about the robbery or Jack Strawman. She wanted to fetch the miniature and present it to him once she had it, not worry him about how she might obtain it. But so far, she was no closer to her goal.

So instead she wrote him about the planning for Louis' party, and Maxie the cat, and the way the leaves were falling from the trees at Heddington Hall. She promised to visit him soon, to bring Cook's best shortbread—after all, West Sussex was not far from Sandhills. One could even go to Petersfield and catch a train on the South Western Railway. Grandfather's doctor had said it would be months before he was seriously ill, perhaps even a year. But she missed him. Heddington Hall was wonderful, but Lufstow Farm was home.

Lady Emma Tentrees' house was less than half a mile away, and Lady Brandon insisted on walking. Amanda had to hurry to keep up with her, carrying the basket of oranges.

"Poor Emma does not have a heated conservatory, so we bring oranges," she had explained, but Amanda had a sense that the real reason was to show which of them had more money. Afternoon calls, she had learned, were partly for sharing gossip, partly for showing one's good taste, and partly for displaying one's superiority. They were the worst part of being a lady's companion, as far as she was concerned.

On this occasion, however, Lady Brandon and Lady Tentrees wished to speak in private, so Amanda was able to stroll in the garden, then sit and think. She did not want to think about Jack Strawman, but it was difficult to put him out of her mind. She had felt threatened, certainly, both when he'd reached toward her in the study and when he had kissed her. It was inherent in her behavior, she thought, and she couldn't be faulted for that. Her mind cast back to her own history to explain why, to go over what had happened to her when she was nineteen. That horrid man had expected her to want his attentions, to just let him touch her. She still had nightmares about what he'd done, and had told no one except her grandfather. He had understood, and asked Li Jing to teach her how to defend herself.

Li Jing had been her grandfather's loyal servant and friend since 1839, when as a merchant to the British in Canton at the start of the first Opium War he had come to England for his safety. Even as an old man, Mr. Li remembered several fighting techniques from his homeland and had been willing to teach them. Amanda had been an avid pupil.

Amanda had become accustomed to creating a shell around herself and not letting people through, especially men. But in this case, she regretted her actions. Even as she pushed Jack Strawman up and knocked him down, she had felt a different instinct. What would it have been like to accept his kiss? She closed her eyes and turned her face to the sun, imagining his eyes and his touch on her arm, then his lips on hers. If she ever saw him again, she would try to view things differently.

It was only the first hour, but many guests had arrived on time and the party was clearly a success. Laughter could be heard from the room where the children were gathered with the nursemaids, and couples were listening to the band in the ballroom. Amanda had at first been rushing about to check arrangements, but Lady Brandon had told her she was expected to join the party and enjoy herself.

It was here that she found her role as companion most awkward. She was not elite enough to exchange pleasantries with the aristocrats, but nor was she lowly enough to socialize with the servants. At such occasions she often found herself with a child or an animal, but the children were all together and Maxie was, as usual, asleep upstairs on her bed.

Amanda wandered into the library, closing the door, and took a deep breath. The fire had not been lit in here, and it was chilly. But she felt best in this room, with its endless shelves of knowledge and diversion. She was often here to select a book to read to Lady Brandon, but perhaps today she would find one for herself. She might want to read *Robinson Crusoe* again, and she remembered there was a copy here of *On Liberty*, that radical work by John Stuart Mill. As she started to look, she heard the French doors to the garden open. A cold draft blew into the room, and Jack Strawman stepped in, his coat thrown over his shoulders.

He stopped as soon as he saw her, his expression turning from surprise to pleasure. Yes, she thought: those lips, that mustache. It took her a moment to remember she had wanted to speak with him.

"Mr. Strawman," she said, with a tiny curtsey.

He bowed ridiculously, extravagantly. "Miss Goodwin."

"I had been hoping to speak with you."

"You had? So you could knock me down again?" He grinned.

"I didn't knock you down. It was a leg sweep," she corrected.

"I seem to recall finding myself on the ground."

"I do apologize for that. You took me quite by surprise."

"And you took me quite by surprise. Where on earth did you learn to do that?"

She had no intention of telling him about Li Jing.

"A woman must defend herself."

"I see."

This was not going well, she thought. He seemed to think it all so amusing, and she felt at a distinct disadvantage.

"Mr. Strawman, I would like to know whether you told anyone of my presence at Mr. Soffitt's house last Thursday?"

"Well," he said, drawing himself up. "I certainly would not have told anyone about your so-called leg sweep. That would have embarrassed me greatly."

"Of course, and I apologize again. I mean about me being there at all."

"Ah, I see, Miss Goodwin. You do not wish it to be known that you were there searching for the miniature. Be assured I have told no one. I am a gentleman."

She almost laughed at that. "A gentleman would never be so forward with a lady."

He stepped toward her, and she did not step back. If he were trying to intimidate her, she would make sure he wouldn't succeed. He was so close she could see the individual hairs of his mustache. Just a few were gray.

"I could not resist the animal attraction," he said softly.

She was about to retort regarding who was playing the animal in this scenario when they heard voices outside in the corridor. Amanda went over to close the door fully. By the time she looked back into the room, Jack Strawman had gone.

4 - A Theft

Amanda looked out the garden door, but could see no one. Where had Mr. Strawman gone, leaving the cold night air coming in? She closed the door and left the library, her mind full of what had transpired. She hoped she could trust him not to reveal her nighttime activities at George Soffit's house. The voices outside the library door were getting louder.

"Stolen? What do you mean, stolen?"

"What was it?"

"From here?"

"Have the police been called?"

The small group in the corridor didn't notice Amanda as she made her way to find Lady Brandon. What could have been stolen, and from whom?

She found her employer deep in conversation with Forsythe, the butler, and she seemed very grateful to see Amanda.

"What on earth has happened?"

"It's Marjorie, Lady Vance," Lady Brandon whispered urgently. "She went up to her rooms to fetch her fan and discovered her necklace has been stolen."

"Her necklace? Was it valuable?"

Lady Brandon looked shocked. "Of course it was valuable, Amanda. We should call in the police, although it will disturb the party. First, I'm asking Forsythe if it would be advisable to have the staff search the house."

"And?" asked Amanda, looking at Forsythe.

"I have recommended against it, Miss Goodwin."

"Send for the police," sighed Lady Brandon. "But quietly, and not too soon. Everyone will go home after dinner, I'm sure."

"I'm sorry, milady, but the police may want to talk with the guests."

"Absurd. I won't let that happen. Send for the police at eight o'clock, please, Forsythe. I will go up and placate Lady Vance."

Amanda touched her arm. "I'm afraid the Morgans and Miss Blythe already know. I heard them talking in the corridor," she said.

Lady Brandon sighed. "Then I'll placate them first. Forsythe, please send Penelope up to Lady Vance with some smelling salts and a cup of tea. I'll be up shortly."

When dinner began, Amanda found herself seated with the lady's maids and nursemaids, none of whom she knew. As she ate, she listened to their conversation, which at one point turned to George Soffitt.

"He died alone, they say," said a trim woman with her fair hair plaited in a circle around her head. "That would be awful, wouldn't it?"

"Alone, in that big house?" said a young, dark-haired girl.

"Well, I wouldn't work for him. Who would?"

"I hear," said a large woman with a watch pinned to her dress, "that the only reason the cook stays is because she has nowhere else to go."

"She's left, too."

"Whatever happened to his son?"

"Left long ago. Changed his name, they say."

"Even more interesting," said the fair-haired woman, leaning forward as if in confidence, "have you seen his solicitor?" The other women shook their heads.

"Oh, he's a delight to look at. Handsome as the day is long!"

"Do tell!"

"He came to the house with some papers for Lady Vance. Taking over for his uncle, who can't get about much anymore. Tall, blond, eyes of periwinkle blue."

"Oh, Clara, you do go on!"

"I swear it's true! He gave me just a little smile, and my heart—" Clara fanned herself with her hand, then held it up as if to stop her own prattling. "But I must go up to milady. She's in her room taking a rest."

The others groaned that she wouldn't finish her story, but their conversation turned to other things. Amanda rose, walked past the parlor, caught Lady Brandon's eye and raised an eyebrow, but her employer just nodded, meaning she could be excused.

Rather than go to her room, Amanda paced the corridors. She'd hidden it well, but she was very disturbed by Lady Vance's necklace being stolen. Was it Jack Strawman who'd taken it? Is that why he was here, to rob the house? Certainly she hadn't seen him before or after their sudden encounter in the library. He was obviously not an invited guest.

The police would come and might want to question her. She should tell them about him. All about him.

Except that then she would have to say how she'd met him when she had broken in to Soffitt's home. Honest to a fault, Amanda felt her stomach clench at the idea of lying, especially to the police. She wished she could disappear, just vanish until the police left. But that would be highly suspicious. She could lose her position if she didn't answer questions, and the same would happen if she answered honestly. Suddenly, the beef soup, roast duck, and almond pudding were not settling so well in her stomach.

She'd walked the gallery, the terrace, and the hallways several times before she heard the guests taking their leave. She should go see whether Lady Brandon needed anything; she must be exhausted and would need help if police were going to extend the evening. It would be a good time to bring her a tonic. Amanda accordingly went to Lady Brandon's rooms to fetch the pink bottle. As she entered the dressing room, she felt an odd feeling. Everything looked to be in place, but she could sense that someone had been here. Taking the tonic, she went into the boudoir and had the same sensation. Had Jack Strawman been in here? Had he stolen anything?

Quickly checking the jewelry boxes on the dressing table, she noted with relief that nothing appeared to be missing. And certainly if things had been moved, they had been carefully replaced. It was just a feeling, she told herself. It's entirely possible no one had been in here at all. It had been an odd evening, and her nerves were surely to blame.

Lady Brandon was waiting on the blue settee in the parlor to meet the police when they arrived, and was grateful for the tonic. Forsythe was in attendance in the hall. Penelope, as a secretary who lived out, had left shortly before dinner, and most of the staff were working in the ballroom, dining room, and kitchen.

"Where do you wish me to be during the interview, Lady Brandon?" she asked.

Lady Brandon looked closely at Amanda.

"You look a bit overwrought, Amanda," she said kindly.

"I am a bit tired," Amanda agreed. "But I am happy to do whatever you need me to do."

Lady Brandon sighed. "I do wish Lord Brandon were still alive. He was much better with this sort of thing."

Amanda refrained from asking why that would have been the case and simply nodded in sympathy.

"You will do very well, Lady Brandon," she said.

"Very well," she repeated. "Yes, I suppose I shall. Please do ask Lady Vance's maid to help her come downstairs, and then just stay in your room until I send for you. I anticipate needing help to retire for the night."

"Yes, Lady Brandon," Amanda said with relief. She went upstairs, found Lady Vance's maid unpacking her ladyship's attire, and gave her the message. The letter to her grandfather remained unfinished, and she sat down to complete it but was unable to keep still. She began pacing the room, wondering what was being said downstairs.

She took the back stairs so that she could hear from the servant's door to the parlor. Sleepy servants were busy or on their way to bed, and no one paid the least attention as she passed. She crouched down at the door to listen.

"Inspector Hawk, I am so pleased that you are taking on this case personally," Lady Brandon was saying. "I knew your father. Portsmouth is quite a journey, and I appreciate you coming yourself."

"Of course, Lady Brandon," said a deep voice. "My father spoke highly of you. Now, Lady Vance, if I could have a description of precisely what was stolen?"

Lady Vance sounded haughty, as if she did not appreciate having to speak to a policeman.

"It was a necklace, Inspector, with a gold chain and three sapphires, each surrounded by small rubies. It was a gift from my husband, and was made for me at Mappin and Webb in London."

"And how much would you say it was worth, your Ladyship?"

"I have not had it valued recently, but I would think at least three hundred pounds."

She heard a gasp.

"Lady Vance," said the Inspector. "You brought a necklace worth three hundred pounds to a birthday party?"

"I bring it if I'm away from home overnight," said Lady Vance's high-toned voice. "What business is it of yours where I choose to bring my jewelry?"

She heard an intake of breath, and then Lady Brandon said smoothly, "I'm quite sure the Inspector is not questioning your actions, Marjorie. I myself had no idea you carried it with you, or I would have provided a footman to guard it for you."

"That's very kind, Constance. You're quite right. I should have informed you."

"Now, Inspector," said Lady Brandon. "Have you more questions for either of us? If not, we are rather tired. It has been an exhausting day."

There was a pause and a rustling of papers.

"Of course, my lady. My sergeant and I have taken a room for the night down the road at the Travers Inn. We shall return in the morning to question the servants. But if I could see tonight where the necklace was kept, that would be most helpful."

Amanda heard people rising and crept quickly back up the stairs to her room.

5 - The Inspector Calls

Inspector Hawk arrived at ten the next morning. Amanda sat next to Lady Brandon in the parlor as the day was arranged.

"I will talk to the senior staff personally, of course," said Inspector Hawk. "Sergeant Farrow will talk to the maids, gardeners, and grooms."

"My household has been in turmoil since last night," said Lady Brandon. "So the sooner we finish this, the sooner we can all get back to our normal tasks. I leave it completely in your hands, Inspector."

"Thank you, my lady." He gestured to Sergeant Farrow, a ginger-haired man with a lean face, to go out to the stables. "I would like to speak first with you, then your secretary, then your companion."

Amanda left the room. Panic was starting to set in. If she told the police about Jack Strawman, they would arrest him. If she didn't mention him, she was lying, which was against her principles.

It did occur to her that Mr. Strawman did not have the same compunctions about lying, that he would protect something with an untruth without blinking an eye. She had never been that way; on the contrary, being truthful was her specialty, usually before she could think to do anything else.

She tried to suppress her feelings toward Lady Vance. In truth Amanda had never liked her. She had overheard a conversation last year, when Lady Vance had come for tea. Lady Brandon had expressed admiration for Lydia Becker, the founder of The National Society of Women's Suffrage, and Lady Vance had taken umbrage. The only role for women in politics, she had said with great emphasis, was to support her husband's views. As a widow, Lady Brandon should do as she was doing and support only those causes her husband had supported. Lady Brandon's polite reply of "naturally, Marjorie" set Amanda's teeth on edge.

Lady Vance seemed to enjoy making people feel uncomfortable and putting them in their place. Her probing questions tended to make Lady Brandon question her own decisions. If one were to associate with people and call them friends, Amanda thought, then one should not associate with people who made you feel badly about yourself or your actions. She was having trouble caring whether Lady Vance got her necklace back or not.

But when Inspector Hawk sat her down for questions, the urge was to be as cooperative as she could be, to answer everything fully and completely.

"Miss Goodwin, you have been companion to Lady Brandon for two years?"

"Yes, Inspector."

"I see. Were you aware that a necklace had been stolen last night?"

"Not at the time, no. I became aware when Lady Brandon told me."

"And did you see anything suspicious during the party?"

Amanda had given this a great deal of thought, trying in advance to think how the Inspector might phrase the question, and how she could get around it without lying. She had been unable to figure it out.

"I'm not sure about suspicious, but I did find an unexpected guest in the library, someone who hadn't been invited."

The Inspector flipped to a fresh page in his notebook, his pencil poised and ready.

"And who was that, miss?"

"He told me his name was Jack Strawman." As soon as she'd said it, she regretted it. A pain passed through her heart.

"And he was not invited, you say?"

"That is correct."

"Did he say what he was doing in Lady Brandon's house?"

"No, he did not." That was truthful, Amanda noted with relief. She had no idea why he was there, unless he was stealing the necklace.

"What time did you see him in the house?"

"About five in the afternoon, but only for a few minutes."

"Do you know anything of this man? His address, for example?"

Amanda was happy to be able to say she did not.

"Can you describe him?"

"Yes. He is tall, with wavy dark hair that falls at the collar, and he has a scar under his right eye. He has a very tidy mustache, but no beard or side whiskers, and a look in his eye as if he's always amused." She realized as she saw him in her mind's eye that she was describing him rather sympathetically. Or perhaps she was just nervous. One did not get interviewed by the police every day.

The Inspector tilted his head and looked at her.

"You're very observant, miss—thank you. Have you any reason to believe he would have stolen Lady Vance's necklace?"

Now here was the question she had feared. Had she any reason? Aside from her knowing he was a thief? Did that mean he had stolen the necklace? She thought it likely, very likely. But that was not the Inspector's question; it was whether she had any reason to believe he had stolen it. She had a personal reason for believing so, but no evidence that he had—indeed, she had never actually seen him steal anything.

"He was in the house when he shouldn't have been," she said, in a tone that suggested this was an answer. The Inspector nodded, put his pencil away, and closed his notebook. Amanda fought not to show her relief or change her expression. She rose.

"Thank you, miss. We will let you know if we have more questions. You have been very helpful."

Not too helpful, Amanda thought as she left the room. And then she was ashamed. The man was a thief. If he was caught, it would be justice, wouldn't it?

As she went to the kitchen to get some tea, her nervousness faded and was replaced by resentment. How dare Jack Strawman put her in this position? How dare he rob a house she was in, as he obviously knew she was? Her pang at naming him to the police began to lessen.

It had occurred to her that he might help her regain the miniature, if he were telling the truth about not reporting her own actions. She needed the skill of a thief. But if he was going to go around robbing everyone, particularly the friends of Lady Brandon, that wouldn't work. She had actually been thinking he could help, and now he had ruined it with this robbery.

6 - Funeral in the Rain

Although West Sussex can be a sunny place in summer, in the winter it may be as miserable as anywhere else in England. The day of George Soffitt's funeral dawned cold and damp, yet the little chapel on the grounds of his estate at Naedre Manor was full of people paying their respects.

The vicar was unknown to anyone, having been called in from Chichester for the day, since the chapel hadn't had a vicar in many years. He performed a suitable, if not to say perfunctory, service, noting the deceased as a man of great standing in the community, and one worthy of respect. There was a murmur in the congregation as the service ended and the group separated. Some went directly to the Manor to stay out of the wet, while a handful of others attended the coffin to the grave site.

Lady Brandon, accompanied by Amanda, made her way across the wet lawn to the Manor, her umbrella at the ready. Amanda felt strange as they approached the house. She chided herself for her nervousness, which undoubtedly arose from having been there before in the middle of the night, trying to steal the miniature. She hoped today might allow her the opportunity of seeing whether it was on display somewhere more obvious than the study. Lady Brandon had wanted to attend the wake to hear the gossip and see the inside of the Manor, which had been closed to callers for a number of years.

"What a large amount of people," Amanda said. Having followed Soffitt's activities over the years, she knew that he had little family and was disliked in the extreme. The wake was being hosted by Soffitt's solicitors, Birch and Comstock. She suspected that many were here because they owed him money, and were hoping to find out whether their debts would now be expunged. For her part, she wanted to know how much time she had before everything he had owned would be sold.

"I suspect they all owed him money, or were being blackmailed by him," murmured Lady Brandon. She shared the popular opinion of George Soffitt.

"There are an unusual number of young ladies among them," Amanda noted. "What on earth could he blackmail a girl of sixteen about?"

Lady Brandon frowned. "I have no notion. Young people these days have such ideas."

They entered the great hall, nodding to people as Lady Brandon maneuvered toward the refreshments.

"Not much of a wake," she said, casting a critical eye over the limited offering of small cakes. "Of course, if the solicitors are paying, it's no wonder. Ah, there is the vicar."

The vicar from Chichester was standing in a corner balancing a cup of tea and looking awkward. Being a woman of some standing, Lady Brandon moved toward him to introduce herself, but just then there was a stir in the hall and Amanda turned toward the front door.

A man was entering, a man of extraordinary beauty. He was tall, with a trim physique and impeccable clothes. Straight blond hair hung attractively to his shoulders, and his blue eyes were kind and gentle. As he entered, he was approached immediately by two of the young ladies, one with a cup of tea in her hand and the other with a piece of cake. He smiled becomingly and greeted each in turn.

"So that explains the abundance of young women," snorted Lady Brandon.

"Who is he?" asked Amanda, a trifle breathlessly. He really did look like he'd stepped out of a painting of Adonis.

"Oh, goodness, not you too! That's Julian Birch, of Comstock and Birch. Took over for his uncle just a few months ago."

So that was who Lady Vance's maid had been talking about. Amanda could see the reason for the irregular heartbeat. At just that moment Mr. Birch looked up, as if scanning the room for someone in particular. When he saw Amanda's face he stopped. She could swear his eyes sparkled as he gave her a brief nod and a small smile. She caught her breath and wished she had brought her fan, however inappropriate it might be for a funeral.

"If you'll excuse me," she said to Lady Brandon, and began to move quietly through the downstairs rooms, looking for display cabinets that might hold miniatures. In the study, now that it was light, she saw a cabinet with several drawers along the wall opposite the desk. They appeared suitable for maps or large papers, but could also hold miniatures. Since there was no one in the room, she tried the top drawer. It was locked. She tried a few underneath it, but none would open. There must be a lock on the entire cabinet, but she was unable to find it before she heard the tread of feet entering the room. Two young women came in with their teacups, looking for a place to sit. Amanda pretended to be examining some books on the shelf.

"Yes, I'm quite sure he's unmarried. But a solicitor is not a good choice for a girl of your rank," said the first woman, sipping her tea.

"Of course not," said the second. "But one can always enjoy a small flirtation."

"True."

As their conversation turned to the intricacies of managing servants, Amanda quietly left the room and continued her search. Soffitt was quite a collector and each room boasted some furniture for display. The parlor had a large cabinet with glass doors filled with Japanese teapots and small jade figures. The morning room contained white marble busts and sculptures on tables, and the withdrawing room had paintings covering the wall, their frames practically touching. But she saw no miniatures.

There was nothing special about the miniature of her grandmother, except to her and her grandfather. But it was known that Soffitt collected them, yet they weren't on view. The likely place was the locked cabinets. Perhaps they were too small to make for a good public display. But she'd need to open the drawers to know for sure.

There was only one solution: Jack Strawman. He was obviously a professional burglar, and most certainly the only one of her acquaintance. If she could find him, perhaps she could hire him or, if that wasn't affordable, plead with him to help her. As she returned to the hall to find Lady Brandon, she heard a voice that sounded familiar. A man was talking to the vicar, who was still standing in the corner. Amanda recognized his voice as that of Inspector Hawk. What was he doing here?

7 - An Arrangement

Jack had taken a chance going to the funeral and wake of George Soffitt. Although he had spent the previous several years in London, it was not out of the question that he could be recognized here. The tweed cap and farm coat should make that less likely. He had tried to survey the assembled visitors from the back of the chapel, and was only able to discern two people he knew: Inspector Hawk and that delightful fellow burglar, Amanda Goodwin. She must be here looking for her miniature.

She was an extraordinary woman, he thought, even though he had only encountered her twice. Examining his motives for kissing her that first night had been useless; it had been an instinctive thing to do. Miss Goodwin was not that pretty, not attractive in the usual sense. Her eyes were large and lovely, but her jaw was a little too square, her face a little too strong for fragile femininity. And of course he'd never known a woman who could floor him with a leg kick. Or, frankly, who would want to.

He'd been relatively successful with women in his forty years. Women had told him his scar, which ran from the outer edge of his right eye, added a bit of danger to his strong face and dark eyes. He could be imposing if he wanted to be, and there was a certain type of woman who found that attractive. Unfortunately, he didn't find women who liked imposing men to his taste. They tended to be passive and contributed little to witty conversation.

The first love of his life, Mabel, had been that way. He was so young that he found her dependence on him flattering. She had a country beauty that appealed to him, and in his desire for her he neglected to realize that they had little to say to each other. He had escaped, but in breaking his promise to marry her he had destroyed his reputation in their small town, and had left for London. She went on to marry a wealthy owner of a shipping line, and had been very happy, but he could never return.

The papers. He must look for them again, but with this many people in the house the conditions were poor for recovering them. He could at least survey the downstairs rooms, to see if anywhere other than the study looked likely. Grabbing a piece of cake in the hall, he avoided the vicar and the inspector. Stepping into the withdrawing room, he found a small writing desk. There was only one in the room, and a quick check of the single drawer yielded only letter-writing paper. As he stepped back into the hall, he saw her.

She was wearing a dark gray dress with an over-jacket. The buttons made a straight line down the front, and the cinched waist accentuated her figure. The brown curls had been tamed somewhat into a low, modest bun at the nape of her neck. She said something to Lady Brandon, and then went out the front door. Jack followed her at a distance. It had stopped raining, although the day was still gloomy and a breeze was pushing gray clouds across the sky.

Amanda strode across the lawn toward the stables, and he watched as she went in. Walking slowly so no one would suspect he was following, he made his way to the stables and entered. She was feeding something to a horse, who was whinnying quietly to her.

He made his steps firm so he would not surprise her, and she looked up as he approached.

"Your horse?"

Her eyes were wide as she looked at him, then narrowed as he got closer. He reached over and gave the horse a stroke on its jaw.

"No," she said. "We've just met." Her tone was icy.

"It's interesting to see you again, Miss Goodwin," he said. "I can't suppose you were a friend of the deceased, since we met robbing his house."

"I am not, Mr. Strawman." She was glaring at him now.

"Miss Goodwin, I cannot help but note a less friendly tone than when last we met. May I ask what has caused such displeasure?"

"You should know very well, Mr. Strawman. You stole a valuable necklace from my employer's house."

"Ah, yes, I heard about the robbery. Lady Vance, I think it was?"

She stared at him, saying nothing.

"Well," he continued, "that had nothing to do with me."

Amanda sputtered out, "Oh, didn't it? You are a liar and a thief, Mr. Strawman."

This much was clearly fact, he thought. She looked terrifying when she was angry.

"Please forgive me, Miss Goodwin. I suppose you are only a thief."

Amanda was about to explain, but her anger thought better of it.

"Why are you here, Mr. Strawman? If you did not find what you wanted before, you have certainly had time since."

"I'm afraid I have not, Miss Goodwin. I have been forced to continue my search."

"Then I should say you are a liar and a very poor thief, Mr. Strawman."

He was starting to get angry, and he fought to control his temper.

"Perhaps so," he said between gritted teeth. "But I assume you have not found your miniature either?"

"No. But at least I haven't been robbing Lady Brandon's friends."

"Neither have I."

"I am quite sure you have. Why else would you be there?"

"I was there hoping to find you, not to rob Lady Vance. It is unfortunate that you have yet to find your miniature."

She continued glaring at him, but her head gave a slight shake.

"I suspect that the miniatures are locked in a cabinet in the library. But I can see no keyhole and of course have no idea where a key might be."

Before he could stop himself, he said, "I am very good with locks of all kinds, you know."

He saw the hope leap into her eyes before he could gainsay it.

"Would you help me?" she asked, her voice quiet and calm.

"Why should I?" he asked, lowering his and stepping closer to her.

This close he could see the waves of her hair. If he took out the pins, it would trail over her shoulders in little shapes he could twirl with his fingers. Her eyes were looking at him with a mixture of suspicion and resolve.

"You would have the privilege of assisting a woman in some distress."

She didn't look distressed, he thought. She looked competent and strong, ready to march back to the house or mount a horse and leave, as she wished. She needed his help, however, and the idea that she would be in his debt was quite appealing.

"I won't do it for you," he said, turning away. He heard her sigh and turned back. "But I will do it *with* you. You, of course, must help me in return."

She blinked, and he could tell she was trying to keep her expression neutral.

"And how could I help you?" she asked.

"What I am looking for may require a diversion. When the time comes, I'll ask you to be that diversion."

8 - Midnight in the Orangerie

There had been no will reading as far as anyone knew, so speculation became a sport. To whom had Soffitt left Naedre Manor? Everyone thought he'd had a son, but he'd been gone for years. Would the firm of Birch and Comstock know where to find him? Some had heard he'd been transported to Australia for horrible crimes, others that he had left for America and made a fortune. Several people had heard his death reported. The truth was that no one knew.

The wake had been an opportunity for half of West Sussex to see what George Soffitt had owned, purchased with what everyone knew must be ill-gotten gains. Would they be auctioned off, the house closed? For now, the manor had been secured, an empty house locked up against intruders, with a sign posted on the door giving Birch and Comstock's business address. Anyone with a claim to the estate was directed to contact them.

To Amanda's mind, she had a claim, but she knew it wasn't a legal claim. She had come to know quite a lot about the law, about contracts and such, from her grandfather. The contract with Soffitt, in return for the sale of her grandparents' precious items, was an entail. Her grandfather could live at Lufstow Farm until his death, then it could be inherited by one of his progeny only if they were unmarried and thus could bear no children. After that person died, the Farm would revert to Soffitt property.

Since Amanda's parents had died eight years before, she was the only progeny left once her grandfather died. It was something she didn't want to think about, but the older her grandfather got, the more she had to. They could pay the expenses of the farm because of her income, and it was her home, the place where she felt most herself.

But now it was her grandfather's home, and she had promised herself to bring him the miniature of his wife. She had been surprised to receive a note that afternoon from Jack Strawman. He had apparently taken it upon himself to enter Naedre Manor secretly shortly after the wake. Although he had succeeded in opening the drawers she had mentioned to him, the miniature wasn't there. However, he had seen several crates of Soffitt's collections boxed up to be shipped to Birch and Comstock's offices in Petersfield.

At this point it was necessary to devise a plan, so he asked her to meet him in the Heddington Hall orangerie at midnight.

Amanda caught herself that evening lingering over the decision of what to wear, before realizing that was a foolish preoccupation and putting on a plain woolen gown and sturdy boots. It had been a typical day with Lady Brandon, calling for her tea, sitting and embroidering together, taking some fresh air as my lady did her letters with Penelope. She had tried to interest Maxie in playing with some yarn, but the cat gave her a look like she had taken leave of her senses, stretched, and went back to sleep.

She had also had time for reading. Since her parents died, Amanda had been studying agriculture. Not content with current magazines on farming, she had begun reading older texts, including those of the ancients. She particularly liked Cato, with his steadfast advice on the use of manure, although she realized much of the book on olive growing didn't apply. England was no place to grow olives.

Amanda had also acquired an edition of Jethro Tull's work on horses and tillage, but she was particularly excited about the new book *Chemistry of the Farm*, which Lady Brandon had kindly asked one of her footman to obtain for her. It was far more detailed than the sporting magazines that talked about farming, but Amanda had trouble concentrating knowing what would happen that evening.

Getting out of the house was easy at the late hour, and she made her way to the orangerie. Although the night was quite cold, the orangerie would be warmer. As she approached, she saw a glimmer of light through the windows; Strawman must have lit a candle. She entered from the back of the building to find him sitting on a wicker bench reading a newspaper by candlelight. The candlelight caught the gray highlights in his hair and made them glow.

"Mr. Strawman," said Amanda.

"Ah, Miss Goodwin," he said, rising and folding the newspaper. He looked at her and his eyes seemed to burn with a dark intensity. Amanda felt the heat rise to her face.

"I . . . I received your note."

He smiled, his moustache lifting. "So I see." He motioned to the place next to him on the bench. She sat down, trying not to get too close.

"First," he said, "may I apologize for being unable to retrieve your miniature? The drawers did indeed look like a possible place, but I am afraid they contained nothing but maps. I know you are disappointed."

"I am, Mr. Strawman. And perplexed. Where else could it be?"

"Unlike a large painting or sculpture, a miniature, or even a collection of them, could reside almost anywhere, even in a plain box, if properly fitted inside."

"Yes, I suppose so."

"And as I said, any number of crates are being transported to the solicitors' office in Petersfield."

"Are you suggesting we follow them? How on earth would we search the crates, even if we could get access to them?"

"I'm not sure that will be necessary, Miss Goodwin. What we need are the manifests, the lists of which items are in which crates. I am sure Birch and Comstock will have been most helpful by creating one. There is no way to keep track of all the items otherwise. They left for Petersfield yesterday."

Amanda thought about this for a moment. "Then we must go to Petersfield."

"Very likely."

It occurred to her that she had no business going anywhere with Jack Strawman, that in fact it was not only socially irresponsible to do so, but personally dangerous. Even thinking about a close ride in a carriage with him made her rise from the wicker bench and begin pacing instead. She was not a child any longer, she thought. If he made an effort to compromise her, she would of course resist, but there must be no discussion about it.

She wanted him to be trustworthy, but asked herself how verifying that would even be possible. She'd met him when they were both thieving, regardless of the fact that her crime was only to try to retrieve the miniature. But she had serious questions for him.

"Sir, I must ask. While I am grateful for your willingness to help me in my quest, I still do not know what you were looking for that night, and may be looking for still. Or were you merely robbing the house?"

She had thought about this a lot, that he might be searching for something, as she was, rather than just stealing valuables. His expression changed in the flickering candlelight, and he leaned over, putting his elbows on his thighs as he looked at the floor and gave a deep sigh.

"You are right, of course," he said. "I wasn't just robbing the house of whatever valuable items I could find. I too was looking for something specific."

"And that was?"

"Papers, Miss Goodwin. There are some papers which have been in Mr. Soffitt's possession that I need to claim. Papers to do with my family's good name." He sounded miserable.

She sat down next to him, and without thinking put her hand gently on his knee, saying quietly. "And if you get these papers will your good name be preserved?"

He nodded, feeling the heat of her hand on his knee. He put his own on top of it, but she jumped up again and paced.

"And would these papers be in the crates, do you think?"

"It's possible." He didn't sound either certain or optimistic.

"We will find them!" she said, determined.

He smiled at her determination. Amanda looked up at him, and his smile was sad. She found herself looking at his scar, wondering how he got it. She knew so little about him.

There was a sudden noise outside the orangerie, and it sounded like footsteps. Through the glass they saw lamplight swinging to and fro as someone approached the building. Jack extinguished the candle.

"Who it is?" he whispered.

"The constable who's been assigned to watch the house."

"A constable's assigned to watch the house? Why?"

"Because you robbed it, that's why!"

"Oh." A pause. "Does he usually come in to the building?"

"How the blazes would I know? I'm not usually out here at midnight." She looked around at the citrus trees. Not much to hide behind.

They waited, but the lamp began moving onward toward the back gate.

"Let us be off to Petersfield tomorrow," he said.

Jack Strawman could be the most infuriating man, Amanda thought.

"Unlike some people, I cannot just run off to Petersfield any time I want. I am a lady's companion. I have a half day on Saturdays—that is all."

"I will bring my carriage for you Saturday at one," he said. "I mean, I'll hire a trap to take us."

Amanda thought a moment. Jack Strawman was a thief. Having him fetch her for a trip to anywhere was unwise. Lady Brandon would be scandalized if she knew, and the servants wouldn't stop talking.

"No," she said. "I shall meet you at the cross-roads at the bottom of the hill."

"Very well," he said.

"May I ask a favor?"

"Anything you like."

"Would you please stop robbing people until our business is concluded?"

He pursed his lips in displeasure.

"How am I to eat, my dear, if I don't get money?"

"I am not your dear. And I cannot continue to associate with a practicing thief. We have constables around the house now, and I have a task to complete. While I am delighted to have your help, given your skills, it is more than my reputation is worth to be known as a—a—"

"An accomplice?"

"Or worse. So, will you promise me?" She was not happy, but she knew that she should be nice when making a request, so she tried a winning smile.

He laughed. "Well, Miss Goodwin, that is quite the grimace. But having made the effort, I will promise. I won't rob anyone in West Sussex until our business is concluded."

Amanda noted the qualification, but decided to let it pass. "Thank you."

9 - A Visit to Portsmouth

Friday was Lady Brandon's day to go shopping, and Amanda went along to carry packages, give advice when asked, and generally provide her with company. This meant a journey into Portsmouth, and Lady Brandon spending time strolling the High Street before having tea with her friend Lady Martin, who had, like herself, been the sister of a sea commander.

The first visit was to Miss Eliza Shepard, boot and shoe maker, for winter boots. Lady Brandon liked shops owned by women, and Miss Shepard's was a favorite.

"Now, Amanda, you must have a pair, too," said Lady Brandon. "We can't have you accompanying me in old boots. How old are yours?"

"Three years old, my lady." Amanda loved her old boots; she had worn them on her last visit to the farm. But if Lady Brandon was feeling generous, she certainly wouldn't mind wearing a new pair when in her presence.

After the boots were ordered, the next stop was Charles Cullingworth, the furrier, where Lady Brandon purchased a new sable coat, packaged in a large box that was difficult to carry.

"Amanda, why don't you take that package to the carriage while I visit Mr. Saunders. Perhaps," she said, reaching into her reticule and handing Amanda six shillings, "you'd like to stop by Mr. Henry's next door? I will come fetch you when I have finished."

Amanda smiled. Considering that Lady Vance had been robbed in her house less than a week before, Lady Brandon was in an excellent mood and happy to have a shopping day. They kept up the pretense that Amanda didn't know why Lady Brandon visited Mr. Saunders, the chemist. He provided her with laudanum in a lovely violet bottle that looked like perfume, and laxative pills dipped in chocolate, and a balm for her arthritis. Although her usual doctor visited Heddington Hall, she preferred to procure remedies herself from an apothecary she could trust.

Returning from the carriage, Amanda was more than happy to spend time in Mr. Henry's bookshop. She knew the way to the agricultural section, but she'd already read everything and it was starting to make her unhappy. How could she use the knowledge she'd gained if she was only a lady's companion? Her dream was to be in charge of Lufstow Farm, and she'd missed so much being unable to be with her grandfather the past several years. Earning money was important, but she missed her home. She drifted into the botany books, and saw several that interested her, but instead of buying anything she pocketed the six shillings and decided to save it. Lady Brandon was not likely to notice.

She stepped outside to find Lady Brandon coming over from next door.

"One last call before Lady Martin's," she said with a smile and a tap of her cane. This was the instrument dealer, Mr. Burdett. But he was more than just an instrument dealer, with his bugles and harps. He had been a concert pianist in London in the 1860s, and was a frequent guest at Heddington Hall. Long after the other guests had gone, Lady Brandon would sit in the parlor with Mr. Burdett, talking about music. At least, that's what Amanda assumed they were talking about. She was usually dismissed for the evening when he was visiting.

"Good afternoon, Mr. Burdett."

"Good afternoon, Lady Brandon." Mr. Burdett had curly white hair and a round, rosy face accentuated by round spectacles. His face suffused with pleasure on seeing Lady Brandon, Amanda noticed, and he rose to find her a chair.

"We are in town for some shopping." Amanda could have sworn that Lady Brandon blinked her eyelashes a few more times than necessary. Her cheeks seemed rosy too, but perhaps that was from her visit with the chemist. Then suddenly it occurred to Amanda that these two were attracted to each other, perhaps even in love. How could she not have noticed it before? She immediately felt like an intruder.

"Excuse me, my lady, but I forgot something at the bookseller's. I'll return in a few minutes?"

Lady Brandon waved her away, and Amanda walked out into the High Street.

It was true that her employer had been widowed many years before, but Amanda had been under the impression that she valued her independence. Lady Brandon did as she liked, whenever she liked, answering to no one. Amanda's grandfather had admired her and had supported Amanda becoming her companion.

"It's hard to find an independent woman these days," he had said. "As you know, your grandmother was a great admirer of Mary Wollstonecraft's work, and joined the suffragists to get women the vote. Lady Brandon will be an excellent model for you, even if she is aristocracy."

These were the values Amanda had grown up with, and she had thought that some day if she fell in love it would be with a man who believed in the equality of women. Instead she had been brutally manhandled by a man she had trusted. Of course, she had been nineteen. Lady Brandon was in her sixties. Perhaps one learned as one got older whom to trust.

She crossed the street to walk through the large church, knowing that Lady Brandon would not miss her. Her thoughts turned to Jack Strawman, and whether she could trust him. She knew she shouldn't—there was no getting around that he was a thief. He said he hadn't stolen Lady Vance's necklace, but was that even possible? Amanda had seen him at the house. And now they were planning to go to Petersfield together. She was older now, and her instinct told her she could trust Strawman even though his activities could hardly be called gentlemanly. She didn't even know where he lived, or who his people were. The arrangement they had, one had to admit, was very odd.

And what had possessed her to put her hand on his knee last night in the orangerie? She had never reached out to touch a man other than her father and grandfather, taking their hand in hers. But when Jack Strawman had mentioned his family's honor, there was such longing in his face. She felt pity and kindness toward him, and touching him had seemed a natural thing to do. She should be more practical. If he could help her reclaim the miniature of her grandmother, then he was useful. And perhaps she could return the favor helping find his papers. Anything else should be put aside as out of the question.

She returned to Mr. Burdett's shop to find Lady Brandon taking her leave, a packet wrapped in brown paper in one hand and the other on Mr. Burdett's arm. The two of them were laughing together and promising to meet again soon. He was saying he would come to Heddington to play for her if she didn't return to town within the week. He caught sight of Amanda.

"Ah, there she is! Now you take good care of Lady Brandon, Miss Goodwin. Make sure she has some music each day." He winked at her.

Tea with Lady Martin was quite dull, the women talking clothes and home furnishings. But Lady Martin had a good library, so Amanda usually spent her time reading. The maid, Louise, brought her tea there.

"Have you heard the latest?" Louise asked Amanda. "There has been another robbery!"

"What do you mean, another robbery? Since Lady Vance's necklace was stolen?"

"Yes! Only this time it's a bracelet and tiara, from Mrs. Beekman."

"When?" Amanda could felt herself sicken.

"Last night. Right out of her house it was, here in town. The police have been asking questions everywhere."

Amanda was unable to listen to the rest of what Louise was saying. All she could think was, "how could he?"

"I heard they are questioning someone. Wouldn't it be exciting if they arrested him?"

"Oh, yes, very exciting," said Amanda in a low tone.

On the way back to Heddington Hall in the carriage, Lady Brandon inquired whether Amanda was feeling quite well. "You've been very quiet, my dear."

"Yes, Lady Brandon. I am sorry."

"Perhaps it will cheer you to know that the Portsmouth police have arrested someone. He stole Lady Beekman's jewelry last night, and might be the same person who stole poor Lady Vance's necklace."

Amanda blinked. "They've captured him?"

"That is what Lady Martin told me. And Estelle does have her ear to the ground here, as they say. Didn't give a name, though."

Lady Brandon continued chattering all the way home, about her visit with Lady Martin, and how much Portsmouth had changed over the years since she was there as a young woman, and how the boots they had ordered should be ready in a fortnight. Amanda responded in the right places, but her mind was on Jack Strawman. If he'd been arrested, he certainly wasn't meeting her tomorrow at the cross-roads to journey to Petersfield. She hadn't found the miniature, and now he was in jail. At the moment, she wasn't sure which bothered her more.

10 - A Trip Alone

There was nothing for it; Amanda would simply have to journey to Petersfield on her own. A thought had occurred to her in the night. What if Soffitt had sold the miniature before he died? She wouldn't know how to find who had purchased it. But at least if it appeared on the manifest, she would know where it was. So either way a trip to Birch and Comstock was needed, and the sooner the better.

Her privileges as companion did not include use of a carriage, and she had not wanted to ask to take the trap. Instead, she found Vesta in the stable and prepared for an afternoon out. She had Lady Brandon's shillings to tip a groom, and she could shorten the journey making her way across the fields from the back of the house until she got to the main road.

Amanda arrived in Petersfield a little over an hour later and made her way to The Square at the center of town. The offices of Birch and Comstock were across The Square from the George Inn, where she left her horse. As she walked across she realized that her ride had made her sweat, and that her skirts were dirtied. She wouldn't win any prize for elegance, but she had not had much choice. She dusted off as best she could and entered the small building.

The front of the office was small, and a dapper man in a trim suit and spectacles raised his tonsured head, then stood to greet her.

"Good afternoon, madam. How may I be of assistance?"

Amanda did not bother to correct his address.

"I have come about the disposition of Mr. Soffit's estate," she said, smoothing back an errant strand of hair over her ear.

The man looked her up and down, raising an eyebrow at her appearance.

"I see. Allow me to introduce myself. I am William Comstock, at your service."

While not exactly crestfallen, Amanda was perturbed that she was not greeted by the attractive Mr. Birch. Mr. Comstock smiled.

"Allow me to apologize for not being Mr. Birch, who is managing the Soffitt estate. He stepped out and will return shortly." She caught an amused twinkle in his eye. "May I ask if you have a claim on the estate of Mr. Soffit?"

"In a manner of speaking, I do," said Amanda firmly. "I am seeking a miniature of my grandmother that was in his collection. I was hoping you might have a manifest of the items you've taken in to storage."

"I am sorry but that information is only for family members. Are you family?"

"No. My understanding was that he had no family."

"We are currently in the process of gathering information to help us find his relations."

He was being very kind, Amanda thought, but she was making no progress.

"Would it be possible for you to look at the manifest and tell me if the miniature is there?"

"I am sorry. I believe there are some miniatures, but they would have been merely counted rather than detailed."

"So there would be no way to know which one was mine without opening the crates?"

"That is correct. And you would need permission from Mr. Birch to have us do that."

Amanda tried not to sound impatient. "And when did you say he would be back?"

Mr. Comstock looked up at the clock and frowned.

"He should have been back by now. He went over to the Old Drum." Mr. Comstock pointed straight out the door. "It's across The Square, then over on Chapel Street."

Amanda considered for only a moment.

"Then I shall go find him. Thank you for your time, Mr. Comstock."

"Ah, Mrs. . . . ?"

"Miss. Goodwin."

"Miss Goodwin, I wouldn't recommend that. Why not have a seat and wait? He really should be back any moment."

But Amanda was already out the door and heading across The Square. Chapel Street was easy to find, and The Old Drum wasn't far along. The building looked like a large house, with a public house on the ground floor and rooms above. As she approached, Julian Birch came out the front door, smoothing his hair and putting his hat on. He was still tying his cravat as he walked, which Amanda thought odd, but the thought of him without it made her heart skip a beat.

He saw her at that moment, and a smile lit up his face, showing straight and even teeth under the blond mustache. His eyes crinkling delightfully at the corners, he stopped in front of her.

"We have never met," he said, "but I saw you at Lady Brandon's party. I have been trying to discover your name for a week." He bowed. "I'm Julian Birch."

"Yes, I know," she squeaked out, then felt embarrassed. His smile broadened. This was not the way to behave, she thought. "My name is Amanda Goodwin. I came to find you. Mr. Comstock told me you were here."

"Oh, he did, did he? Well, then, I am forever in his debt. Miss Goodwin, you are enchanting."

Amanda could feel herself blushing, which made her even more embarrassed. He held out his arm.

"May I accompany you back to the office? Or was your business of a more personal nature?"

Amanda stared at his arm. She couldn't, she really couldn't. He shrugged and they began to walk toward The Square.

"The office, please." Somehow she had lost the firm tone she had used with Mr. Comstock. "It's about . . ." For a moment she forgot what her inquiry was about. She shook her head as if to clear away a dream. "It's about Mr. Soffitt's estate. He had an object that belonged to me."

"Did he indeed? What would that object be? A love letter, perhaps?"

Amanda knew he was teasing.

"No, a miniature of my grandmother."

Birch stopped and looked down at her, the sun catching the glints in his blond hair.

"Under what circumstances would such a delightful woman lend a picture of her grandmother to someone like George Soffit?" he asked.

"I didn't lend it to him." She was too truthful to say that Soffitt had stolen it, though in a way he had. "My grandfather was forced to give it to him."

They had arrived at the office. Comstock rose when he saw them come in and grabbed his hat.

"Ah, Miss Goodwin. I see you found Mr. Birch. I'm off on an important errand, so if you'll excuse me?" He bowed quickly and left.

"That was sudden," said Amanda.

"My partner had an unerring sense of when it's best that I be alone with a client," Birch said. "It is most gratifying. Please take a seat, Miss Goodwin."

She sat on a wooden chair upholstered in red leather. Looking around the office for the first time, she saw that all the furniture, wallpaper, even the rugs were of high quality and in excellent condition. The firm must make quite a bit of money.

"Your office is lovely," she said.

"We like it," he replied, seating himself behind the desk. "Now, you say Mr. Soffitt did not take the miniature on loan from your grandfather, but that he was forced to give it to him. So how did that happen?"

"My grandfather owed a great deal of money in the Lesgus Scheme."

"Yes, I understand George Soffitt set that up."

"We were one of the families ruined by it. My grandfather gave Mr. Soffitt jewelry and valuable items to pay his debt."

"And one of those items was the miniature?"

"Yes."

"Why would he give up a picture of his wife?"

Amanda looked up and hoped the tears in her eyes didn't show. "She had just died. He was grieving."

Mr. Birch looked at her kindly.

"I do wish there was something we could do," he said.

"There is! It could be in the boxes from his estate. I asked Mr. Comstock for the manifest, but he said only family could see it."

Birch was looking at her closely, first in her eyes. Then his eyes dropped to her lips.

"Mr. Birch, are you listening to me?"

Birch looked up but said nothing. He seemed to be trying to see into her soul. She felt herself blushing again, and spoke with her eyes lowered.

"Mr. Birch, I need to get that miniature back. My grandfather is a very old man, and he wants to see his wife's picture."

Birch stood and came around to the front of the desk. He pulled over the other wooden chair close to her. She daren't turn her body toward his. His being this close to her felt dangerous, and she looked about the room as she recalled there was no one else in the building.

"I think," said Birch, his voice low, "that can be arranged."

She looked up at him. "It can? That's wonderful, Mr. Birch. May I see the manifest? When can I see whether my grandfather's miniature is in the crates?"

"I said it could be arranged. The arrangement would require that you allow me to take you to dinner."

Amanda looked at him. His face was friendly again, guileless and charming. The feeling of danger must have been her own, because he'd gotten so close. Why could she not get over what had happened so long ago? If she could, perhaps she could enjoy being with a man like Mr. Birch.

"I would be delighted," she said, though she had to choke out the words. "But could it be soon, please? If the miniature isn't here, I need to keep looking."

"Of course! More than happy to oblige. Would this evening do?"

Amanda paused. She had come on horseback, and shouldn't ride in the dark on the roads or through the fields, even with the moon to light her way.

"Mr. Birch, I would be happy to, but as you can see my clothes are dusty. I came on horseback, and would need to return soon."

"And where is your horse now?"

"At the George Inn."

"Well, he'll be well taken care of there. And then after dinner, I can take you home in my trap, with your horse on a lead."

She was not sure what to do. Mr. Birch's physical beauty was blinding; she wanted to stay with him, talk with him, have him look at her the way he was looking. But a dark ride home, in a trap, alone? Was he a trustworthy gentleman? Surely he would not be able to continue his business as a solicitor if he were not. People trusted solicitors with the most important things in their lives.

"Very well," she said. "But when may I look at the manifest?"

"I shall bring it along to dinner," he said, rising. "As for your appearance, the George Inn keeps a retiring room for ladies on the first floor. If you tell the proprietor I sent you, he will let you in so you can get tidy and have a rest. I shall call for you at six, if that is all right?"

11 - Dinner and a Trap

The wife of the innkeeper at the George Inn led Amanda up the stairs, and she was able to sponge her dress, neaten her hair, and do some of the stretching moves that Li Jing had taught her. Feeling much more clear-headed, she went downstairs to meet Julian Birch.

"Excuse me, miss?" said the innkeeper's wife. "There's a gentleman waiting for you in the front parlor."

"Thank you," said Amanda. There was a man in the front parlor waiting for her, but it wasn't Mr. Birch. It was Jack Strawman. Her eyes narrowed as she approached him.

"What are you doing here?" she said between gritted teeth.

"Waiting for you." He rose and folded his newspaper. "I spoke with Mr. Comstock, and he told me a woman had been in asking about the crates. I saw your horse being watered in The Square and found you."

"I thought you were in jail in Portsmouth." He didn't look like he'd spent the night in jail. His hair was neat, and his clothes clean.

"I was *at* the jail in Portsmouth for a bit, yes." He smiled. "They let me go."

"Why? Did you give them back Lady Beekman's jewelry?"

"I never had Lady Beekman's jewelry. Without proof, they had to release me. No evidence, no arrest—that's the wonderful thing about the British justice system."

Amanda realized what that meant.

"Oh! Were you at the cross-roads?"

"I was. You weren't. And I even hired a carriage."

Amanda was angry, but didn't know it was at herself.

"I suppose you can afford it after selling what you'd stolen," she hissed.

"I can afford it, yes."

His expression was affable, which just made her angrier. She was about to say something scathing, when Julian Birch appeared at her side, looking quizzically at Jack Strawman.

Amanda forced her face into a polite expression, but her insides had begun to twist.

"Good afternoon, Mr. Birch. May I introduce Mr. Jack Strawman?" Then it occurred to her she should say how she knew him. "He was at my employer's party last week."

She saw Jack blink, and remembered that he had not been a guest at that party, but an interloper. Julian Birch hadn't been there, so surely it would be all right?

"Sir," said Birch formally, bowing slightly to Strawman. Jack responded in kind, his eyes showing his amusement.

Mr. Birch turned toward Amanda. "Shall we proceed?" he asked.

"That won't be possible, Mr. Birch," said Strawman.

"Why not, may I ask?"

Amanda was sensing that Julian, despite his calm exterior, was deeply displeased.

"Because I have been sent by Lady Brandon to come take Miss Goodwin home, since it is getting dark."

Amanda was stunned. Lady Brandon could not have sent him; she didn't even know him. He was lying. Again. But by claiming he'd been sent, he had won. Julian Birch realized this too.

"If I may have a moment with Miss Goodwin before you leave, Mr. Strawman? It's a matter of business. Perhaps you could wait outside."

Jack bowed while continuing to hold Julian's gaze, then left the room.

"Mr. Birch, I am so sorry—" But why was she apologizing? She was here to find out whether the miniature was in Petersfield. The charming Mr. Birch was the one who had made dinner a requirement.

"It's quite all right, Miss Goodwin. But I am afraid your question will go unanswered until your return."

Amanda was angry, for the third time that day, but she bit her tongue. She would need to think through what was best to do. And it was difficult to curse at someone who looked so angelic. Instead, she left to find Jack.

He said nothing, but walked with her to the stable to fetch Vesta. He reached for her lead, but Amanda grabbed it from him.

"My horse, you may recall."

Jack laughed.

"My carriage," he said, gesturing toward a large, plain black carriage. The driver got down, took Vesta's lead, and tied her to the back.

"It will be a slow ride," the driver said to them. "But we'll get there afore two hours has passed. I know the roads."

Amanda tried, given her temper, not to flounce into the carriage, but she sat down so hard it hurt. Jack sat opposite her, riding backward. They were soon headed out of the town and back toward Heddington Hall. It was getting colder.

"May I tuck this around you?" asked Jack, holding out a wool blanket that had been on the seat beside him. She took it from him and put it in her own lap.

"Lady Brandon didn't send you," she said, crossing her arms like an angry child.

"Of course not. But I did not think it wise for you to continue your evening with the comely Mr. Birch."

Amanda decided not to ask why not.

"I was with him to get the manifest. That is why we were coming here, wasn't it?"

"Ah, the manifest. Yes."

"Did you have any luck with Mr. Comstock? He told me only family members could look at either the list or the crates."

"Yes, he told me that too."

"So, since you wouldn't let me have dinner with Mr. Birch, how do we get the manifest?"

She had put him in the wrong, she thought, which was exactly where he belonged. If he had let her be, they would have the list.

"Oh, you mean this manifest?" he said, taking a packet of papers from inside his jacket.

Amanda was aghast.

"How—? When—?"

"Birch's coat was hanging by the door of the inn. As I was leaving, I simply looked in the pocket while he was talking to you."

"And you just took it?"

Jack smiled. "I am a thief, you recall."

12 - The Manifest

Jack watched her face as she perused the list, holding it to the window to try to catch the light from the carriage lamp. With her brow furrowed in concentration and little wisps of her hair escaping from her bun, tipping her spectacles up and down to try to peer through them, he was reminded of his childhood schoolteacher Miss Simmons. But Miss Simmons had never made his heart beat stronger, had never made him want to tuck those wisps back in with his finger.

"I can't see well enough to tell if it's here," she growled. He found her temper amusing, but he also enjoyed how passionate she became about things. The miniature was important to her, so important she was willing to associate with a thief to obtain it for her grandfather. Loyalty was a fine quality, he thought. Although sometimes it could be misplaced.

He wondered about Julian Birch, and felt his mood darken. He had been at the wake, of course, and must have seen Amanda there. Did he know her already? Perhaps Lady Brandon used his services. Amanda must have come to Petersfield on her own, so perhaps Birch had gotten the wrong idea when she arrived unaccompanied. He didn't like the man. He especially didn't like the way he looked at Amanda.

Which, of course, was ridiculous. Who was he to Amanda but a useful acquaintance with skills she needed? Her response to his kiss was certainly not something he'd care to repeat, even if the kiss was. She was very prickly, this Amanda Goodwin. Perhaps she had been through something in her past, or perhaps her personality was just different from other women he'd known.

"Damn, damn, damn," she said, slamming the manifest down in her lap.

"I am sorry. I should have arranged for interior carriage lighting," he said smoothly.

She looked up and glared at him.

"Unless," he said, "you would care to stop at a tavern. We could have dinner and look over the list together."

"That is an excellent idea," she said, her face brightening. "Where?"

Jack looked out the window. They seemed to be about half-way back to Heddington Hall.

"Driver!" he called out the window. "Pull up at the White Hart and there's a beer in it for you!"

In a few minutes they arrived at a white half-timbered building with lights blazing in the windows. Jack asked for a table and a lamp, and they were shown to a corner of the inn, near the fire. Without even noticing her surroundings, Amanda opened the manifest on the table and began running her finger down the listings.

"A lot of furnishings . . . some large paintings . . . potted plants. Who on earth would care about potted plants?"

"Maybe the pots are valuable," Jack suggested.

"Huh ... bathroom fixtures ... armor ... a halberd. Goodness, he had a halberd?"

"Perhaps he liked to keep people at a distance."

"I sympathize. Wigs? Oh dear, how revolting. Pens ... books of maps ... a rosewood box with papers."

Jack jumped and grabbed the list.

"A rosewood box with papers? I didn't see such a box."

Amanda grabbed the list back.

"You must have missed it. It's in crate number twelve. Now ... rings ... seals with crests ... miniatures! Here are the miniatures! Crate twenty."

She looked up at him. Her cheeks were flushed and her eyes flashing. He had never seen anything more beautiful.

"Here you are, sir. Two porters and two veal pies." The food had arrived.

"I'm ravenous," said Amanda, casting the list aside and smiling at the woman wearing the apron.

"You will enjoy this, then," she said, but she was looking at Jack and leaned forward a bit as if to whisper, the top of her breasts revealed in her tied blouse. "Best pie in the South Downs."

"I'm sure it is," said Jack with a grin. The woman winked at him and left. The words "brazen hussy" occurred to Amanda, and she wondered what Jack would do if she dressed like that. Was that the kind of woman he wanted? And why should it matter to her if it was?

As they ate, Jack flipped through the list, but there was no other mention of papers that sounded like what he needed. They ate in silence, listening to other people talking and laughing. Then Amanda took the manifest back.

"How can we get this back to him?" she asked.

"Sorry? What do you mean?"

"To Mr. Birch. It's his list. We should return it."

Jack almost choked on his last piece of pie.

"We stole it."

"You stole it."

"Yes, I did, for us to use. We don't need it anymore. Let's throw it in the fire."

Amanda shook her head. "It's not ours. It belongs to Birch and Comstock. They need it to dispose of Soffitt's worldly goods."

"Soffit's worldly goods were mostly stolen or coerced from other people."

"All the more reason to return the list to the solicitors."

He took a sip of his porter and considered her. She continually surprised him. Not just her honesty and openness, but her way of looking at things. She was not at all naïve, but seemed to live in a world of just actions that he had abandoned long ago.

"And how do you suggest we do that? I have no intention of returning to Petersfield."

She looked up at the ceiling for a moment. "We can post it back."

As bizarre as the idea was, Jack saw that it was a rational suggestion. Sent from here, the theft could not be traced back to them. He called for the serving woman, who was more than happy to return to the table.

"Yes, sir? What can I do for you?" It was clear from her look she was willing to do quite a bit.

"Just a pen and some sealing wax."

She pouted.

"For now."

He winked at her and she went to fetch the items.

"Do you wish to bed her?" Amanda asked irritably. "I can take Vesta and ride home from here."

It was a shocking thing to think, and even more shocking to say. Jack was dumbstruck for a moment.

"As delightful as that might be, my mission is to return you safely to Heddington Hall. Do you think I bed every woman who gives me a smile?"

The pen and sealing wax was brought by the burly barman instead of the woman. He frowned at Jack, and Amanda thought he was no more amused at the flirtation than she was.

When he left, Amanda laughed. "Apparently not, when they are guarded by barmen."

She saw the edges of his mouth twitch, although he pretended to be concentrating on folding and sealing the manifest, then writing the address upon it. He gave it to the barman with a nod as they were leaving, asking that it be posted to Petersfield as soon as possible.

They were at Heddington Hall within a half-hour, and Amanda untied Vesta and began walking her to the stable. Jack asked the driver to wait and trotted after her.

"You understand we have thieving to do," he said.

"I suppose so. Will the crates remain at Birch and Comstock, do you think?"

"It's likely they will until someone claims them, or a court decides what to do with them. We need to get there first. I don't want the papers revealed, and you don't want the miniature sold."

Amanda began brushing Vesta down.

"That's true," she said. "Can we do it soon?"

"Tomorrow would be a good time. The law offices will be closed. Are you required to go to church, or could you leave?"

Amanda considered. Lady Branford hated going to church, which is why she insisted Amanda go with her. Once Amanda had been in the middle of her courses, and asked if she could be excused. She supposed she could do that again.

"Yes, I think so."

Horses would be fastest, they decided, and this time they would actually meet at the cross-roads.

13 - The Gauntlet

"The police are being very slow," complained Lady Vance, seated on the best sofa in Lady Brandon's withdrawing room. "I've lost a valuable necklace, and all they have done is talk to people."

It was Saturday afternoon, and the weather had been mild. Little country calling had been done the week before because of the rain, but visiting had now resumed. Lady Brandon much preferred her calling days to her home days, because they were more fun than sitting and receiving visitors, even if one's own home was on display.

She would have rather gone into the garden on a day like this. She could prune down the last of the roses, put the leaves down on the flower border, potter about in the shed. All with her cane, of course. The doctor had warned her not to walk about without her cane. Instead, she'd had to stay home to callers. It was exhausting.

"Constance, are you quite all right?" asked Lady Vance.

"I apologize, Marjorie: I was thinking of something else. You were saying?"

"I was saying the police are being very slow solving the theft of my necklace."

Aware now of where the conversation might go, Lady Brandon was concerned, but she tried not to let it show.

Forsythe had brought in tea, and Lady Vance loved Cook's tea cakes.

"I am quite sure the police are doing their very best, Marjorie. The inspector talked to all my household staff. The only one who saw anything untoward was Amanda, my companion. She even gave them a name: Jack Strawman."

"Whom the police have been unable to find," grumbled Lady Vance. "And they had to let that fellow go, the one they thought stole Lady Beekman's jewelry. Not doing a very good job in Portsmouth, I'd say."

She paused for a moment, nibbling her cake.

"Your cook makes the best tea cakes," she said, then returned to the subject without looking at Lady Brandon. "I believe you are acquainted with the inspector, Constance?"

"I knew his father. He was in the navy when I frequented Portsmouth with Gerald."

"Is it possible," said Marjorie, taking a sip of tea, "that he is trying to save you embarrassment?"

"How do you mean?"

"The necklace was stolen in your house, during your party."

We might as well have this out in the open, thought Lady Brandon.

"Are you saying that Inspector Hawk is deliberately conducting a slow investigation to save me social embarrassment?"

Lady Vance gave Lady Brandon a look that bordered on pity.

"You must admit it is somewhat embarrassing. How could some man no one knows just enter your house and steal something? It does speak to a certain kind of carelessness."

Lady Brandon had been friends with Marjorie since both their husbands had died within a year of each other. They visited each other, and had traveled together to see places like Holy Island, Wells Cathedral, and Lyme Regis. But they did not share many confidences.

"Of course," continued Lady Vance, "I suppose it could have been one of your guests?"

Lady Brandon tried not to bristle and instead appeared to consider this seriously.

"I suppose that is possible. I would say, however, that it's unlikely. There were only six children at the party, and twenty-three invited adults, plus four lady's maids and three footmen. It was a rather small party, and everyone there was known to me except the maids and footmen, who were interviewed thoroughly by Sergeant Farrow."

"Yes, of course." Lady Vance rose. "I must be off to make my other calls, Constance, but I hope to see you at the Naval Festival Ball?"

"That is Friday, isn't it?"

Both of them knew it was Friday. Like everyone else, they were each having a special gown designed for the event.

"It is," said Lady Vance. She stopped and turned at the door. "Constance, you should know that I have said little about the robbery to spare you talk among our friends. I even asked Miss Blythe and the Morgans to keep the secret. But I was thinking that if my necklace, or the miscreant who stole it, hasn't been found by the time of the Naval Festival Ball, I will begin speaking about what happened to more people. Perhaps others have had something similar happen to them, and could be helpful to the police."

After Lady Vance left, Lady Brandon had another cup of tea. The gauntlet had been thrown, she thought. I cannot simply sit back and wait for Vernon Hawk to solve this case. While she thought her social standing was likely safe in general, she did not like talk, particularly talk indicating she was a careless hostess. The impact on her own soirees would be enormous.

Amanda was a trustworthy person, Lady Brandon reflected, and had provided the only clue to the police. Why hadn't they found this Jack Strawman? Were they in fact moving too slowly? It was a necklace, after all, not a murder or a horrible accident. On the other hand, they had arrested someone almost immediately in Lady Beekman's robbery, even if they got the wrong man and had to let him go. And if Hawk were protecting her social standing, he needed to know it was being threatened more by not solving the case quickly.

She went to her writing desk and wrote a quick note to Inspector Hawk, asking him to visit at his earliest convenience with news about the case. Then she rose and gazed out the window for a few minutes. Perhaps she could do more than just question the inspector. She had friends in Portsmouth, men who had known her husband. If they knew something about this Jack Strawman, she wanted to know. She sat down again and began writing more letters.

14 - Crates and Boxes

It was Sunday morning, and Amanda had to admit that if she was going to be a thief, it was much nicer in the daytime. The sun had come out, and the ride to Petersfield had been invigorating. It seemed to have improved her companion's temper too. When Jack gracefully dismounted at the George Inn, he had a sheen of sweat on his forehead and tousled hair. She wondered if he looked like that in bed, then shook her head at her own imaginings.

She had in fact been having very odd dreams. In one, she was riding Vesta across miles and miles of fields, all the way to her grandfather's house. In another, Mr. Birch appeared, and then his head turned into a dragon's head and he breathed fire. But the most disturbing dream had been last night, when she dreamed of Jack Strawman. She'd been in the front parlor at Heddington Hall, arranging the little statuettes on the mantle, when he had come up behind her, wrapping his arms around her in a warm and familiar way. She rarely dreamed of anyone touching her, and when she did those dreams were nightmares.

There were few people in The Square, and one groom took both of the horses at the inn. Amanda assumed most of the town would be at church or working. Nevertheless,

Strawman led her around the back of the empty offices of Birch and Comstock. Behind the office building was an outbuilding with a padlock. As Amanda kept watch, Jack kneeled and worked on the lock. It took him only two minutes. Amanda was impressed. At least he hadn't lied about being good with locks.

He closed the door behind them and lit the bulls-eye lamp he'd brought. The shed was large, with crates and boxes stacked against the walls. All had labels, and since they'd arrived recently, most of Soffitt's goods were near the door. Number twenty was closest, so Jack pried it open with a bar that was hanging near the door for that purpose. The crate was filled with boxes of various sizes. One by one they took them out, opening and examining the contents. One box had buttons made of ivory and jet. Another had small ivory figures, each wrapped in cotton wool.

"Netsuke," Jack said.

"What?"

"Japanese ivory figures, for attaching a purse to a kimono."

Amanda wondered how he knew that. It seemed rather esoteric, even for a burglar of fine art.

They went through all the boxes, but none were of miniatures.

"Bloody hell," said Amanda. "It said a box of miniatures on the manifest."

"Perhaps the manifest isn't accurate. Or," he said with a sigh, "someone has taken them."

"Some bastard has stolen them, you mean?"

"Or sold them. Perhaps these solicitors aren't as honest as they appear."

"Bloody blue damnation!" Amanda sat down hard on the floor and tried not to scream in frustration. All this effort, all this way, and nothing.

"It is your fault, Jack Strawman," she said, her eyes narrowing. "Your sneaking about has called attention to what we're trying to find, I warrant."

"Oh, do you?" he said. "I find that highly unlikely, Miss Goodwin. And you were the one who asked for help."

"A stupid thing for me to do, obviously. I told them about you, you know." She wanted to hurt him now. Her disappointment was choking her.

"Told who what?"

"The police. I gave them your name."

"Did you indeed? Then I am sure they will be here any minute, to arrest both of us." But she could see the hurt in his eyes.

She had said too much, so she just sat there trying not to cry.

"Do not concern yourself, Miss Goodwin," said Jack with some sarcasm. "I shall find crate number twelve myself."

He opened it and went through all the inside boxes until he found the rosewood box. It was filled with various papers: deeds to property, promises of payment, architectural sketches, maps of the fictional Lesgus, and even some letters pleading with Mr. Soffitt for more time, lower payment, or just some grace. But the paper he was looking for wasn't there.

Jack sat down on the floor too.

"Nothing?" asked Amanda.

"Nothing of use to me," said Jack. "And it doesn't make sense. The document I'm looking for would be of use only to me. Unless…"

"Unless what?"

"Unless someone is considering some sort of blackmail. But surely Soffitt would have already exhausted that possibility while he was alive. Perhaps it's in another crate."

She saw him look around the many crates, the desperation evident on his face. He looked crestfallen and for the first time Amanda felt sorry for him, felt badly that with all his thieving talent he was getting no further than she was.

"Tell me about these papers," she said softly.

He looked at her closely, searching her face.

"I'm not sure I should trust you. You told the police my name."

Amanda realized she had been wrong to do so. "I am sorry. I am a very honest person. It is a fault these days, I fear."

"Why did you tell them?"

"They asked if I had seen anything unusual at the party, and of course I had: you."

He said nothing, then stood up and dusted off his trousers. As he was replacing the crates where they had gone, he suddenly gave a start.

"What is it?" Amanda asked.

"The manifest." He took it off one of the crates in the corner and showed it to her. It was the same one he had taken from Birch and they had posted back.

"But we meant it to be back here, didn't we?" she asked.

"Yes, but he's had it in here. One of the solicitors must have been looking through the crates either late last night or early this morning. We need to get out of here."

They left everything where they had found it and peered out into the yard. No one was around. Jack locked the padlock and they went round the back of the George Inn to get their horses, tipping the groom generously not to reveal they had been there. They were about a mile away before they felt comfortable.

"I would like to know about the papers," Amanda said as they continued side by side down the road.

Jack sighed, looked up into the afternoon sun, then over at Amanda. His expression was unreadable.

"Perhaps another time. We need to think on what to do next."

There was a pause, then Amanda spoke.

"Perhaps you could tell me how you got your scar?"

"Why, does it repel you?" He glanced over at her.

"Not in the slightest. But I am curious."

A carriage was approaching, so they led their horses to the side of the road so it could pass. As it went by, the passenger peered out the window at them. With horror, Amanda recognized Lady Vance.

"You've turned white as a ghost," said Jack. "Whatever is the matter?"

"That was Lady Vance. She's seen us together. Damn and blast."

The implications of this gradually sank in as they returned to Heddington Hall. Lady Vance would recall who she was, and that she was riding with a man. She might report this to Lady Brandon, or share the information with her friends, or the police. Jack would be recognized and arrested. She'd given his name to the police.

"Well, it has been a pleasure getting to know you, Miss Goodwin," said Jack as they approached the cross-roads. "I regret to say that given that the police know who I am, and the victim of the theft just saw us together, I will need to remove myself from the public eye. Our adventures have been unsuccessful, which is very unfortunate, but may I say that I will never forget you. I wish you the very best finding your miniature. You are an extraordinary woman."

And with that, he rode off down the road. She watched until his horse disappeared over the ridge. He hadn't looked back.

15 - A Conversation Over Embroidery

"Now, Amanda," Lady Brandon said after they were settled together with their embroidery. "I need you to tell me everything you can about the man you saw at my house the night Lady Vance's necklace was stolen."

She asked as if it were a casual request at conversation, but Amanda knew it was not. This was the moment of truth.

"Yes, my lady."

"All right," said Lady Brandon, biting off a thread and selecting a cerulean blue from her basket. "How did you know his name was Jack Strawman?"

"He told me."

"Why?"

Amanda knew that Lady Brandon was talking only about the day of the party, so without mentioning that she had met Jack Strawman at George Soffitt's house in the middle of the night, she could answer without lying.

"Because I demanded it of him."

Lady Brandon suppressed a smile. "Well done," she said. "Was it your impression he was there to steal?"

"I assumed he was," said Amanda. "Why else would an uninvited guest be in the library, entering through the garden doors?"

"Yes, that is what you told the police. And you described him to them, but they have been unable to find him. I have demanded speedier action from Inspector Hawk. I will tell you confidentially that Lady Vance has threatened some damage to my reputation if this isn't solved quickly."

"Oh, dear." And here Lady Vance had seen her on the road!

Amanda thought as she pushed the needle in and out and the clock ticked on the mantle. She had not been as honest as she should have been, as her stomach was telling her. The best thing would be to confide in Lady Brandon. But if she lost her position, she could not help her grandfather at Lufstow Farm, and she would be unable to get a good reference. She supposed she could be a governess, but she did not get along well with children. Horses, yes, but not children.

"What is even more odd," continued Lady Brandon, "is the man they caught in Portsmouth and let go."

"The one everyone thought stole Lady Beekman's jewels?" Amanda's fingers were getting clumsy; she kept poking her finger.

"Yes. No one seems to know who he was or why he was released. I am hoping to ask Inspector Hawk about it when he comes."

Forsythe appeared at the door.

"Milady, Inspector Hawk awaits you in the front parlor."

"Thank you, Forsythe." Lady Brandon rose, put her palms on her lower back and stretched. "You needn't continue with embroidery if you don't want to. I will be with the Inspector for a half hour, I suppose. I do not plan to ask him to stay for dinner."

She looked out the window.

"Would you please gather some flowers for the table? The sun seems to be favoring us today."

"Of course, milady."

Amanda's stomach was jumpy as she went out into the garden, fetching the basket and secateurs from the shed. Wind had blown most of the flowers, but she did find a few hearty roses and a few mums to gather. In the herbaceous border she cut some rosemary to fill out the flowers. It smelled glorious, that heady spicy smell. Rosemary is for remembering, she thought.

How unfortunate it was that she was remembering Jack Strawman. She knew he was the man arrested in Portsmouth. He had told her he had been released for lack of evidence. That must mean he didn't have the bracelet and tiara on him. She imagined him wearing a tiara and almost laughed. It would look ridiculous in those dark curls, with that scar on his cheek.

He had ridden off, she thought, like one of those romantic heroes in the novels. It occurred to her she had no idea where he lived, and she still suspected he had another name. If she wanted to find him, she couldn't.

Why on earth would she want to find him? she chided herself. The man's a liar and a thief, and even if he is attractive you have seen what men do. He likely stole Lady Vance's necklace and Lady Beekman's jewels, and sold them or gave them to an accomplice. Did he have an accomplice? If he did, was it a man or a woman? Surely she wasn't jealous of an accomplice?

Stealing was dangerous work, usually at night. One sound and you could be caught. Amanda had to admit it had been exciting, though. Breaking into Soffit's house, even if she had stubbed her toe and been surprised by Jack, had been thrilling. Concealed in the shed opening crates, hoping against hope the miniature would be there, had made her breathless.

No, she thought. If she was going to have a man, and she wasn't at all sure she wanted one, it should be someone with stable employment and a socially acceptable demeanor. Someone like the solicitor Julian Birch. Upstanding, attractive, secure in the profession of law. He had seemed interested in her, but she was a bit suspicious. Amanda knew her attractiveness lay in the quickness of her mind and the strength of her spirit, not her physical beauty. Her jaw was too square, and the spectacles made her eyes look too large. She looked like a schoolteacher and she knew it.

In her experience, people gravitated toward those of a similar level of beauty. Julian Birch was surely out of her league. But he had wanted to take her to dinner . . .

As she came into the morning room and arranged the flowers, Forsythe came in with a letter.

"For you, Miss Goodwin," he said.

She assumed the letter was from her grandfather, but when she opened it she saw it wasn't.

> *Dear Amanda,*
>
> *I regret that our last meeting in Petersfield was cut short. Would it be possible for me to send my carriage for you on Tuesday?*

*I am having a small gathering of friends at my
house for dinner. My cook makes an excellent
roast joint and we will be serving at eight. I live
at Wharton House along the Petersfield Road.*
Yours,
Julian Birch

Amanda's first thought was that the suggestion was outrageous. To go to a single man's house for dinner? There were two thoughts that stopped her from rejecting it out of hand. One was Birch's handsomeness, of course. It would be at the very least aesthetically pleasing to see that face over dinner. But the other was the idea that if the miniatures weren't in the crates, then Birch might know where they were. She had told her story to Comstock; perhaps he had relayed the information, but perhaps not.

It was presumably a mere formality to ask Lady Brandon if Amanda could go out for an evening, but Lady Brandon issued a caveat. Amanda would go in her own carriage, with her footman staying to wait for her. And he would have orders to bring her home at ten, ostensibly so that Amanda could help Lady Brandon to bed. At first she thought such precautions unnecessary, because she could defend herself, but by the next day Amanda was glad Lady Brandon had arranged them.

16 – Dinner for Two

Wharton House looked perfectly respectable, thought Amanda as she stepped down from Lady Brandon's carriage. She had again chosen her plain gray wool, as it was only a small gathering and the night was cold. Her spectacles had fogged in the carriage. She felt rather foolish as the footman prepared to wait with the driver, a meal in a basket their only supper. No other carriages had stayed.

Amanda was let in by a butler rather younger than she had expected and shown into the parlor. The house wasn't large, and she could hear the clattering of plates in the kitchen. A roaring fire had been laid, and the warmth made Amanda sleepy.

Julian Birch joined her within minutes, his smiling face beaming at her.

"I am so glad you decided to come," he said. "I wondered whether my invitation was too forward."

"Not at all, Mr. Birch," she said graciously. "I have business to discuss with you when you are not busy with your other guests."

A look of confusion crossed his face, then changed to earnestness.

"The other guests, I am sorry to say, declined. Two had previous engagements, and one is ill. I am afraid my invitation was rather sudden."

"I see."

She was alone with him. Well, perhaps not alone, with a house full of servants and two of Lady Brandon's men outside the door. She considered bringing this fact up now, then decided to wait. The precautions were somewhat embarrassing.

"However, my cook has been working all afternoon, and has quite the feast ready early. Are you hungry?"

"I am indeed."

In reality, Amanda had no idea if she were hungry. Mr. Birch's courtesy and manner were so wonderfully smooth and friendly, she wondered why Lady Brandon would have been concerned. He radiated an invigorating kind of energy that filled the room.

The table was large, with only the two place settings. Mr. Birch sat at the head, with Amanda to his right at the corner. A man in livery entered and served the soup and filled her wine glass.

Why, thought Amanda as she ate, would a solicitor have a liveried servant? And in such a small house? He must earn rather more money than she thought.

"Miss Goodwin, do tell me what you do with your days. Is it interesting being a companion?"

As she talked about her daily tasks, Mr. Birch listened attentively, interjecting questions that made her job sound more interesting than it was. She began to feel rather proud of being a companion. Over roast and potatoes and more wine, he asked her about the books she read, and whether she followed politics.

At first the undivided attention flustered Amanda. As a companion, she was accustomed to being on the side in conversations. Her place was always understood. Here with him, she wasn't sure. She recalled the conversation between the two women at the funeral, where Birch was considered a flirtation rather than a marriage prospect. Why, as charming as he was, had he not found a wife?

Wine was served with each course, and Amanda became less unsure of herself as they continued to converse. Over pudding, she introduced her subject.

"Mr. Birch—"

"Call me Julian, please." He leaned forward, his eyes holding hers.

"Julian." She took a deep breath. "I do not know whether Mr. Comstock told you about the miniature I am seeking. I believe it is among George Soffitt's items, which are in your firm's custody."

"No, he did not. What miniature?"

As she explained about Grandfather, his expression followed her own emotions. He looked concerned and shook his head as if a wrong had been done to her.

"Forgive me, Miss Goodwin—may I call you Amanda?"

She nodded without thinking.

"Amanda, do forgive me. I knew nothing of this. I have been concerned, however, because there seem to be others who are also interested in Mr. Soffitt's goods. I have had the items list stolen from me, and the shed that contains the crates full of his property has been burgled."

Amanda made every effort to look surprised.

"Most importantly, I supervised the packing of most of the crates, and do not recall seeing any miniatures at all. I cannot imagine how painful this must be for you, with your grandfather wanting so much to see his wife one last time."

His voice was so sympathetic, his face so concerned, that Amanda felt tears forming. She had no handkerchief; she had never needed one. Julian took one out of his pocket and handed it to her gently, then put his hand over hers as she dried her eyes. All the emotion of the search threatened to come out, and she did not want to start sobbing with a man she barely knew.

"I can see you are overwrought, and no wonder," he said, rising. "Let me get you some brandy, and let us sit somewhere more comfortable."

He led her into the back parlor where there was a small sofa, then went to the sideboard to pour her a brandy. Amanda rarely drank more than a glass of wine with dinner, or a bit of port in the evening. She drank a sip and a knot began to untie inside her, a knot she hadn't known was there but that she must have had since her quest began.

"Then I suppose it's hopeless," she said. Her spectacles were fogging so she removed them. Julian took them and put them on a side table.

"It is an object," he said, philosophically. "Perhaps our experiences in life are more important than objects. Your grandparents must have had many happy years together that he can remember."

"Yes, they did," she sniffed. "I suppose that will have to do."

"Experiences are what life is made of," he said, beside her on the sofa now. He took her hand and lifted it to his lips. Her heart beat faster, and she looked up at him. Such a beautiful face.

He looked into her eyes and his were serious now.

"I would give you so many beautiful experiences," he said softly. "Whatever you desired."

Through the fog a memory hammered through, and she took her hand away, standing to cross the room to fetch her spectacles. She put them on and faced him stolidly.

"What I desired when we met," she said firmly, "was the list of Soffitt's items. You would not give me that list unless I agreed to dine with you. When that wasn't possible, you refused again. Now you say the list has been stolen. Mr. Birch, I do not believe you are being honest with me."

He rose and picked up her glass.

"You are upset," he said kindly, "and I understand. Perhaps more brandy would settle your nerves."

"I do not need my nerves settled," she said more fiercely. "What I needed from you was some help retrieving an item of importance to me. Yes, I know it is just an object to you, but to me it is also a promise, a promise that would help rectify what George Soffitt did to my family."

"Amanda—" he began.

"I am Miss Goodwin to you, sir. Would you please inform your servant that I am ready to leave, and would like my coat?"

There was a pause as Birch stood, the glass in his hand, his eyes narrowing as he observed her. His face changed, no longer placid and friendly but more intent, as if he were deciding something.

"Of course, Miss Goodwin. I am so sorry to have offended you." His tone was formal. He pulled the bell on the wall, and the servant appeared with her coat.

As she stepped into the carriage, the footman said, "You must have been watching the clock, miss. It's exactly ten." Lady Brandon may have been wrong about her needing male watchmen, but she'd been right about the time.

17 - Another note

It would not be correct to say that Jack had been expecting the blackmail letter. He had assumed that Soffitt's death might put an end to them. But now he realized that this was unlikely; however much Soffitt had taken from people, there would always be someone to take his place. Perhaps he had just hoped it would take more time than this. The man had only been dead a fortnight.

While phrased differently, the intention of the note was the same.

> *Dear Sir,*
>
> *This letter is to inform you that your previous business arrangement with Mr. Soffitt has resumed, and that I have been assigned to accept the payments from this point.*
>
> *Please remit £20 to the post office and savings bank in Portsmouth, Queen Street, care of Soffitt and Sons. The same will be expected each month, delivered on the 20th of the month as usual.*
>
> *Yours.*

There was no signature, just as there was no Soffitt and Sons, and Jack was not amused by the name the new blackmailer would use to retrieve the funds. It was as if it were a blackmail company. The price was more than before; it now amounted to two months wages for a skilled tradesman. Jack was not a skilled tradesman. He had the money, just. But every time he paid it he ground his teeth so much his jaw hurt.

If he could only find the papers, there would be nothing to blackmail him with. But if they weren't among Soffitt's things, where were they? Was there someone Soffitt trusted enough to give them to for safekeeping? Soffitt's only sibling, a sister, had died a spinster years ago. She had run a branch railroad she had won in a card game, making her as devious as her brother. No one had mourned her death either.

The doctor? Jack had met him for only a few minutes, having entered Naedre Manor as he was closing the old man's eyes. He had been the village doctor from Nyewood, and when Jack asked he confessed he had never met the old man. One of the maids for hire had contacted him because her mother knew his wife. One would hardly trust a village doctor with something so important, and surely one more item held for blackmail would have no particular import. For Soffitt, it had served its purpose.

Jack put the letter away. He would not pay this one immediately. It was only the 11th. There was still time to find the papers and put an end to this arrangement. Still time to clear his family's name before its origin was revealed to all and sundry.

And it was time to concentrate on preparations for the Naval Festival Ball. It was one of the highlights of the autumn season in Portsmouth. Anyone even remotely associated with the Navy would find a way to be there. Women would be dressed to the nines, wearing their finest jewelry. He returned to the list he had been making.

Lady Vance was at the top. She was sure to be wearing the sapphire necklace her commander husband had given her for their 15th anniversary. Lady Denver always wore her agate and diamond bracelet to every event that had dancing, because it sparkled as she moved. Several captain's wives were known to have broaches of high value. The daughters of the local naval elites would wear smaller pieces. The temptation, Jack thought, would be very strong. Inspector Hawk and some of his men would certainly be on duty.

Lady Brandon rarely wore valuable jewelry, but she was sure to be there. It would be very likely that Amanda would accompany her. Jack had vowed to stay away from her after they had been seen together, but this couldn't be helped.

Then it occurred to him. Since he didn't want to be seen, he should adopt a disguise. A naval officer, perhaps? No, he would be a stranger to the other navy men and their wives, and they would ask questions and be suspicious. But he needed a way to circulate through the crowd. A servant might work. No one ever looked at those serving them food or drinks. The Royal Naval Seamen's Club in Landport would be closed for the day, and the servants from there would be helping at the ball. He could join them and no one would notice.

He knew one of the waiters at the Club, and that he only worked there on Fridays and Saturdays. The rest of the week he was at the Greenville Inn, just down the road. Good, Jack thought, he hadn't had dinner yet anyway.

By the time he arrived, the moon was coming out and the night was chilly. It would frost tonight, he thought. He liked being aware of weather patterns. When he was a boy he'd wanted to be a farmer, but life hadn't worked out that way. He ordered a beer at the bar, then a chop and potatoes at a small table at the back. Long ago he'd developed the habit of sitting at the back, facing the middle of the room. It made it easier to see everyone.

Will was here, bringing food out of the kitchen, his tall frame making him easy to spot. Jack called him over.

"Good evening, sir," said Will. "Nice to see you again."

"Thank you, Will. I've come in to talk with you. May I have a moment?"

He explained to Will that he needed to help serve at the ball. Will agreed to talk to Mr. Hope, who was organizing the staff, but they could certainly use more help. The ball always needed extra servers; they often went begging for grocers' boys and beer retail workers.

Warm and well-fed, Jack rode home, but his mind wandered. If he was lucky, he could be in the ballroom with Amanda without her being aware of him. If he were honest with himself, he wanted to see her. He hadn't seen her since Sunday, when he'd left her at the cross-roads.

But he'd thought about her every day, picturing her in his mind. He'd look up and imagine her glaring at him, then asking for his help. Her quixotic nature enchanted him, compelling him to switch moods at her whim. He suspected that inside she might be afraid, that her heart had been bruised at some point in her life. And now, despite the risk, he would see her at the Naval Festival Ball. But the ball was no place to make love to her–he had serious work to do.

18 - The Naval Festival Ball

It was the social event of the season, well worthy of London but with a Portsmouth seafaring attitude. Held at the Naval College, the ball was a chance to wear one's uniform and medals on a society occasion rather than a funeral or something more formal. And for the women it was an opportunity to show one's taste with a dress expressly made for the occasion if one could afford it. The ball capped a week of festivities that including the spectacle of crowds on the beach watching the ships sailing in the harbor, visits by vessels from other countries, and a parade of troops. Despite the welcoming of ships from other nations, the massive fortifications made it obvious to all that England was not to be trifled with by foreign powers.

The chandeliers were ablaze in the college's ballroom, which was large enough for several hundred people. It was impossible for everyone to dance, however, so for most of the evening over half of those in attendance were conversing in small groups instead. The crowds came as a shock to Amanda, but Lady Brandon seemed in her element, using her cane to navigate and gently push people out of her path. The chairs at the sides of the room seemed to be full, and Amanda had to keep herself from laughing as Lady Brandon went directly to the chairs in the quietest corner and just glared at the two young ladies occupying them. They stood immediately and giggled their way onto the dance floor.

Amanda was relieved to have a seat, but her task was to make Lady Brandon comfortable.

"May I fetch you a drink, my lady?"

"That would be very kind, Amanda," said Lady Brandon, looking about for people she knew.

Amanda saw no refreshment table in the ballroom, but she could see waiters in black and white uniforms, taking orders from guests. She caught the attention of one of them, and he came over to her.

"Yes, miss?"

Amanda gasped, then dropped her voice to a whisper. "Mr. Strawman! What the hell are you doing here?"

He gave a small bow. "My job, Miss Goodwin. May I help you with something?" His eyes were amused, but they were also searching hers.

For a moment she wasn't sure what to say, but was aware of how glad she was to see him. She felt herself smile even though she didn't want to.

"I thought I wouldn't be seeing you again," she said.

"One never knows, Miss Goodwin."

Someone bumped into Amanda from behind, no doubt making their way to the door. She was pushed into Jack, and he reached out to help steady her. Her eyes widened, but he didn't remove his hands from her waist. She stepped back.

"Thank you, Mr. Strawman. I am quite all right now." But she realized with surprise she hadn't really minded.

"Good. I don't think there's enough space in here for one of your leg sweeps."

Amanda made a face at him.

"I came to find a drink for Lady Brandon," she said.

"Of course! Where is she sitting?" he asked, in his best waiter manner.

Amanda gestured toward the wall.

"Excellent. I will get you both something suitable." And he left the floor.

She made her way back to Lady Brandon, still wondering what Jack was doing there. As she approached, she saw that Lady Vance had taken her seat. Lady Brandon was admiring her necklace.

"And those beautiful sapphires, Marjorie! So nice to see them again." Her tone indicated that she had seen them quite a lot.

"Thank you, Constance. I see you are wearing your second-best broach." Lady Brandon had chosen an enamel broach shaped like a lily.

Lady Brandon was about to reply when she spotted Amanda.

"Ah, Amanda! Were you able to find drinks?"

"The waiter will be here in a moment, Lady Brandon. Lady Vance," she said, nodding at her.

Lady Vance did not reply, and gave Amanda a look.

"I sense that I've interrupted your conversation," Amanda apologized. "I believe I will step outside for a breath of air?" Lady Brandon nodded.

Leaving them to spar, Amanda made her way outside. Jewels. That must be why Jack Strawman was here. She did not believe for a moment he was making extra wages working as a waiter. He wanted to steal from these wealthy women.

But he had promised! Or had he? He had promised Amanda that he wouldn't rob anyone in West Sussex, but this was Portsmouth. What a louse! She began walking faster. Should she report him to the Portsmouth police? There was no point just yet, of course. He hadn't stolen anything, as far as she knew. But once he did, she would tell the police who he was.

It occurred to her she'd already done that, already given his name to Inspector Hawk. They had been unable to find him. But here he was. Perhaps if she found a constable, she could explain that the Jack Strawman they had been looking for was right there in the ballroom, serving drinks. Then they could arrest and question him.

Or, she thought, I could just wait. Perhaps I could catch him doing it and be a witness when they caught him. Yes, a much better idea. She proceeded quickly to the ballroom and returned to Lady Brandon. Lady Vance was gone and Jack was handing Lady Brandon a glass of punch. Amanda sat next to her, and he handed her one too.

"Thank you," she said, not looking at him.

"You're welcome," he said, and she could feel him looking at her.

He left, and they sipped their punch and listened to the distant strains of the Royal Marine Light Infantry Band playing a tune for a quadrille.

"Who was that?" asked Lady Brandon quietly.

"I'm sorry, my lady?"

"The waiter fellow. You know each other." Amanda looked at her, appalled. "I am not blind, my dear, only old."

Amanda debated what to say to her. Anything she could come up with would be a lie.

"That's Jack Strawman."

"I thought as much." Lady Brandon took out her fan and fanned herself. The room was getting rather warm.

"You did?"

"I did. Is he here to relieve some of these women of their jewelry, do you think?" She touched her lily broach.

"I don't know, but he could be." She was relieved to be telling Lady Brandon, even if the whole thing was shocking. "Should I tell the police?"

"Have you seen him doing anything untoward this evening?"

Amanda had to admit that she had not.

"Then do not be concerned, my dear. Inspector Hawk is around here somewhere; I saw him earlier. I am sure he will apprehend Mr. Strawman if he does anything. Perhaps he is only being a waiter." She took a sip of her punch. "But Amanda, if he is up to no good—"

"Yes, my lady?"

"Tell him to start with Lady Vance."

19 - Off to London

My dearest Amanda,

It is my fond hope that you are enjoying and learning from your time as Lady Brandon's companion, and that you are having both time to read, which I know you love, and to continue your studies of agriculture. Although not an exciting life, being companion to such a strong woman should be an enjoyable experience.

Life here at Lufstow continues as always. Thank you for the money you sent last week; it shall go directly to the repair of the barn, which has a leaky roof with the holes covered in oilcloth. The cows are doing well, and all the grain and hay have been stored, so it is important to fix the roof.

Our helpful neighbor Mrs. Lowry has insisted that I include in this letter a report of Doctor Kirk's visit on Friday last. He is unhappy about my swollen legs, which force me to sit down when I would rather be out working in the fields. He has leeched them once, which was helpful, but says with his 'scope he

*can hear my heart working too hard and has
diagnosed dropsy. I now have digitalis drops
each day, and feel much better.
If the weather holds, I hope you will be able to
visit for a winter holiday, but Lady Brandon
may have need of you there.*

I remain,

yr loving grandfather

Amanda put the letter in her lap. The letter had arrived this morning, and she'd taken to reading her grandfather's letters outside the house, this time in the orangerie. Some of the letters, like this one, brought tears to her eyes even when they were cheerful notes.

She was aware of the dangers of dropsy, however, and although she was reassured somewhat by the foxglove remedy, she knew that the ailment meant her grandfather was finding it harder to grow old. Amanda remembered Mrs. Lowry, who lived on the farm next to Lufstow. Without her, Amanda would worry a good deal more about her grandfather being alone. Mrs. Lowry was a widow with a number of workers on her property year-round, and she had agreed to share their labor with Grandfather. He thus had few worries about hiring more people each season; he simply shared the expense.

Sometimes Amanda wished that Mrs. Lowry could write to her too, so she could know what was going on with her grandfather from another person's point of view. It was hard not to be there herself. How difficult were things for her grandfather? Was he able to get dressed to work each morning, make a hot breakfast, remember his new medicine? But Mrs. Lowry did not know how to write, and she could not observe him all the time. She had her own farm to run.

Time could be running out for Grandfather, thought Amanda. The feeling of time pressure to find the miniature was inescapable, but she was glad she hadn't told him she was trying to reclaim it. If she had, her failure would have made her even more miserable. He assumed it was gone forever, and while he may be right, Amanda still felt she might find it, if she could only think where it might be. Jack Strawman had been less help than she had thought.

She looked out the orangerie windows and could see the sun was getting high in the sky.

"Oh, hell," she mumbled, walking as quickly as she could back to the house. It was Saturday, when Lady Brandon liked to take a long walk in the gardens after breakfast. Although her routines were not inflexible, if no other activity had been planned the usual ones would prevail. She got back to the house as quickly as she could, but instead of waiting for her in her coat and hat, Lady Brandon was upstairs at her writing desk.

"There you are, Amanda. I've decided we should arrange to go up to London soon for the next few weeks, instead of waiting until Christmas. My niece will be there for the Season, and I would like to see her and my sister. Penelope will make lists of what to take with us for the house, but as I still don't have a lady's maid I'd like your help with gowns and jewelry."

Amanda was surprised and then chagrined. She had thought they weren't going up to London until the 20th of December, so she hadn't thought about it. But now it was a problem. She wanted to visit her grandfather, and she was hoping to find the miniature first. How could she search for the miniature if she was in London? How could she see Jack Strawman? This last thought made her jump—why should it matter whether she saw Jack Strawman?

"I would be happy to, my lady. May I inquire why we are going sooner?"

"Oh, several reasons. First is that Lady Vance has begun her talking campaign, and I would rather not be in West Sussex for it. Too many callers will come just to be snide. I am also looking forward to the townhouse, which can be kept warmer than here. My rheumatism, you know. I am thinking of consulting a Harley Street doctor."

Amanda had not known of any firm diagnosis, but she had seen the increasing use of the cane and the tiredness, so perhaps that was the reason for it. If another doctor would help, that would be a good idea.

"And of course several of the Portsmouth traders spend time in London. Mr. Burdett, in fact, will be in Town soon to assist with the tuning of instruments for the Kensington balls."

Ah, thought Amanda. Now we get to a genuine reason to go to town. She was rather glad she had figured out the relationship between Lady Brandon and Mr. Burdett.

"Yes, my lady. I will begin with the gowns."

Amanda did not mind doing lady's maid work, although she wasn't trained for it. Lady Brandon made far fewer demands than she had expected, and always treated her with respect. And although her ladyship was far from infirm, she could use the help.

The morning of their departure, crates and luggage were loaded into the carriage and the wagon, and Amanda was just settling Lady Brandon in her seat when Mr. Birch appeared. He approached the carriage and, seeing Lady Brandon, removed his hat, his blond tresses moving slightly in the breeze.

"Good morning, Lady Brandon. What a beautiful day for a journey."

"Good morning, Mr. Birch. We are almost underway."

"I have come to talk with Miss Goodwin, but I promise I will only keep her a moment."

"Amanda?" Lady Brandon asked.

"Very well, Mr. Birch," said Amanda. "But I only have a moment."

He took her a few steps away from the carriage.

"Miss Goodwin, I want to tender my sincerest apologies. I know I offended you when you visited my house." His earnest face looked truly contrite.

"I forgive you, Mr. Birch."

"I also want to apologize for not being more help to you, finding the miniature. I have looked at the manifest and through the boxes, but they aren't in there."

Amanda already knew this, so she just looked at him.

"I see."

"I want us to part as friends, and I hope to see you again when you return to Heddington Hall."

Amanda looked at him closely. Perhaps she should give him another chance, but all the same she was glad she would be in London for a while.

"But I also wanted to warn you," Birch continued. "That man you were with in Petersfield. I don't for a moment believe Lady Brandon sent him for you," he said, nodding toward the carriage. "You introduced me to him as Jack Strawman, and I heard that the police were looking for him in Portsmouth. So I asked my legal friends in the area and discovered something I came here to tell you: that man is not Jack Strawman."

"He isn't?" asked Amanda, her brow creasing in concern.

"That's why the police couldn't find him. His real name is Peter Joshua, and he's a high-stakes gambler in London. I cannot tell you what he was doing in Portsmouth, but do be careful, Miss Goodwin. It wouldn't do for you or Lady Brandon to mix with that sort of fellow."

He bowed over her gloved hand, gave her a gentle smile, and left.

20 - A Chance Encounter

Amanda had been to the London townhouse the year before, and enjoyed her visit very much. The city was exciting, with its bustling traffic, theatres, concerts, and amusements. But this year, by the time they arrived the rain was pouring and the afternoon was cold. The footmen struggled to get the cases and crates in from the mews, while the staff lit fires in the kitchen, parlor, and Lady Brandon's bedchamber. As soon as it was warm enough, Amanda helped her up to bed for a rest.

She then sat down to write her grandfather and tell him her address for the next few weeks. While the library at the townhouse was smaller than the one at Heddington Hall, it still had a good number of volumes, including Thomas Hardy's *Under the Greenwood Tree*, so Amanda was able to read for the rest of the afternoon.

But she had trouble concentrating, as her mind drifted to Julian Birch and Jack Strawman. They were alike in their intensity, but different in every other way. Birch was attractive, smooth, and polished. She had played that evening at his house over in her mind several times, each time balancing Birch's winsome personality with his refusal to help with the miniature unless he was given the opportunity to seduce her. She had allowed that situation to go as far as she intended to allow it to go.

Jack Strawman, on the other hand, was continually amused by her, and argued with her, and yet he had never taken advantage of her or made her feel uncomfortable. However, he was not who he appeared to be, but rather a gambler known here in London.

The ridiculousness of the situation had not escaped her. In a sense, Birch was the more open and honest of the two. It was quite clear what he wanted. He seemed to be neither a thief nor a liar, while Jack was both. Birch was so attractive he made you catch your breath. And yet, when she closed her eyes, it was Jack's face she saw. He had tried to help her find the miniature, and he had even done for her things he clearly thought unnecessary, like posting the manifest back to Birch and Comstock.

On the other hand, he wasn't Jack Strawman. She suspected that, of course, since the beginning. But somehow she had wanted to believe that he was only a common thief who was clever enough to avoid being caught, or a Robin Hood who stole from the rich to give to the poor. Was he only stealing to feed his gambling habit? That added another bad mark to his character. Gamblers were selfish, and they could be violent about debts unpaid. How could he be so angry about Soffitt's swindle when he was a swindler himself? Is this the secret Soffitt had held over him, the information that would ruin his family name?

The next day, Mrs. Brandon had invited Mr. Burdett to the townhouse for luncheon, and he had accepted. The rain had stopped, although the sky remained gray. Once she had eaten, Amanda excused herself but her exit was hardly noticed. Feeling trapped in the house, she decided to go for a walk in Regent's Park. There were a few brave souls like herself, wrapped in mufflers and wearing woolen caps, trudging along the paths. Chilly or not, it was a place with grass and trees, and Amanda felt she could think better in the open air.

Because she was thinking about him so much, she fancied that she saw Jack Strawman everywhere. Oh dear, she thought. I must change the name. Peter Joshua. She thought she saw Peter Joshua everywhere. Then she'd get closer and realize it was her own wild imagining.

This could not be what Grandfather meant. She was supposed to be an independent woman, not a lost soul meandering in the park. London was a source of information, she thought. Perhaps there were people who knew where miniatures from country estates would be sold. Perhaps someone here knew more about George Soffitt—most of his victims were here in town, after all. She could ask about, find others who had suffered at his hand. She felt embarrassed that she hadn't thought of that at the funeral.

Her other task, she reminded herself, was to be of use to Lady Brandon. A lady's maid might be found more easily here in town than in West Sussex, and a Harley Street doctor might help her get around more easily.

Amanda began to walk with longer strides, and more determination, her head down. There was no point in mooning about. London was a large city full of gossip and information. Things could be learned here if she kept alert and took advantage of what the place had to offer.

She was so busy thinking that she bumped directly into a gentleman in a large wool cape and top hot. They both stopped, and she looked up to apologize.

And there he was. Not an imagined Jack, but the real Jack. But not Jack, she reminded herself. His face lit up as he looked at her. She looked at him first in surprise. Then her eyes narrowed.

"Pardon me, Mr. *Joshua*," she said, biting off each word even as she apologized.

He blinked.

"Miss Goodwin. I am delighted to see you." But it came out more like a question.

"Are you indeed, Mr. Joshua?"

They were in the middle of the path. Other chilly walkers were grumbling as they were forced to walk around them.

"May I suggest we sit on this bench, Miss Goodwin?"

She looked around, then marched over the bench and sat down firmly, crossing her arms in front of her chest, staring straight ahead. He sat next to her and she could practically hear the wheels turning in his head as he decided what to say.

"Are you inventing another lie, Mr. Joshua?" she said smoothly.

"No," he said, and sighed. "I am trying to think how to apologize, and to tell you why I was using another name."

"Because you didn't trust me with your real one, obviously. And do you know something? I knew it all along. A straw man isn't real, is he?"

"True, but I am very real, I assure you."

"A straw man is one devoid of integrity. Most appropriate." She turned her face away from him but did not really see the woman and child crossing her field of vision, hurrying down the path.

"Miss Goodwin, I had no choice. I could not use my real name in West Sussex or Portsmouth."

"Because there were people there that you had cheated out of their money at the gambling dens?"

"I never cheat, Miss Goodwin."

Amanda let out a sound that was very close to a snort.

"Then why the false name, Mr. Joshua?"

"Please don't say 'Mr. Joshua' with that tone, Miss Goodwin. I needed the other name to protect my interests."

"Of which you have many, I'm sure."

"I wish I could explain further. There were a few gentlemen in town and country there who owed me money, and were pretending not to have it when they were here in London. By traveling under an assumed name, I could find them without them knowing I was looking."

That sounded logical enough, thought Amanda. But he was still a double-damned liar.

"And were you successful, Mr. Joshua?"

"Somewhat, yes. I found one of them."

"Good for you. So the papers and Mr. Soffitt—that was all a lie?"

"Not at all, Miss Goodwin. I am still most serious about the papers."

"Then why are you in London?" she asked, turning and looking him in the face.

Their eyes locked. Oh yes, he was much more handsome than Mr. Birch, in a reckless sort of way.

"I was hoping to find the papers here. I discovered that Soffitt had a bank box in the City," he said gently.

"Where would that be?"

"At the National Safe Deposit Company vaults in Queen Victoria Street."

Amanda's curiosity won out over her anger.

"You don't suppose my miniature could be there too?"

Peter Joshua looked out across the park. "I am sorry, but I think that is unlikely. As you told me, there was nothing special about that miniature. However, if it is there, I will find it."

"But you are a gambler, sir. If you find it, how do I know it will be returned to me?"

"I give you my word."

The word of a man who used to have one name and now had another. The word of someone who lied like most people breathed. But it was all she had.

21 - Safety Deposit

The building at One Queen Victoria Street was right on one of the busiest corners in the City, at Poultry near Cornhill. But Peter Joshua, formerly known as Jack Strawman (a name he now regretted as too obvious), was stationed at the corner of Mansion House across the street. Deciding what to wear had been tricky. A working man standing around might cause no comment, but if necessary he needed to be able to enter the building. So he had decided on a modest banker's suit and one of the new bowler hats.

He found the hat quite silly compared to the caps he usually wore while in disguise. Apparently bowlers were first adopted by toffs who didn't want their hat knocked off by tree branches while chasing foxes. But it was becoming the preferred style among young clerks and bankers in the City, so he was less likely to be noticed. He easily adopted the behavior of a man waiting for someone. He was less sure that he could keep that up all day.

The National Safe Deposit Company opened for business at ten, and Peter watched as clerks came and went. The occasional Important Personage would dismount from a carriage, usually carrying a box, and scurry in. Everyone knew the deposits were utterly secure.

The building was the first to be both fireproof and burglar-proof. It had three sub-basements sixty feet into the ground which housed the vaults. The walls were ten feet thick and reinforced with steel, and it took three officers to open the vault doors. Any attempt to circumvent the security system flooded the vaults with water.

Peter had no way to access the vaults, much less Soffitt's safe deposit compartment. Only wealthy people could afford such security. Instead, he stood on the corner and waited. Within an hour, he saw a figure who could only be Mr. Birch approach the door. How gratifying to know that Robert, the doorman at the hotel and a friend, was correct about Birch's movements. For the next half hour Peter continued to pretend to wait, checking his tarnished old pocket watch and looking up and down the street occasionally. His next move would be fairly simple, but he'd like to perform it further away from the Lord Mayor's house, maybe even out of the City Police's jurisdiction.

When Birch left the building, Peter followed. His prey walked swiftly down Cornhill, then turned suddenly into an alley. Peter turned and could not see where he had gone, but there was only one door before the alley ended, so he knocked on it.

A large man in a tall hat opened the door.

"Good morning, sir."

"Good morning. I would like to speak with Mr. Julian Birch, please, if I may."

"There is no one here of that name, sir," the man said smoothly. Peter realized his whole body was blocking entry into the building.

"But I believe I saw him enter less than a minute ago."

"Are you a member, sir?"

Peter knew that if he asked a member of what, he obviously wasn't one.

"No."

"Then I am sorry, sir. Good day." He closed the door.

There was nothing to do but wait again. He stood on Cornhill across from the alley for two hours, until hunger gnawed at him, but no one came out. Perhaps Birch had gone in to meet someone for early lunch, if this were some sort of club. Or perhaps he had gone out the back, or there was another exit from the alley.

My skills are getting rusty, thought Peter. *He must have known I was following him.* There was nothing for it but to lurk instead in his hotel lobby, so he searched along the busy street for a hansom to return to the Clermont when he heard a voice.

"Mr. *Joshua,* what are you doing?"

He turned in shock to see Amanda, in a thick woolen cloak with a muff. Two clerks passing almost bumped into him.

"Miss Goodwin! Whatever are you doing here?"

"Following you." She squinted at him.

"For heaven's sake, why? And how? Don't you have companion duties?"

"Lady Brandon didn't need me today. She said I could explore the city. You told me you were going to the Safety

Deposit building, so I waited where you couldn't see me and then followed."

A man passing by hit Peter's foot with his umbrella.

"We are blocking the people walking again," said Peter.

They began walking slowly along the pavement.

"You lost your quarry," said Amanda. "Who was it? I didn't see."

"You didn't?"

"I was too busy following you. I am not accustomed to following people. It takes a great deal of concentration." He noticed that her face was somewhat flushed. She removed her spectacles and wiped them on her cloak, replacing them on her nose.

He was so busy staring at her that he didn't notice the man stopping beside him. Before he knew what was happening another man appeared on the other side of Amanda. His arm was grabbed.

"Right you are, Mr. Joshua. Now you two just come along with us and won't nobody get hurt."

"Just what in hell do you think you're doing?" Amanda squeaked.

The men flanked them, pushing their way through anyone in their path. They were forced down a different, narrower alley, and turned toward a yard at the back of a pub where there was a shed.

Peter could hear the sounds of laughing and singing from the pub, but the yard was deserted. They were closely escorted into the shed, the shift from daylight to darkness blinding them. Peter was pushed to sit on the ground, and his hands and ankles were tied with a cord.

The other man did the same to Amanda, firmly but more gently.

As the men closed the door and left, it occurred to Peter that his disguise might not have been so good after all.

22 - *In a Shed*

"Why the blazes didn't you struggle, or yell at them?" Amanda demanded, shifting as her bottom became uncomfortable on the shed floor.

"I think you were doing enough of that for both of us," said Peter.

"But we might have escaped!"

"I doubt it. They were both very large and very determined."

"So you just did nothing?"

"I was trying to make sure I knew exactly where we were."

"Why?"

"So we can escape without the inconvenience of dealing with the two gentlemen. And miscreants tend to tie bonds more loosely when you don't resist."

"That's ridiculous," grumbled Amanda, pulling on her very tight bonds. She hadn't thought she could be angrier with him than when she believed he'd stolen Lady Vance's necklace. Then she found out he was using a false name. And now she was tied up with him on the floor of a shed somewhere in the City.

"You're just angry because you didn't think fast enough to use your leg sweep," he said.

He could feel her fuming.

"Will Lady Brandon be looking for you?"

Peter was trying to slide his way toward the back of the shed.

"Not until she needs help preparing for bed."

"And when would that be?"

She could hear him puffing his way across the floor.

"Ten o'clock. Unless Mr. Burdett is at the townhouse. Then it would be eleven." She continued to twist at the bonds, but they seemed to get tighter whenever she did.

"Why does she need help preparing for bed?"

Amanda was getting the feeling he was trying to distract her from their situation. It had occurred to her that the men might come back and kill them. But if they had wanted to do that, surely they would have done it already. No witnesses had been in the yard when they were brought here. Nevertheless, Peter's voice was calm and reassuring.

"She has trouble with her legs, and sometimes her shoulders. Lately she's been calling it rheumatism. She uses her cane more now."

"Yes, I saw how she used it at the Naval Ball. Quite effective."

"What exactly are you doing?" Her eyes had adjusted and she could see the shape of Peter near the back of the shed.

"Looking for something sharp."

"Oh," said Amanda. "Would anyone be looking for you?" She knew nothing about this man. Perhaps he had a big family, or was married. Her stomach became upset, and not just because she hadn't had lunch. Perhaps there was a Mrs. Strawman—no, a Mrs. Joshua—somewhere.

Unsure why she was suddenly curious, Amanda was nevertheless aware that the question had top priority. What was the etiquette here? How did one ask a man whether he was married? How did one ask a man such a question when you were both tied up in a dark shed, with an uncertain fate? Why did she care what the etiquette was, anyway?

"Are you married?" she raised her voice so he could hear her at the back of the shed.

"I beg your pardon? Ooomph," he said as she heard a bump.

"Did you find something?"

"Just a rather heavy crate. Nothing useful yet."

He hadn't answered her question. Now she wasn't sure she could ask it.

"Well, damn," she said. "How are we supposed to get out of here?"

"You could consider helping," he said. "Try moving to the edge of the shed. Perhaps there are tools in here."

"That is rather difficult in a dress, Mr. Joshua. But I will try." She tried to put her heels down so she could slide on her bottom. Peter could hear the ripping sound across the shed.

"Blast it all!" she spat. "Why do women have to wear such impractical clothes?"

"I suppose you prefer trousers?"

"I was wearing trousers when we met. They are much easier to move in."

"You were? I don't believe I saw—"

The shed door was pulled open, the afternoon light shone in, and there stood Julian Birch. He looked frantic.

"Oh thank heavens! I thought it was you, but I couldn't believe—"

He rushed over to Amanda first, untying her bonds. She sat up and stared at him.

"What in hell are you doing here?"

Birch was busy untying Peter.

"How could this have happened?" Birch said. "I left my club and visited the pub here to have a drink. I came outside to"—he glanced over at a wall convenient to the back door of the pub—"um, came outside, and I thought I heard your voice, Miss Goodwin. It seemed impossible!"

"We were brought here by two men and locked in. What is this all about, Birch?" said Peter. Amanda thought it sounded like he was clenching his teeth.

"I don't know," said Birch, returning to help Amanda to her feet. She stood and clutched the torn part of her dress in her fist. "My God, did they—?"

"No, Mr. Birch. They only put us in here and tied us up. They did not threaten my virtue."

"Thank heaven. Are you all right?"

"Yes, thank you. Dirtied, but all right."

"Are you unhurt, sir?" he inquired of Peter. "Shall I call the police?"

"That won't be necessary, Mr. Birch. Thank you for your timely assistance. I will accompany Miss Goodwin home."

"I wouldn't hear of it. Please allow me to hail a cab and get you both home." He was leading them back through the alley toward Cornhill. "Where are you both staying?"

"I am staying at the Clermont Hotel," said Peter.

"That's where I am staying too," smiled Mr. Birch. "What an interesting coincidence. And you, Miss Goodwin?" He waved at a cab.

"Lady Brandon's townhouse in Mayfair."

A cab pulled to the curb to collect them.

"Then we shall go to the Clermont first, so your companion can get himself in order, then I shall escort you to Mayfair."

Peter bristled as he sat down across from Birch.

"No, Mr. Birch. We will take Miss Goodwin home first, so she can rest. Then we may proceed to the Clermont."

Amanda quickly became aware that this could turn into a brawl.

"Oh, yes, if you please, Mr. Birch. I am most uncomfortable."

He could hardly refuse. She called up her address to the cabman, instead of waiting for one of the men to do it.

"Yes, ma'am," the driver replied, and they took off. She had achieved the age where regardless of her status, she was called ma'am. It annoyed her, but it could have its advantages.

She mounted the steps up to the townhouse, holding her bedraggled dress closed at the tear. Forsythe came down the steps when he saw her.

"Miss Goodwin! What on earth has happened? Are you all right?" He offered his arm, and she took it. She was suddenly very tired.

"Yes, Forsythe, thank you. I am all right. Where is Lady Brandon?"

"She is resting in the back parlor, miss. She didn't want to go upstairs."

"Then I shall be very quiet as I go up to change. Please, Forsythe, do not tell her the state I'm in. It will only worry and upset her."

Forsythe said nothing, but Amanda was sure she could trust him. Only after she'd gotten to her room, washed, and changed her dress did question Mr. Birch's choice of pub.

23 - Tea at the Clermont

On Saturday afternoon, Peter Joshua watched from the front parlor window as Amanda Goodwin approached the Clermont Hotel. It was perfectly acceptable for women to dine at a hotel, and she was coming for tea, but curious eyes watched as she entered on her own. Peter rose as she approached the table, amused at the formality given what they had been through.

Since their adventure in the shed, he had been considering her safety. But he had also recalled that she had managed the experience with courage and fortitude. And swearing, of course. He hadn't really expected less. And she looked today as though nothing had happened, and she was all business.

"Mr. Joshua," she said curtly.

"Miss Goodwin," he said with a smile, resuming his seat.

She removed her gloves. Had he seen her wear gloves before? She hadn't during the robbery, nor with the horses. Surely she must have been gloved when he met her in the park, but he couldn't recall. Her gown was plain blue but quite lovely, he thought, the dark color bringing out the deep brown of her eyes through the spectacle lenses. Oh, those spectacles.

"May I ask, Miss Goodwin, if you truly need those spectacles, or are they simply convenient to hide behind?"

She stared at him, then simply removed her spectacles and handed them across the table to him. He raised them in front of his eyes and turned toward the window. Everything appeared so blurry that he couldn't tell where he was.

"You need them," he said, handing them back.

"Mr. Joshua, if you are finished examining my eyeglasses, I would like to discuss a possibility with you."

She was about to launch into an explanation when the waiter asked if they would like to place an order for tea. As soon as he left, Amanda resumed.

"I have been asking about the city for information about miniatures. If they were not in Petersfield, and before that were not in Mr. Soffitt's house, and you haven't found them, they might have been sold. If they were sold here in town, I have it on good information that they could be at the South Kensington Museum."

"Why would that be?"

"Because they have been collecting miniatures for some time now, and have a large number of new acquisitions. Some of these, of course, would be from private collections, and feature miniatures from the 16th and 17th centuries, but they have also been acquiring more contemporary pieces."

Peter was careful not to make his admiration show, but he was impressed with her research.

"The problem is," she continued, "that many of them would not be on display, and in fact the recent acquisitions may not have been catalogued. While I could just go to the South Kensington Museum and try to get an appointment with the director, I wanted to ask you first if there was an easier way."

"Why would you need an easier way?"

"Because although you may not have noticed, I am a single woman, and men in positions of standing will not necessarily agree to discuss their business with me. I have previously had trouble with bank managers, doctors, and farmers."

Farmers? Now he was intrigued. Why would she be discussing business with farmers? He struggled to focus.

"I see. And what makes you think that I, a mere gambler, could assist you in this regard?"

The tea arrived and the table was laid with sandwiches and cakes, and a pot of tea. Amanda looked in the pot and decided to wait a moment.

"You seem to know a great many people in your different guises," she said, looking at the teapot rather than him.

Peter considered this. He did know a great many people. Although he was not acquainted with Sir Francis Philip Cunliffe Owen, the director of the South Kensington Museum, he did know Frank Clive, who was in charge of deliveries, who knew the exhibition organizer, who knew the secretary to the curator.

"I shall be happy to undertake your request," he said. "I can visit the museum on Monday morning."

"Excellent," she said, pouring the tea for both of them. "Now what can I do to help you with your quest?"

Peter Joshua had not considered that she might be of service in his search, at least not since they had arrived in

London. And in light of recent events, he thought it a terrible idea.

"Miss Goodwin, we still do not know who put us in the shed. But I am quite sure it was related to my quest rather than yours."

"Very likely," she agreed.

"I think it would be best if I continued on my own rather than endanger you."

There, he thought, he had been a gentleman. And deep inside, the thought of her getting hurt because of him caused him distress. He did not bother to examine this feeling too closely, but he was sure it wasn't only because she was a woman. Now that she knew there was danger, he was quite sure her leg sweep would be of use next time.

Seeing Amanda with her torn and dirtied dress, knowing she was tied up and he could do nothing to help her, had affected him. She could easily have come to harm, either at the hands of those men, or by slow starvation if they hadn't been able to escape for days. Although it had not bothered him at the time, that night and during the nights to come he had been haunted by what could have happened to them, but most particularly to her.

"I don't agree," she said firmly.

"Miss Goodwin, I do not require your consent to engage my own business. I am happy to help you with yours, but someone is obviously most unhappy with mine. I need to find out who that is and why."

"Precisely," she said. "You may recall you said you would need me as a diversion? I am ready for that."

He knew there was no point in arguing. The incident in the shed had caused him to dismiss his plan of using her to divert those who might see what he was doing. Now he didn't want her in that position, which could put her in harm's way. Luckily, he thought, her job kept her occupied much of the time, with the exception of Saturday afternoons.

"And that is why," she continued in a reasonable tone, "I will be informing Lady Brandon of both our quests. I think she will understand and if she does, we will have two advantages we don't have now."

"And those are?"

"More time for me to join you in searching, and access to Lady Brandon's societal connections."

Peter was horrified.

"You'll tell her about being tied up in a shed?"

Amanda wrinkled her nose. "I might omit that part."

"I thought you hated dishonesty."

"That's true. Perhaps I will tell her, then."

"You will lose your position," he warned.

"I do not think so. She can forbid me to do it, of course. But she's always been very kind to me."

During the silence that followed, they ate their cakes and drank their tea, listening to the murmur of conversation around them. She was giving him time to think, thought Peter. How unusual. And she hadn't used a single curse word since she arrived. Also unusual. She must want this very badly.

He considered, aware that a number of things he'd done had been with the purpose of spending time with Amanda. He had shown up in unusual places, where she didn't expect him to be. Admitting that he wanted to be near her wasn't the problem, although he had to wonder why. She was infuriating, and frequently infuriated with him. Yet he had never truly lost his temper with her. Even now when every part of him was screaming that he not permit this collaboration, he knew he was going to agree. But it wouldn't do to make it too easy.

"I do not agree. I think this sort of collaboration would be a terrible idea."

"I was sure you would say that. But I think you may concur after Monday, when I will accompany you to the Museum. I shall see you there at ten."

24 - A Letter Arrives

Sunday dawned bright and cold, and Amanda found herself in the small garden of the townhouse, holding a basket for a bundled up Lady Brandon as she pruned the roses.

"The key to good roses, Amanda, is to trim off all the leaves. The walls here," she said, gesturing to the brick walls surrounding the garden, "keep the warmth in. That is good in the summer, but in fall can make them vulnerable to frost."

"Yes, my lady."

Amanda had little interest in flowers, but there was an apple tree in the garden and one day she hoped to have a grove at Lufstow.

"I read that apples and roses are related, being both of the Rosacaea family. Should we also trim the leaves off the apple?"

"An excellent idea, Amanda. But I would like to finish tidying up the garden today. Tomorrow morning I want to go to Chelsea, with you accompanying me. Your help will be invaluable."

"Why is that, my lady?"

Amanda's heart sank. She had practically ordered Peter Joshua to meet her at the museum at ten, but she would not be able to be there.

"We are going to visit the Physic Garden. I'd like you to take notes and help me navigate the narrow winding paths."

Amanda had to admit that she was more than interested.

"Oh, my lady, that would be delightful. I could learn so much about herbs."

"I only hope there is enough left of the garden to enjoy. I haven't been there since before they built the Embankment. We are due to meet with the curator, Thomas Moore, at ten." She put the last leaf in Amanda's basket.

There was no way to send a note to Peter Joshua to tell him she wouldn't be there, not without Lady Brandon or Forsythe seeing it. Mr. Joshua would likely know it was duty that called her away. All the same, she had wanted to meet him.

"You look far away, my dear," said Lady Brandon. "Why don't you take me up to my room for a rest, then you can trim the apple tree."

After she pruned off the apple leaves, Amanda went into the house to read. Forsythe came up to her with an envelope.

"Miss Amanda, I found this on the steps by the front door. It is addressed to you."

"Thank you, Forsythe."

Amanda's heart beat a little faster. Perhaps it was from Peter Joshua. Then she felt silly getting so excited about a note. She sat down on the settee in the back parlor and opened the envelope.

My dear Miss Goodwin,

As I promised, I have made inquiries to discover the whereabouts of the miniature of your grandmother. Although I did not realize it when I spoke with you, Mr. Comstock had found a record of its likely sale from the day before Mr. George Soffit's death. A box of miniatures was purchased by Peter Joshua on October 24. Mr. Comstock has it on good authority that it was then sold on to an art dealer in Portsmouth.

Your friend,
Julian Birch

She couldn't believe it, but it did not improve on second reading.

"What bloody cheek!" she said to no one in particular. "That bastard!"

All this time he had claimed to be helping her find the miniature, and all this time he had bought it himself the very day they had met, then sold it along with other miniatures even after she told him about her quest. Peter Joshua was just as untrustworthy as Jack Strawman.

She paced around the parlor, furious. How could he? Well, that was obvious. He was a liar and a thief. She had known that from the beginning. But over time she had believed his pitiful statement about harm being done to his family unless he recovered those papers. She had very little information about that. He had never said what kind of harm, or why.

But she had been a font of information for him! She had told him about the miniature that first night and had given him her name. Her real name. Within a few days he had discovered who she worked for and where she lived. But she had never known where he lived until now, when she knew he was at the Clermont Hotel. She was tempted to go over there and show him some of the other moves Li Jing had taught her. No, she'd rather just pummel him.

Maybe she could find those men who had tied them up and help them put him in a shed. Maybe she could drug him and shave off that impossibly perfect mustache while he slept. Maybe she could just find a sword and run him through. Thank goodness she hadn't revealed anything to Lady Brandon. This was all just too embarrassing.

Wait, if he had found and sold her miniature already, what the hell was he going to do at the museum tomorrow? Just laugh at her as they tried to get information, she supposed. He must think this was awfully funny, that she was just a person to be laughed at. Poor Miss Goodwin, how very amusing. Big spectacles but she cannot see what is right in front of her. She was suddenly very glad she was unable to join him tomorrow.

In fact, she planned never to join him again, for any reason. Make fun of her, would he? She would get so angry at him, and he would just smile. A continual source of amusement. Never again. When Lady Brandon returned to West Sussex, she would search the shops in Portsmouth. He could manage his own quest himself, damn him. There was no need to speak to him again.

She was still pacing the room, the note crushed in her hand, when Forsythe came in and told her Lady Brandon required her assistance. She thanked him, took a deep breath, and went upstairs.

25 - Mr. Joshua's Monday

It was well after ten, but Amanda hadn't come. Peter Joshua was beginning to feel quite foolish standing outside the South Kensington Museum. Finally he decided not to wait any longer. Perhaps Lady Brandon had needed her this morning. She had sounded very certain that she could get away, but she might have been wrong. Although she always sounded quite certain when she spoke, Peter was very aware of Amanda's ability to be wrong.

The secretary to the curator sat at his desk trying not to look impatient. He had important duties this morning. A new crate had arrived without papers, and he was supposed to direct its opening and disposition. The exhibition organizer, Daniel, had not come in to work because his wife was giving birth to their fourth child, so he would have to supervise the moving of the cabinets in the main room.

But instead he was waiting for a Mr. Joshua, because Frank Clive in deliveries had asked Daniel who had asked him. It was a simple favor, but one which was becoming more annoying by the moment. When Mr. Joshua was shown in, the secretary struggled to smile, but he rose and motioned Peter to a seat in front of his desk.

"Mr. Payne, it is a pleasure to meet you," said Peter as he took a seat.

"Thank you, Mr. Joshua. I am afraid we have quite a busy schedule today, so if you find it acceptable to ignore the niceties, I would like to inquire what I can do for you."

"Yes, of course. It is about some miniatures, one in particular, that might have made its way into your recent acquisitions. It is a more modern piece, made during the 1820s or 30s, of a woman in blue."

Mr. Payne took out a packet of papers and began to look through it.

"When might we have acquired it?"

"Possibly last month."

Mr. Payne ran his finger down the columns.

"Here we are. Two receipts of miniatures. The first, from a private collection, is all 17th century, with a bit of 18th. The second appears to have only 18th century items." He looked up. "I am sorry, Mr. Joshua, but I do not think we can help you."

Peter stood and thanked Mr. Payne, then left and walked down Exhibition Road. It was a long shot, he knew, that the miniature would be here, but it was worth a try. He couldn't help looking for Amanda as he passed people on the road. Why wasn't she here?

Of course, his own quest he intended to manage without her, but for the moment he had reached an impasse. The papers were not at Naedre Manor, and not at Birch and Comstock. It was possible that, like Miss Goodwin's miniatures, the papers had been sold. The blackmail note, then, would have come from the new owner, the one using the Soffitt and Sons moniker. They would hardly be listed in the Register of Companies. It was a name invented to send a message.

The opportunistic blackmailer would have to realize the significance of the papers. That narrowed down the field, surely. And what about the men who had tied up Miss Goodwin and himself? Did this new blackmailer really have that kind of manpower? It seemed unlikely. Most blackmailers refrain from getting their hands dirty, or hiring thugs.

The only thing he could think of at this point was to advertise. Many problems were solved simply by putting a listing in the *Times*. Hailing a cab for the four-mile journey to the offices of the *London Times*, he considered what his listing should say.

"Would whoever is blackmailing Mr. Peter Joshua please contact this correspondent at . . ."

Not likely. How about:

"Witnessed two unsavory men leading a couple into an alley in the City on Thursday last? Reply to . . ."

That one is possible, he thought. Or:

"Do you know Soffitt and Sons? Please send a letter to . . ."

Perhaps he should try all three.

Having paid for his listings, Peter decided to go to Mayfair instead of returning to the Clermont. Amanda Goodwin had not appeared for their appointment this morning, but perhaps she had been occupied. It was now late afternoon, a time when Peter Joshua imagined older ladies might have their nap. He searched in his pocket for his calling cards. This one? No, that said Jack Strawman. The one with the curlicues? No, that was better for evening. This one was best, the one that just said Peter Joshua.

He knew the townhouse from returning her home after the shed incident. He had been hoping that perhaps one day he would be able to visit like any other caller, only to call on her. For the past several days he had considered whether a traditional wooing, with calls and courting, would be appreciated. Although he had decided that it wouldn't, he felt it would be a good way to let her know he was serious. He let out a sigh. Was he serious? How could anyone be serious with an exasperating woman like Amanda Goodwin?

He certainly found her fascinating, and when she wasn't nearby, he wished she were there. Her directness, her confidence, even her swearing he found refreshing. She made him smile, and it had been years since a woman had made him smile. He had no news that would please her, but it would be logical that he would call to tell her what happened at the South Kensington Museum. Yes, he could have sent a note, but—

Knocking on the door and then stepping back a bit, Peter looked up at the townhouse. While not imposing, it was elegant. He assumed there was a large garden at the back, and thought he might like to see it. It was a bit chilly, but perhaps they could sit in the garden.

A tall man with gray hair answered the door.

"Yes, sir?"

"I would like to see Miss Amanda Goodwin, please." He proferred his card. It was unusual for anyone to call on a Sunday, but the butler showed no look of surprise.

Expecting to be invited in to wait, Peter began to step in the door, but the butler stepped directly in front of him.

"If you will wait here, sir." The butler closed the door and left him, quite literally, out in the cold. Why? he thought. Miss Goodwin was only a companion, not the lady of the house. Was she treated this regally by Lady Brandon? Peter doubted it.

The butler returned. "I am sorry, sir, but Miss Goodwin is not at home."

Peter was stunned. He knew that "not at home" meant she might be home but did not wish to see him. He tried to remember if anyone had ever refused his card, and he couldn't recall a single time. He looked at the butler, who returned his gaze implacably.

"When might she be home to callers?" he asked.

"She does not have receiving hours," the butler answered.

That was true, thought Peter. A companion does not have receiving hours. But in this case he felt he was being fobbed off. She clearly didn't want to see him. Why, for God's sake? He had spent the morning trying to find her miniature, and now she wouldn't be home to him? He thanked the butler and left.

There must be a simple explanation, he thought. Perhaps Lady Brandon forbid her companion to have callers. Could it be that Amanda just didn't want to see him? No, he thought, shaking his head. That made no sense at all.

26 - The Chelsea Physic Garden

The garden had once been larger, going all the way to the river where it got its water. But the construction of the Embankment had put an end to that. The large causeway along the bank of the river, with pipes and tubes underground and a smooth surface on top, provided a lovely promenade but separated the garden from the river. But the Worshipful Society of Apothecaries, whose garden it was, had continued their efforts in the smaller space, and now the gardens were a destination for students, herbalists, and pharmacists. It was also a place for patients like Lady Constance Brandon.

Thomas Moore, the curator, met them at the big ornate iron gates. He was a gentle-looking man of medium height, his beard becoming a line at his jaw and his hair combed neatly back. His suit looked comfortable, almost rumpled, as if, like Lady Brandon, he would rather be gardening than sitting behind a desk.

"Welcome to the garden, Lady Brandon. I apologize for the disarray, but we are still working with the limited space and changing light. Allow me." He had spotted her cane and was offering his arm on her other side. Amanda followed with her notebook.

"We have a large collection of medicinal plants and other herbs, all carefully labelled, and a small library of books. We train apothecaries' apprentices and students from the medical schools. The numbers of medical students has expanded extraordinarily. We used to have only two hundred. Now we have over a thousand."

Lady Brandon replied, "May I assume that is because the Apothecaries now allow women to study medicine?"

Mr. Moore nodded sagely. "Yes, indeed. The women have expanded the numbers of formal students. But there have always been women healers making use of the gardens."

He gestured at the carefully laid out beds, each with a cluster of related plants.

"This area, for example, is herbs for pain. We have here the willow tree, whose bark is most useful."

"Yes," said Lady Brandon. "I have been availing myself lately of willow bark drops. They are quite helpful for the rheumatism."

Mr. Moore would not have dreamed of introducing the subject, but now that Lady Brandon had referred to her infirmity, he could speak with more confidence.

"I think then you might be more interested in this garden bed," he said, leading them along the path. "This is turmeric, which can help with the swelling of what Dr. Garrod calls 'rheumatoid arthritis'," he said, pointing to a clutch of green leaves. "The root is the part that is most effective. May I interest you in a consultation? I have some books I would like to access if you don't mind?" He pointed toward a small building at the edge of the gardens.

"Yes, that would be a good idea. Amanda, why don't you study some of the plants here, and I will return shortly." She continued on Mr. Moore's arm as they proceeded to the building. In the meantime, Amanda went around the entire garden, taking notes of which herbs were good for which conditions. Meadowsweet for digestion, lavender to help sleep, foxglove for heart problems, poppies for pain. She decided that when she had her farm, she would cultivate a corner for medicinal plants.

At least that part of Amanda's life was, in a sense, secure. With or without the miniature, she would inherit Lufstow so long as she didn't marry and have children. Although she wouldn't be able to pass it on, that had never been a consideration. But she was in no hurry. She loved her grandfather, and they simply did not have enough money to run the farm without her work. This meant that when he died, she would need to find a way to finance the farm without his help. She would likely have to find a tenant for it, and continue to try to save money. But she could still dream that one day, she would have the farm and be able to support it. She had so many ideas she'd like to implement. New plants, more animals, even some machinery. But it all took money.

Lady Brandon was returning with Mr. Moore, who was saying, "We are very grateful that you have decided to become a patron, Lady Brandon. The garden is of great use to the training of doctors and chemists, and despite its smaller size we want it to be useful for many years to come."

"You are welcome, Mr. Moore. Not only is the cause worth supporting in general, but in my case it may be of direct assistance. Are you ready to leave, Amanda?"

"Of course, my lady."

"Then it is time to find me a lady's maid."

Amanda watched the city pass by the carriage window. The traffic was heavy, and they were stopped several times on their way to Mayfair because of carts and omnibuses. This was the one disadvantage of London, thought Amanda—the time lost getting from place to place. It was such a large metropolis. It was easy to get lost. And it was easy to know someone and never see them again, even when you were both in the same city.

When next she looked over at Lady Brandon, she could see she had fallen asleep. Her ladyship had not been her usual self the last few weeks, getting slower and needing more rest. Although she was not a young woman, the decline seemed more rapid than Amanda had expected. Perhaps Amanda had been wrong thinking that visits with Mr. Burdett was the real reason Lady Brandon had come to London. The visit to the Physic Garden and to Dr. Garrod may well have been more important, although Lady Brandon would have been ashamed to admit it.

Just like Grandfather. The miniature, Amanda thought as they stalled again behind an omnibus. It would make her grandfather happy to see it. But even if she hadn't found it, she wanted to be able to go see him, and spend some time at the farm. That wouldn't be possible until a lady's maid was found for Lady Brandon, so that should be her priority.

Upon their return to the townhouse, Amanda busied herself with writing the requirements for a lady's maid, then checking the list with Lady Brandon before her afternoon rest.

"Yes, this looks like a good description," said Lady Brandon. "Let us send Penelope to the employment agencies, just the best of them, you understand. She may collect the inquiries, and you and I will conduct the interviews together. I would like to have someone by Friday."

"That leaves only the rest of the week, my lady."

"Yes. Mr. Moore has obtained an appointment for me to see Dr. Garrod on Wednesday, so we should do the interviews on Thursday and decide. I hope to return to West Sussex on Saturday."

They had been in London less than a fortnight. Even if Amanda had been able to work with Peter Joshua, if he hadn't turned out to be such a rat, she would not have had time to do so now. So she must not think about it, but just help Lady Brandon as best she could.

27 - Lady Brandon's Plans

Penelope returned by luncheon the next day with a handful of papers as Amanda was sitting with Lady Brandon in the morning room. There was a nice fire in the fireplace, and her ladyship had found it easier to stay downstairs.

"My lady," said Penelope, "there are quite a number of applicants already, most with excellent references. You could probably begin interviewing tomorrow if you've a mind to."

"Excellent," said Lady Brandon, rising from her chair to walk slowly to the table. She was using her cane at home now too. Penelope laid out the papers.

"I am placing them in three stacks," she explained. "These are young women with experience, who will expect to be paid more, but almost all are prepared for immediate employment. This stack is younger women with less experience but whom we could pay less, all also employable this week. The third stack is a mix: all have indicated a desire to leave London, but some cannot do so until the end of the month."

"Perfect. Amanda, we will begin with the first stack. I do not mind paying more for the best person."

They sat at the table, going through the dozen or so names, putting those with references known to Lady

Brandon on top. Luncheon was served, so they pushed aside the papers. After lunch Amanda helped Lady Brandon upstairs to the desk in her boudoir, where she penned notes to the references she knew and had Forsythe have them delivered.

During Lady Brandon's rest in the afternoon, Amanda found she did not have enough to occupy her mind. The lady's maid search was at a stopping point for now, there was nothing she could think to do about the miniature, and she did not want to ruminate on her misfortune over Peter Joshua. She went out to the garden, but it was too cold and wet to enjoy. Reading or writing a letter to Grandfather would be possible, but she could not concentrate her mind.

Forsythe came in with a calling card.

"Mr. Joshua again, Miss Goodwin." She almost heard him sigh. It was not the butler's job to deliver calling cards to a mere companion. He liked Amanda, but he was already working more due to Mr. Burdett's visits and these calls were interfering with his routine. He was very much looking forward to returning to Heddington Hall, where there was a larger staff.

She did not want to see him, of course.

"Forsythe, I am sorry to ask this, but would you wait a few minutes while I write a reply? He has become bothersome and I want to forestall more visits."

"Yes, miss. I will return shortly."

Amanda went into the parlor quickly in case the insufferable man was trying to peer in through the glass panel at the front door. She took out paper and wrote:

Dear—

Good heavens, no. Not "dear".

Sir,

I regret to inform you that our association is at an end, having discovered through a mutual acquaintance that the miniatures were in your possession from the start of our quest. I wish you the best of luck—

No, she didn't, not without the tone of sarcasm she would use if she were speaking to him. She crossed that out and changed it to:

You may proceed on your venture alone.

She thought of adding that he should not call again, but thought that was clear in the first sentence. Should she sign it? No, that was silly.

For a moment she experienced a pang. He was right outside the door, not ten yards away from where she sat, with the waves in his hair and that intriguing scar and his insouciant smile. Would he be angry at her note, or just go about his business? How would she know? How would she ever know?

She had seen a picture once of a woman, with an angel whispering into one ear and a demon into the other. The angel told her that one does not associate with liars and thieves, especially those who conceal things and play one along. The devil told her that Peter Joshua, despite his innumerable faults, was a fascinating man and that she really wouldn't mind being tied up in a shed with him again.

"Miss?" It was Forsythe, waiting for the note.

She grabbed another piece of paper and wrote:

Albert Memorial at eleven.

"Thank you, Forsythe," she said as she folded it twice and handed it to him.

Mr. Burdett came for dinner, and Lady Brandon had asked if she would mind having dinner with Penelope. Amanda liked eating in the kitchen, although the townhouse kitchen was much smaller than that at Heddington Hall, and conversation with Mrs. O'Reilly and Penelope would be a welcome change.

Mrs. O'Reilly was the cook and loved having people eat in her kitchen. The grooms and maid-of-all-work had eaten earlier, and Forsythe ate in his room, so it was just the three of them. Mrs. O'Reilly was always good for a bit of gossip to go along with the food.

"And did you hear about the new bridge? They say it sways too much. Just finished it but someday soon it will have to come down and be rebuilt. Can you believe it?"

"But there aren't any tolls now," said Penelope, who knew London better than Amanda. "So how will they pay for it?"

"Dunno," said Mrs. O'Reilly, serving both of them more potatoes with their roast pork. "You girls want more spinach?" Every female was a "girl" to Mrs. O'Reilly, except Lady Brandon.

Amanda was having trouble getting any food down at all. Her stomach was fluttering like there were crickets inside it. What on earth had she been thinking? Going out to meet Peter Joshua late at night by the monument was insane.

28 - Moonlight at the Albert Memorial

As she walked to the irresponsible rendezvous, she planned out what she should say. She should refuse to see him again, and avoid being persuaded by what were sure to be lies. As she approached the Memorial, she saw him standing by one of the four large pillars. The moon was waning, but was very bright, and the night air was so cold she could see her breath. Peter Joshua was wearing a large broad-brimmed black hat and a black cloak with its hood up, shrouding his face. But she knew by his stance, leaning against the pillar, that it was him.

"What are you dressed like that for?" she couldn't resist asking.

"Good evening, Miss Goodwin. An assignation late at night requires suitable clothing, I decided. It wouldn't do to be seen."

"Mr. Joshua, anyone who would see us at this hour would not himself wish to be seen."

"True," said Peter, and threw back the hood of the cloak. His face was pale in the moonlight, the dark curls patterned around his face and the mustache, again, perfect. For a moment she forgot how angry she was with him.

"Mr. Joshua," she said with what she hoped was firmness, "you must not call upon me."

"I understand. It's a risk to your position."

That gave her pause. Was it best for him to believe that, or not?

"I shall instead send you notes," he continued. "That will provide less embarrassment, and clearer communication."

She stared at him. Is that what he thought this was about?

"Mr. Joshua, I asked you to meet me because I have come to understand that you already possessed my miniature when I met you, and have since sold it."

She could see his mustache turn downward in a frown.

"Who told you that?"

Amanda had no intention of telling him. "A friend."

"Why would I go to the museum today if I already knew your miniature wasn't there?"

He was being awfully casual about this, and her blood began to boil. She stamped her foot.

"Because you are a bloody liar and a cheat, and I never want to see you again."

She turned away from him, crossing her arms over her chest. She wasn't cold anymore.

"Miss Goodwin, I am on my own search, as you know, for some documents related to my family. I do not need to waste time on yours."

She turned on him.

"You, sir, are avoiding this issue. Did you sell my miniature?"

"No."

"Did you sell any miniatures at all from Mr. Soffitt's house?"

"Yes."

"Then my case stands," she growled, and turned her back on him again.

"Miss Goodwin," he said as he came up behind her. "I see that you are angry with me, again. It seems that you are always angry with me. Can I do nothing right to win your regard?"

Amanda caught her breath. She didn't turn, but said, "Why the hell would you want to do that?"

"Because ever since I met you, I cannot rid you from my thoughts."

She turned slowly, her eyes narrowed. "You are trying to distract me from the point."

He stepped toward her. "And that is?"

He was inches away from her face, his eyes dark.

"Mr. Joshua, I—"

He kissed her, wrapping her in his cloak as he did. Then, suddenly, he jumped back.

"What?" Amanda said, breathless.

"I do not wish to be leg sweeped."

Amanda's heart was pounding. She reached out to slap him, but he caught her wrist.

"None of that, Miss Goodwin. Your instinct to attack on the least approach is, shall we say, somewhat disconcerting. It is like trying to get close to a cobra."

Her feelings high up in her throat, Amanda was tempted to scream in frustration. What would he know about unwanted attentions, about the feeling of powerlessness? She felt powerless now, but she realized it was because she wanted him to keep kissing her. She had stopped him instinctively.

They both heard the tune being whistled at the same time and looked toward Kensington Gore. A constable was walking his beat past the park.

"You'd best take my arm, Miss Goodwin. At this hour, standing in this oppositional posture, the constable will think I am attacking you. We need to look like lovers on an assignation, not boxers ready to begin the match."

She took his arm without thinking, and he placed his hand over hers. They walked along in the park in the same direction as the constable. The constable looked up at them and touched his truncheon to his helmet in greeting.

"I am not sure he believes us," said Peter in a hushed voice. "May I have your permission to be more convincing?"

Amanda, still befuddled, nodded. He turned her to him, wrapped his arms around her waist, and kissed her again. She could feel herself respond, putting her hands up into his hair. His kiss seemed to tingle down her whole body. Everything around them seemed to turn to nothing.

He stopped, but did not retreat this time. Instead, he turned her back on the path, put her arm through his, and continued their slow walk.

Nothing was said for a minute or two. It wasn't that Amanda had never been kissed, but not so many years ago she had been forced to kiss, and it had felt like an invasion. This time, she felt like she wanted to give him more and take more of him. It took more steps, the cold night, and watching the constable turn away from them onto his beat to remember why she had come in the first place.

"I wish I could trust you," she said.

"I understand why you feel you cannot," he said. "Perhaps some day you will."

"For example, you have never told me how you got your scar."

"No, I have not. Is it important?"

Amanda shrugged.

"I assumed it was a duel or something."

"You assume correctly."

They took a few more steps together.

"We return to Heddington Hall on Saturday," she said.

"I am also returning to West Sussex," he said. "I have found nothing here except trouble. All I seem to have done is alert the wrong people that I am looking. I shall return Friday week, and hope that I may call upon you at Heddington?"

"Yes," was all she could say.

That would be less than a week after her own return, but it now felt to Amanda like a long time to be apart. They walked across Kensington Gore and she realized he was escorting her to the townhouse. It was midnight, and nothing was turning out like she thought she would.

29 - Lufstow Farm

The new lady's maid, Evelyn, turned out to be a delight. She was petite, with ash blonde hair arranged in large waves, an obvious demonstration of her skill. She was able to tease Lady Brandon's chestnut hair into a smooth twisted chignon, controlling unruly curls using new Marcel Grateau curling tongs from Paris. She was cheerful, energetic, not given to deep thinking, and not averse to sharing the latest gossip. Lady Brandon found her both useful and amusing.

Having ensured that Evelyn was suitable, Amanda was ready to broach an important subject with Lady Brandon during their next embroidery session.

"Lady Brandon, I have a great favor to ask."

"I think I can guess. You want to visit your grandfather."

They had been back at Heddington Hall for only two days, and Amanda had received another letter from her grandfather that made her unsure about his condition and spirits. Lady Brandon's own condition and spirits had improved. Dr. Garrod, the renowned doctor, had diagnosed rheumatic gout and prescribed colchicum drops and a strict diet. She was already feeling better and moving more easily, although she complained about not being able to eat meat and drink brandy. Her hopeful mood had encouraged Amanda to ask for time off duty.

"You have time that I owe you for being both lady's maid and companion," continued Lady Brandon, "and you have solved that problem as well. Yes, do go visit your grandfather, and give him my best regards. Would you be able to return by Friday?"

Amanda assured her she would.

As she packed her bag, she re-read the note she had received from Peter Joshua the day before.

> *My dear Amanda,*
>
> *I take the liberty of using your Christian name, but I felt that our sympathies seemed to align that night at the Albert Memorial. You have been often in my thoughts, and I hope I may call upon you once I return to West Sussex on Friday.*
>
> *Yours,*
> *Peter*

The "Yours" made her smile. She could not deny she found Peter to be provoking, even exasperating. But she had seen something underneath, and was able to recall several occasions when he had shown consideration for her even as he was teasing her for things she said. But more importantly, he treated her as an equal, not like a fragile flower. She had given up on male company long ago because most young men were like the groom, Timothy, looking to debase her, and most older men expected her to listen to them without speaking much.

They wanted a woman to assure them of their superiority, not counter with their own ideas. It was a role she disliked in the extreme, and one of the reasons she enjoyed being a lady's companion. She was rarely required to dine or converse with gentlemen visitors.

Growing up with Grandfather had made things harder for her, she supposed. He had always respected her opinion and that of her grandmother. Women were people with their own dreams and ambitions, just like men. She wanted to make sure he was all right, but she also wanted to be in his company again, and be at the farm. And she would return on the same day that Peter Joshua would.

Unfortunately, the December day began cold and rainy. Lady Brandon ordered the carriage to take Amanda to the Petersfield Rail Station, but even with her umbrella her gray skirt was speckled with dots of rain when she got in the station. She bought a hot water canister for the ride, to keep her feet warm. The route took her through some of the most beautiful country in Hampshire and Surrey, but she could see nothing with the clouds and rain.

The neighbor, Mrs. Lowry, had sent her worker Johan with the trap to collect Amanda at Witley Station for the ride to Sandhills and Lufstow Farm. Her grandfather was waiting for her in the parlor, where a fire was warming the room.

"Oh, my dear Amanda! Welcome home, child." He rose and opened his arms to embrace her. She smelled the old familiar smells: pipe tobacco, hay, woolen jacket.

"Hello, Grandfather. I am so glad to see you."

He smiled his old smile. Amanda thought he looked a little tired, a little more stooped than when she saw him last. As he walked back to his chair, she noticed he shuffled his feet rather than lifting them. His legs must still be swollen.

"I have the stew on the stove," he said. "Are you hungry?"

The lamb stew was steaming hot and warmed her through. Afterward Grandfather got the bottle of port off the mantle and poured her a glass.

"Now," he said. "Tell me all about life with Lady Brandon."

As she described her life at Heddington Hall, she watched her grandfather closely. There was no slurring of words, no loss of memory. He seemed very much himself, just a little older. Amanda was relieved.

He told her about the farm, how the calves birthed in the spring were all well and ready for winter, how the male calves had already been sold, how the geese were being fattened to sell for Christmas, how Broom the young donkey was chasing around the older cart horse.

"How long can you stay, my dear?" he asked as they rose to go to bed.

"Just a few days, Grandfather. But it is so good to see you."

The next morning the rain had passed, and the sun came out. Amanda's old boots were still by the back door, and she went out to the barn. Grandfather was already there, milking the cows. As she walked around, she looked across the barley fields toward the woods, which she'd always found dark and mysterious. She looked up at the ridge where the two apple trees were and crossed the brook toward the winnowing shed. She heard a few brave birds chirping in the bare trees. She was thinking about Peter Joshua, even though she didn't want to be.

God, how she loved the farm. She had spent too much time elsewhere. It felt like hers, and some day she wanted it to be. As she looked at the birch trees and the meadow and the fences, she was suddenly aware of her ignorance regarding the legalities of the farm. If inheriting it meant she mustn't marry, she wanted some details. Not that she planned to marry anyone, of course. But how could she bring the subject up with her Grandfather? No one wanted to talk about how things might be after they had left this world.

For now, there was breakfast to be made and she should help Grandfather carry the pails of milk to the dairy. The animals were all housed for winter, so they'd need to be fed. There would be no ploughing today given the heavy rain of the last few days, but she could help by churning the milk to make butter and feeding animals.

The sun set a little after four, and by then both Amanda and Grandfather had put in a full day's work. Amanda cooked up some beans with chunks of pork from this year's slaughter and made a salad of beets, endive, and purslane.

"Grandfather," Amanda said as they sat down to dinner, "how can I learn more about the legal situation of the farm?"

"You mean the entail?" His eyes crinkled as he tried to discern what she was thinking.

"Yes, the entail. The conditions under which we can keep the farm."

Grandfather chuckled. "It is all right, Amanda. You want to know about how you keep the farm when I am gone. It has been awhile since I've looked at the entail. Is there something in particular you're worried about?"

Amanda was stymied. She didn't know where to start.

"I want to be clear about the language of the marriage and children portion."

Grandfather finished his salad and put down his fork.

"Amanda, my dear. Why are you worried? Is there something I should know?"

She looked into his bright blue eyes, filled with kindness and concern.

"I—I don't know."

"Then let me get the document itself." He rose and shuffled slowly into the parlor, and returned with a packet of papers, handing it to her.

She removed the plates from their dinner, dusted off the table with her hand, then put down the packet, untied the strings, and opened it flat.

Grandfather thumbed through until he found the page with the entail. He rose again, shuffled back to the parlor to fetch his reading spectacles, and returned to the table. Amanda noticed his shuffling was worse than in the morning.

"What is your question?" he asked, peering at the entail.

"Whether the condition is that the heir not marry and not have children, or whether those are separate."

He raised a white bushy eyebrow, but kept his attention on the paper.

"It says the condition of inheritance is that the heir 'not marry nor produce children'". He took off his spectacles and peered at Amanda. "My dear, are you contemplating marriage?" He said it in a hushed voice, as if the idea were shocking.

"No," she said, then realized that wasn't completely honest. She was considering the idea, which was not quite the same thing as contemplating marriage. "I just want to know what my property rights are."

"Who were you thinking on, then, as you wandered in the fields this morning?"

So he had seen her, mooning about.

"I am sorry to say it's a man, damn it. I think I may have fallen for the absolutely wrong man."

30 - The Entail

Amanda sighed at having revealed her thoughts. Yes, she should tell her grandfather. He wouldn't understand, would tell her she was foolish, would warn her about losing her independence. But he was the one person she could talk to.

"Who is this wrong man?" Grandfather asked.

"Peter Joshua. He is a gambler."

"Goodness, that does sound wrong." Grandfather was very much against gambling of any kind.

"He could, however, be a good man inside. I'm not sure."

"That sounds tricky," said Grandfather.

"I believed he was a liar and a thief. Now I think he might not be as much of either as I supposed."

"Well, I should hope not," said Grandfather.

"I let him kiss me, Grandfather."

He reached out his hand and put it on top of hers. He knew better than anyone why she didn't allow people to touch her, why she was afraid.

"How did it feel?"

"More wonderful than I anticipated."

"I see." Grandfather thought a moment. "You know, my dear, entails can be broken."

"I thought they were unbreakable for generations."

"Well, they are supposed to be. But down the road here in Brook the Morgan farm was entailed, and a solicitor helped them contact the owner and have it revised."

He was not chiding her for being with a man, Amanda noticed. Or for looking into the legal details about marriage and the entail. He was, as always, trying to help with what she wanted.

"But the owner is Mr. Soffitt, and he's dead without issue. Or at least they can't find any children."

"That may make it easier to get it revised. But I don't know any solicitors in the towns around here. I've never needed one. My will is in my desk if ever it's wanted."

Amanda thought a moment, then something occurred to her.

"I know two solicitors," she said. "A firm with two. One I'm not sure I trust at all. That's Julian Birch. But the other, Mr. Comstock, seemed kind and helpful."

"Then you should go see him. If you are sure revising the entail is what you want."

How could she be sure? At first she had thought this was just about the farm, and her attachment to it. But obviously there was more. They were so sudden, these feelings she had for Peter Joshua, and she didn't trust them at all. She could not possibly explain, to herself or her Grandfather, how someone she'd been angry with most of the time could be so important to her.

"It shouldn't be what I want, should it?" she said when they were sitting by the fire enjoying a bit of hot cider. Grandfather reached for his pipe, and Amanda filled it and handed it to him.

"I am not sure we always get to say what should be," he answered. "I have been thinking about this quite a bit lately, thinking on your grandmother. My Emily was a strong and wonderful woman. But it was us, together, that made things work. Not just raising your father, though goodness knows he was a handful. But we built something more than each of us, the two of us."

He took a puff and gazed into the fire.

"But you always taught me to be strong and independent," said Amanda. "You read me Wollstonecraft as soon as I was old enough to understand it. Women have been kept apart from the throng that is dominated by men. We need to be as educated and active as men can be." Amanda was confused.

"Thinking back, I am not sure you wouldn't have been strong and independent, even without that. And I know that any connection with any one person can change who you are. But perhaps that isn't a bad thing. It wasn't for me and my Emily."

Amanda went to bed thinking about that. All this time she had assumed that being on her own and being strong and independent went together. Anything else was a form of dependency, of making herself a lesser person. But if Grandfather were right, that wasn't true. Two people together could make more than either could separately. Not just children, either, but ambitions and dreams.

Her last day on the farm the neighbor, Mrs. Lowry, came over from her farm to see if Grandfather was well and to make lunch. She was pleased to see Amanda.

"I'm making soup, and I will have plenty for all of us," she said, chopping turnips, carrots, and watercress. Grandfather was out feeding the chickens, and Amanda offered to help with the chopping.

"I can't thank you enough for coming over to see to Grandfather," she said. "It eases my mind knowing you're nearby."

Mrs. Lowry gave her a look and lowered her voice. "Much good it will do, me coming over only twice in a week. My own farm keeps me very busy, even with the workers. He really shouldn't be here alone."

"Has he been unwell?"

"He was for a bit, but the digitalis is helping quite a lot. If he could reduce the number of animals, that might be helpful, but he needs them for sale. But he'd have to do much more if you weren't such a good girl, sending the money like you do."

Amanda thought about it. There didn't seem to be a good solution. He couldn't afford to have someone here all the time.

"I would like to move back here, but of course I can't," said Amanda.

Mrs. Lowry patted her hand. "Now, love, don't take me to mean I think you should. Perhaps some day I will convince him to come live with me at my farm. But don't tell him that's my plan, or he won't ever do it." She winked at Amanda.

So Mrs. Lowry did have designs on Grandfather. Amanda was not sure how she felt about that, but it would certainly make life easier for him. On the other hand, Amanda was quite sure he wanted to be independent too, and that he still loved her grandmother. Her conscience began nagging her about the miniature.

Before she left for Heddington Hall early in the morning, Grandfather wrapped the entail papers in parchment and oilcloth, tied with a string.

"Now you take this to that solicitor, Amanda, and don't let him tell you there is naught he can do. I know there is. If this is the same firm working to find Mr. Soffitt's heirs, they can find the one who needs to sign a revised entail, or eliminate it all together. It makes no difference to me, but it could be your future."

Amanda tried not to cry as she embraced her grandfather, then Johan drove her to the station. It was clearer weather today than when she'd come, and Amanda let the fading green fields and brown farmland soothe her as she rode. And tomorrow, maybe even later today, she should receive a visit from Peter Joshua.

31 - The Absent Suitor

It is far too early to be concerned, thought Amanda as she chewed at her fingernail. But the fact was that today was Friday and Peter should have called, or at least sent a note. His note from London had indicated an eagerness to see her, and yet she had heard nothing. She had taken her walk while Evelyn styled Lady Brandon's hair and hemmed her gown, and the walking now seemed to take the form of pacing the library. She had laid out over a dozen books on the library table, and couldn't decide which to choose for reading aloud to Lady Brandon. It would be easier if she weren't so distracted.

There was much to do now that they had arrived back at Heddington Hall. Holiday preparations were beginning. Lady Brandon's relatives, including her young nephew, would be coming to stay in a fortnight, and the closest family would be staying until the new year. Mrs. O'Reilly was in her element in the kitchen. She'd been given a free hand to hire two girls to help in the preparations. The fact that the girls were her friend's children made it even better; they wouldn't dream of not following her directions.

Forsythe was, as usual, put in charge of decorations, a chore he detested and that Amanda detested even more. Nevertheless, he appeared at the door of the library.

"Miss Goodwin, if you would be kind enough to move those books, I need the table to lay out the decorations."

He said the word "decorations" the way many people might say "manure".

"Of course, Forsythe," she said, gathering them up. She quickly decided that it was too early in December for Charles Dickens' *A Christmas Carol*, and chose *Lady Audley's Secret* to place in the morning room and the second volume of Henry Stephens' *The Book of the Farm* to bring up to her bedchamber. The rest she put back on the shelves.

Forsythe went out to bring in the boxes Timothy, pressed into service, had brought down from the attic. Amanda, knowing if she stayed in the room she would be handed candles or the willow wreath and expected to tie in boughs. Already she knew that embroidery would be put aside to sew ivy leaves onto lengths of red ribbon. The best thing to do was make herself scarce, so she went into the conservatory.

The conservatory had been recently renovated. Lady Brandon did not have a great love of indoor plants other than her orange trees, but all the best houses had a conservatory and more callers expected to be shown their friends' latest exotic plants. One of the younger gardeners had been assigned to tend it, and he had made quite a job of it, even going to Kew to look at plant options. It was easier to hide in, now, with taller palms, heliotrope a yard high, and orchids and ferns nearer the ground. Amanda sat in a wicker chair and tried to read the farm book.

She was unable to stop her thoughts returning to Peter Joshua, and his absence. She thought of the farm, then her grandfather, then what he had said about marriage, then Peter Joshua. She played over scenes with him in her mind, at Soffitt's house, in the stable, in the shed, at the Albert Memorial. The words of her book blurred on the page.

It suddenly occurred to her that if Forsythe received a note for her, he wouldn't think to look here, and would be occupied with Christmas decorations. As she went into the morning room, Evelyn found her and told her Lady Brandon needed help for her rest, so she went to help her settle in.

"I am in a mood to be read to," said Lady Brandon as she was settled on the day-bed in her boudoir. "What have you brought me?"

"*Lady Audley's Secret*, my lady."

"Oh, good. I haven't read that one in years." She settled back, closing her eyes. The beginning of the book was all soothing description—the house, the moat, the stagnant well—and before the first character was introduced Lady Brandon was asleep. Amanda looked at her. Perhaps it was just her newly tamed hair, but Lady Brandon really did appear to be in better health. The trip to London had been a good idea.

London, Amanda thought. Could Peter still be in London? Perhaps he hadn't returned at all. Perhaps something had kept him in town. He could have found new information about the papers, or consulted a legal expert or found someone related to Soffitt. Or he could have found more trouble. What had he said? All he had found in London was trouble. The more she thought about it, the more she thought that the men who had captured them, however temporarily, had been looking for him rather than her. They could have found him again.

She chided herself for thinking such drastic thoughts. It was far more likely that Peter was comfortable at home here in West Sussex . . .

And where was this home, exactly? She had first seen him at Mr. Soffitt's house, and after that he seemed to just pop up in places. He had access to some kind of carriage, but it might not have been his own. He was in Portsmouth just as easily. Did he live there? It would be a long way to come to be near Heddington. It started to bother her that she didn't know where he lived. She couldn't even send a note to tell him how perturbed she was that he hadn't contacted her.

Perhaps she had misread his note. Maybe he was just being polite saying he would call upon her. Suddenly she felt embarrassed that she had said anything to Grandfather. Those kisses could just be what he did with unmarried women; perhaps they meant nothing to him. He was a smooth talker, never at a loss for words. He probably told a lot of women he thought about them all the time. It was the sort of thing that could make a younger woman lose her head.

Amanda was not a young woman, and she didn't like the idea that she might have been taken in by a scoundrel. She may have been deluded in seeing something deeper in Peter Joshua. She rose and went downstairs to find paper. The only place to send it was the Clermont Hotel.

> *Dear Mr. Joshua,*
>
> *It is late Friday, so late that this note*

may not reach you until tomorrow. I had hoped to hear from you upon your return to West Sussex, but since I have not I assume you are still in London. Please reply at the first opportunity—

Why? Why should he reply? So that she could make sure he kept his promise? Was it even a promise? She reread the note. It sounded as though this were a business meeting. But she was not ready to lay out her heart on the page if he had just been making midnight conversation. It was so easy to embarrass oneself in a letter.

She decided to just end it:

Please reply at the first opportunity.

And the closing? Not "yours", certainly. "Sincerely"? "Best regards?" No, she certainly didn't wish him the best if he was toying with her.

Regards,

Amanda

She did not want to hand it to Forsythe. Confident that Lady Brandon was napping, she went to the stables, knowing full well that asking Timothy was a bad idea.

"Timothy, could you please take this to the White Hart to put on the mail coach?"

Timothy grinned at her. "And if I do?"

Amanda dug into her pocket and handed him sixpence.

"All right, miss. But next time I will be asking for more." He winked and was about to make one of his inane comments, but she turned and went back to the house.

She wondered too late whether Timothy was nosy enough to read the note, but she couldn't worry about that now. She had done all she could for today.

32 - Meeting with Mr. Comstock

The reply to her note came the next morning from the Clermont Hotel. It was in a large envelope with her own unopened note enclosed within it and only her address on the envelope.

> *We regret to inform you that Mr. Peter Joshua*
> *left the hotel on Tuesday last and did not leave*
> *an address with the hotel for the forwarding of*
> *communications. Our apologies.*

This was not encouraging. Could he have already come to West Sussex? How would she find him if he had? Today was her half-day off, and she was planning to take the entail papers to Mr. Comstock in Petersfield.

Perhaps someone would know at the White Hart. That woman, the one who served their food when they had stopped to look at the manifests, could know. Amanda had been jealous at her open way with Peter. And the barman who took the manifests to be sent back to Petersfield had seemed to know him too. They might tell her where he lived. The White Hart was only a mile out of her way.

The weather seemed like it would stay clear even if it wasn't at all warm, but she took her cloak anyway and made sure the entail papers were carefully wrapped in the oilcloth.

The White Hart was very quiet at that hour of the day, but the door wasn't locked. No one was at the bar or the tables. She went up to the bar and gently rang the bell attached to the post. The woman who had served them before came down the stairs, a man's dressing gown pulled around her shift. She closed the gown and held it together when she saw Amanda.

"What do you want, then?" The look was not friendly either.

"I am looking for—" Amanda remembered that he hadn't been using the name Peter Joshua then. "I am looking for Jack Strawman, the man in my company here several weeks ago."

"The handsome one with the scar?" she asked with a smirk.

Amanda swallowed. "Yes."

"No, he ain't been round here. Lost him, have you?" The woman looked Amanda up and down. "Can't say as I'm surprised."

Amanda struggled to keep her temper.

"Do you know where he lives?"

"No."

Amanda could feel the disappointment show in her face. The girl smirked again but took pity on her.

"He sounds like he's from around here, but I don't think so. Only saw him for the first time a few weeks ago."

A deep, sleepy voice called from upstairs. "Flossie? Where are you?"

Amanda said thank you and left.

Where could Peter be? she thought as she rode. And the woman had said he wasn't from the area, so likely didn't live here. Where was he from, and where did he stay?

She tried to put it out of her mind. People were not necessarily reliable. If he had further business in London, that might have kept him away. She shouldn't be too concerned, and on further thought looking for him at the White Hart was shameful. She hoped that Lady Brandon never heard about it. Time to get back to the business of the entail.

Saturday was market day in Petersfield, and The Square was full of stalls selling cabbages, potatoes, boots, calicoes, tea sets, and more. The groom at the George Inn gave her a smile and took her horse, and she walked over to Birch and Comstock's offices only to find a sign in the window that they were closed for lunch. She bought a cheese and haslet sandwich at a stall, and found a bench just off The Square, wrapping her cloak around herself for warmth as she ate. She had just bought an ale to wash it down when she saw Mr. Comstock come into The Square from St. Peter's Road. She saw him reopen the office and finished her drink.

"Mr. Comstock?" she asked, entering the building. She was relieved to see no sign of Mr. Birch.

"Good afternoon," said Mr. Comstock, his round face smiling. "How may I help you, madam?"

"We have met before," said Amanda. "I am Miss Amanda Goodwin, who came to you about the miniature of my grandmother from Mr. Soffitt's estate."

"Ah, yes," said Mr. Comstock, gesturing her to the seat in front of the desk. "I apologize for my distraction. I have just returned from the magistrate's court, and the morning has been very busy. As I recall, I had referred you to Mr. Birch, who is handling the Soffitt estate?"

"Yes, thank you. Today I am here on quite another matter. It involves an entail."

Mr. Comstock smiled and folded his hands in front of him on the desk. "That, Miss Goodwin, is my specialty. How may I assist you?"

Amanda realized that although many a young woman might want the services of Mr. Birch, Mr. Comstock seemed more trustworthy and was likely popular for entirely different reasons. No wonder their offices were so lavish. She took the packet out and untied it, handing the main document to Mr. Comstock.

"You can see that this entail is originally signed by Mr. Soffitt, but nevertheless my grandfather and I would like to appeal for a revision. It is my understanding that a new agreement could be signed between us and the new owner."

Mr. Comstock perused the document.

"I see, I see," he murmured. "This does relate to the Soffitt estate, indeed it does. But Mr. Birch quite has his hands full with the tangible property, and has not yet had time to examine contracts and such. I believe I can handle this for you, but of course we must find the heir."

"May I ask what happens if an heir to the estate cannot be found?"

Mr. Comstock frowned. "That rarely happens, Miss Goodwin. There is invariably someone with the right to take title." He looked around the office. "Unfortunately, Mr. Birch is still in London, and is not due to return for several more days. I will review what he has done and write to him in London. I will also write to a colleague of mine in Inner Temple and ask him to advise me. How may I reach you when I have more to tell you?"

Amanda gave him her address as Heddington Hall, which caused Mr. Comstock to raise an eyebrow.

"I am companion to Lady Brandon," she said.

"Oh, I see!" She noticed his manner shift slightly, his eyes brighter and more interested behind the round spectacles. "I will contact you within the next day or two. May I keep these papers?"

Amanda thought for a moment. She supposed it was necessary, but she confessed she was nervous about leaving them, and it must have shown on her face.

"Have no fear, Miss Goodwin. We have our safe right here." He pointed to a small but sturdy Chubb safe in the corner. "I assure you it will be protected."

As she fetched Vesta from the stable, dark clouds were rolling in and the air started to crackle with electricity. The horse pawed the ground, eager to be underway. Unlike most horses who shied away from a storm, Vesta found them invigorating so long as she didn't get too wet.

Raindrops didn't fall until they were almost back at Heddington Hall, and she was in time for dinner. Timothy came out to take the horse.

"Back safe I see, Miss Goodwin. Off doing goodness knows what. Off to meet a gentleman, I warrant." He gave her a grin and she ignored him. There was no point answering his insinuation.

33 - The Shed Again

Peter Joshua couldn't help but notice that every possible tool had been removed from the shed. It was essentially empty, except that he'd been given paper and a pen, a Bible, and a worn copy of some of William Wordsworth's poetry. The slop pot was in a corner, and there was a table and a chair next to a cot.

There was no need to tie him up this time. The story had been told about that he was a madman his family was trying to save from the asylum, and after the first day of yelling he realized no one cared. Food was brought to him from the pub across the yard.

After a few days he had memorized most of Wordsworth, and decided he hated him. If he saw one more "O!" he might take off his cravat and hang himself with it. The Bible turned out to be a great deal more violent than had ever occurred to him in church, but at least he could take passages of it and write about them to pass the time.

He also wrote letters, although they couldn't be posted. Pages and pages to Amanda. Then he started writing her letters back to him, but that made him feel like he actually would go mad. So then he started drawing plans. Plans of Soffitt's house, which he struggled to remember. Plans of this part of London. Plans of the roads between Petersfield, Heddington Hall, South Harting, and Portsmouth. Routes from there to London by horse and train.

The men holding him had told him very little, just that they wouldn't harm him if he behaved and he needed to stay there for a while. Nights were difficult. The shed was very tightly built, not just wood for the roof but brick for the walls. Little bits of daylight sky could be seen through tiny slits in the roof, but other than that it was dark and his request for a lamp, which could have set the roof on fire, had been denied. He was a prisoner, and although he had been in jail a few times, that wasn't the same. In jail you had a jailer and sometimes others to talk to. In prison you were alone, in the dark.

He knew that his imprisonment must have something to do with his investigation as he tried to find the family papers. He had a fairly good idea now that they were in Petersfield, but just as he was ready to leave London to see if that were true, he had been captured. His main consolation was that Amanda was not with him this time. As much as he would have enjoyed her company, even her anger, it was best that she was safe in West Sussex. He wished more than anything he could get word to her, but he hadn't figured out how to do that.

If they were feeding him rather than killing him, he had surmised that whatever was going on must be time-limited. They were waiting for something to happen, or not happen, before letting him go. For this reason, although he was frustrated and bored, he was not truly afraid. While he didn't think his captors needed him for anything—he obviously wasn't being held for ransom—he was pretty sure they would let him go in the end.

He'd been there about a full day before he had an idea. If they weren't going to kill him, perhaps he could try to get a note to Amanda. If he failed, if they found the note, he'd have to take a chance that they had no interest in harming him. The worst that could happen is they might take away his paper. So he began:

My dearest Amanda,

Know that I have been captured by the miscreants who put us in the shed, but that I am well. They are feeding me and will, I am sure, release me soon.

He wanted to write something more about his feelings for her, but couldn't think what. If she had answered his previous note, he didn't know about it. He tried:

Do not worry, my love—

No, too much, he thought, and changed it to:

Do not worry, my dear—

Oh, but he had already said "dearest". He told himself this was not literature, and that it might be trod in the mud anyway so there was no point in dallying.

Yours,

Now the name. Just Peter? Peter Joshua? Mr. Peter Joshua? A friend?

Peter

That evening, as the pub crowd was thinning and going home, he put the chair atop the table and managed to climb up to the crossbeams and push the letter through a slit in the edge of the roof. He was not able to see whether it fell to the ground or not, so he listened but he couldn't hear anything.

He did the same the next day, and the day after, then stopped in case his jailers might see a pile of notes on the ground. It had begun to rain anyway. Either someone had taken one and posted it (he had put "Miss Amanda Goodwin, Heddington Hall, West Sussex—Please post" on the front), or they had not. There was little else he could do but wait.

34 - Tiring Vesta

The note from Mr. Comstock was brief and asked whether Amanda could journey to his office to discuss the entail. She asked Lady Brandon's permission for a Monday afternoon off.

"Is this about your grandfather, dear?"

"Yes, my lady. The farm is entailed through my lifetime, but then it would revert to the owner. The owner would be the heir of Mr. Soffitt."

Lady Brandon looked confused.

"Are you saying that Mr. Soffitt owned your family farm?"

"Yes, my lady."

"How on earth would that have come about?"

Amanda was reluctant to say, but Lady Brandon's eyes were kind. She had put her embroidery in her lap.

"My grandfather was taken in by the Lesgus Scheme."

Lady Brandon raised an eyebrow and sighed.

"I see. And the farm's entail was part of the payment owed?"

Amanda nodded, trying not to let it show that tears were starting. She felt like a failure in so many ways. She couldn't find the miniature, she couldn't make her own way in the world, and she had feelings for a thief who turned out to make his living as a gambler. She had lived her life with the conviction that she was an independent woman, as her grandfather had taught her, and now even he was talking about life being better with a partner. And if she had that partner, or in the natural course of things had children, she would lose the farm she loved.

Sitting there in the parlor of Heddington Hall, she assumed that Lady Brandon would not understand. She had a husband years ago, and now owned this house, a London townhouse, property, and money. How could she sympathize with someone like Amanda? But it was clear that she did.

"Where does Mr. Comstock come into the problem?" she asked gently.

"Grandfather said a solicitor might be able to change the conditions of the entail, if the heir to the Soffitt estate could be found. Mr. Comstock said they seemed near to a discovery."

"Then you must go, obviously," said Lady Brandon, reaching for her cane. Amanda stood to help her out of her chair. "It's all right, Amanda. I can do it myself." She rose on her own.

"Thank you, Lady Brandon. I will understand if you withhold my wages, since I have taken several hours for personal business."

"I won't do that. Besides, from the sound of it you may need several more. Do not hesitate to ask."

Lady Brandon's kindness almost brought the tears back.

The next day she rode into Petersfield again. The same groom was there, and Vesta seemed happy to see him.

"She likes you," Amanda said with a smile, handing over some pennies.

"I like her, too," said the groom, showing a gappy grin. "She's got spirit."

Wish to hell I did, thought Amanda as she walked across The Square. Mr. Comstock was behind his desk, his round spectacles pushed up on his forehead. The surface of his work area was covered with papers.

"Miss Goodwin," he said, rising, and gesturing to the chair. His spectacles dropped back onto his nose. "I shall be with you in a moment. May I get you a cup of tea?"

"That would be very kind, Mr. Comstock. I have had a chilly ride."

"Yes, I apologize for being unable to come to you at Heddington Hall, but Mr. Birch is still on business in London and I confess I have been a little overwhelmed. I could use a cup of tea myself. Sugar and milk?"

"Yes, please." He gave a small bow and left the room.

Amanda sat on the leather chair, looking around the room. Everything spoke of good taste, including the painting on the wall, which showed a scene of gloomy brown landscape that looked like somewhere in Scotland. She was surprised by the array of papers on the desk. Mr. Comstock seemed an orderly man, with his brocade waistcoat and dapper shoes. She surreptitiously glanced at the documents, able to read some of the print upside down.

The word "Lufstow" caught her eye. This must be what he was going to tell her about. She got up from the chair and peered out the office door. Mr. Comstock was holding a teacup in his hand, but a woman had come in and interrupted him as he was making tea. She heard him explaining that Mr. Birch was not in, and would not return for some time. She took a closer look at the paper. It appeared as though Lufstow Farm was on a list of properties with Soffitt's name at the top.

Next to that was a form of some kind. She peered closer. It was a form for legal change of name. The handwriting was old, but she was able to discern that someone named Marcus Soffitt was changing his name to Theodore Pennington-Smythe. She was looking for the date when she heard the sound of a spoon in a cup. Without thinking, she quickly took the paper and folded it into her purse, then stepped over to look at the painting as if she were interested in it.

"Oh, do you like it? It's an original Lanseer," he said proudly, stepping in to the office.

"It's gloomy, but I like it," she said as her heart slowed its pace.

He put the cups down and resumed his seat at the desk.

"Very well, then, Miss Goodwin." He selected the first paper she had seen. "I can confirm that Lufstow Farm is on the list of Soffitt's entailed properties."

He looked up at her and she nodded, adjusting herself in her seat as if eager for more.

"And we have reason to believe that we have discovered the possible heir. It seems to be a Richard Pennington-Smythe."

"Oh?" Pennington-Smythe was the name on the change form, but hadn't that been Morris?

"Have you heard the name before? Have you or your grandfather been contacted by anyone of that name?"

"No, not to my knowledge. I can write a letter to my grandfather to be certain."

Mr. Comstock nodded sagely. "I would do that as soon as possible, Miss Goodwin. We have been unable to locate the gentleman to discuss this entail, and have had difficulty finding him or anyone who knows him. He may not be local to the area."

"Yes, I see," said Amanda, trying not to sound crestfallen.

"Do not be concerned, Miss Goodwin. It takes some time to find people, and perhaps your grandfather can be of assistance. I can write him myself at Lufstow Farm if you would like."

"No, that might confuse him. I will write to him."

He was looking expectantly at her, and she realized the polite thing would be to thank him, not grumble about coming all this way to Petersfield for something he could have told her in a note. But it had been another long ride.

"You will be helping us as well, Miss Goodwin. We have a number of matters concerning the Soffitt estate that can not be resolved without him. Your entail is only one of these."

"Yes, of course," she said, and looked down at her hands. Shouldn't the solicitors be the ones finding the heir? Was she a law clerk? She was having to force down anger, but she couldn't keep it all down.

"Mr. Comstock, I have to earn my living as a lady's companion. In future, perhaps you could consider writing me a letter? It takes me an hour to come here on horseback, and an hour to return. I have to get my lady's permission to be gone that long. Lady Brandon is generous, but there are limits."

If she had thought that mentioning Lady Brandon would be helpful, she was right.

"Of course, Miss Goodwin. Please allow me to tender my apologies for causing you to undertake an additional journey. May I purchase some lunch for you before you go?"

"That won't be necessary, Mr. Comstock."

"I can at least pay the groom for your horse." He rose and put on his jacket.

As they walked to the stable, Amanda glanced back at the buildings behind Birch and Comstock.

"Do those sheds belong to the law firm too?"

"Yes, indeed they do."

"What are they for?" she asked innocently.

"Storing goods that don't yet have a claimant."

"Your firm seems to be doing very well, Mr. Comstock."

"I would venture to say we are the finest law firm in Hampshire," he said proudly, "and possibly beyond."

She thought of Mr. Birch and wondered how much of that fine profit was made from wealthy young ladies. Mr. Comstock at least seemed reliable.

34 - Finding Peter

"Amanda, you have stopped your embroidering. Is something wrong? You have been distracted for days."

Quite a few things were wrong, thought Amanda. First, she hated embroidery, but she wasn't going to say so to Lady Brandon. She had written to her grandfather about Richard Pennington-Smythe, but did not yet have an answer. The main difficulty was that it was now Tuesday, four days after Peter Joshua had said he would return, and he hadn't. She wanted to search for him again, which made her edgy and distracted. She would again need Lady Brandon's support and she had just been gone all afternoon the day before to see Mr. Comstock.

"I am sorry, my lady."

"No need to be sorry, my dear. Mrs. O'Reilly said you have been eating little at meals, and I am concerned about you. On Sunday in church you kept looking over at my hymn book to find out where we were in the service. Yesterday after you returned, when you read to me you stopped in the middle of a chapter and stared off into space. Is there something I can do?"

"That's very kind, my lady. The only thing would be to give me even more time off."

"I could, but what would you do? You went to see Mr. Comstock yesterday."

"It is not about the farm, my lady. I am afraid it's about—"

She paused, shocked that she had gone this far. It was not her place to keep troubling Lady Brandon with her problems. She was her employee, not her friend.

"Jack Strawman?" Lady Brandon was concentrating on her embroidery and for a moment Amanda thought she had imagined what she said.

She became aware that her mouth was hanging open when Lady Brandon continued.

"As I told you, I can see what goes on between people. Forsythe told me you went out very late one night last week—he was up polishing silver because he couldn't sleep. Age does that, of course. I sleep in the afternoon when I would rather be awake, and then at night I cannot sleep."

Oh no, Lady Brandon knew she was out at midnight. What must she think?

"I know a man was calling for you at the townhouse. Forsythe said his name was Peter Joshua. I assumed Jack Strawman was not his real name. Straw man, indeed. Is his actual name Peter Joshua?"

Amanda's eyes were wide open as she stared at Lady Brandon, whose eyes were intently fixed on her embroidery. She gulped.

"Yes, my lady."

"And you have no desire to see him? Forsythe says you sent him away."

Damn Forsythe. He seemed to be Lady Brandon's eyes and ears.

"I did see him, my lady, as you say. Very late at night, to talk with him." She thought it best not to mention the kiss, and felt her stomach twinge at the deliberate omission. "He is on a quest to find papers that will restore his family's good name."

"Goodness, that does sound serious. I am afraid I have never heard of the Joshuas."

"Apparently some wrong was done to his family. I was trying my best to help." Again she omitted the time they had spent arguing, the time tied up in the shed, the tea at the Clermont. She felt herself becoming a liar. Just a beginning liar, but a liar all the same.

"And what happened?"

"He has disappeared, my lady. He was to leave London Friday and return here. But he has not. I wrote to his hotel in London and he had left." She did not want to add that she feared for his safety, because then she would have to explain why.

Lady Brandon broke off a thread with her teeth.

"I see. And you want to go to London to find him. How much time do you need?"

36 - The Criminal Element

The train in Petersfield hadn't yet arrived as Amanda arranged to leave Vesta at the station. She was very glad that she still had shillings in her pocket from weeks ago in Portsmouth as she bought a train ticket and boarded within minutes.

By her calculations, if she wanted to return that evening she would have six hours in London to see if she could find Peter Joshua, starting at the Clermont. But her stomach gnawed at her as she pictured the shed where she had been held with him. What if he had encountered those two horrible men? Perhaps she should have sent a note to the Metropolitan Police instead. The trouble was, she couldn't tell them exactly where the shed was. But she was quite sure she would remember if she started at the place on Cornhill where they had stood arguing on the pavement that day when they were taken.

As she stared out the window, she started to feel resentful. Here she was dragging herself this distance just because she felt in her stomach that something might be wrong. If it weren't, she might be embarrassed, but more than likely he'd never know about her foolishness. If she found him lounging around the Clermont, perhaps even with some woman, she couldn't do anything about it. She played the scene in her mind, going into the hotel, finding him sitting having tea with some woman of loose virtue, them laughing at her. This did nothing to improve her mood. She felt her anger begin to build as the journey continued. The worry and anger and despair all seemed to combine in her belly.

The Clermont was steps away from the station. Amanda went up to the desk and inquired about Peter Joshua. No one here by that name, the clerk said. Jack Strawman? No. She had no idea what his room number had been, so she couldn't just storm upstairs. The only option was to believe the clerk and go to Cornhill. It was well past lunch time, but she really didn't think she could eat.

She found the spot easily on the pavement, despite the many people walking along about their business. She and Peter had been arguing here when they were manhandled into the alley. She looked around, picturing that day and the direction they were headed. The alley would be up there, on the right. Then the next alley off that one. She must have gone the wrong way, because she came up against a brick wall. Go back. There it was, the entry to the yard. The shed was right there where she remembered.

It was impossible, she knew. He couldn't be in there. She had no idea who owned the shed, but once again there seemed to be no one around. Then she saw a man, coming out the back door of the pub. It was one of the men who had abducted them before, the shorter one who had taken her arm and then tied her up. She felt the anger swell in her chest. He had touched her, without her permission, and restrained her. Who did he think he was, taking people off the street and tying them up in sheds? She felt her hands ball into fists as she approached him.

He looked up, but did not seem to recognize her. He does this every day, Amanda thought, takes unsuspecting people off the street. She didn't realize until now that she had been waiting for this moment, to encounter one of the men who deserved whatever trouble she could give him.

"You are the man who kidnapped me and my— partner, you bastard," she said through gritted teeth.

His eyes narrowed. "Is that so? And what are you going to do about it?" he growled, reaching for her. She took the stance that Ji Ling had taught her and used his own momentum to throw him to the ground. He groaned and she kicked his shin before he was able to get up.

She went to the door of the shed and banged on it. She could hear nothing at first, then a faint knock on the other side. She looked down at the kidnapper.

"You bastard! He is in there again, isn't he?"

She hadn't heard the other man come up behind her. She tried to kick back but he grabbed her arms and lifted her. The shorter man scrabbled up from the ground, got out keys, and unlocked the shed door. She was bodily thrown at Peter, just as he stood there in surprise. They both tumbled to the ground and the door was slammed and locked.

"Ugh," said Peter. He'd hit the ground hard.

"Ugh yourself," said Amanda, scrambling off him and adjusting her bodice. She looked down at him and became aware she had never been happier to see anyone in her whole life.

"What on earth are you doing here?" His voice was practically a squeak, but he was smiling.

37 - The Shed Yet Again

"How in blazes did you manage to get captured again?" she chided him, then sat down on the floor next to him.

"You just got captured again, too," he pointed out.

She huffed and looked around the shed.

"Can't say as I like what you've done to the place," she said.

"They removed everything. But they've been feeding me, and, as you can see, we are not being restrained."

She put her hands on the brick walls. "I suppose there is no need. But why again?"

Peter put his head in his hands. "I have been thinking about that quite a bit, and have come to the conclusion that they need me out of the way for a certain period of time. In order to accomplish something."

"But what?"

"I have no idea."

They had both regained their breath, and for a few minutes just sat there looking at each other in the dim light coming through the roof cracks.

"Is there a lamp?" Amanda asked, looking around.

"No. I might set fire to the roof with it."

"How long have you been in here?"

"This is my fourth day. I did try to sent a note to you by pushing it through the crack up there, but I don't think anyone posted it." Suddenly it occurred to him. "Oh God," he said. "That must have been why they were waiting for you. They read my note."

"I do not believe that. That short one had just come out of the pub and did not know me at all."

"So what are you doing in here then, if he didn't recognize you? Why didn't you just run and fetch the police when you saw him?"

Amanda sighed. "Because I told him who I was so I could best him and he'd know why he was being punished."

There was a silence, and then he laughed. "Oh, Miss Goodwin—your temper! Did you use a leg sweep?"

"No, I managed to throw him down, but the other one came up behind me."

Amanda stood up, dusting off her dress and adjusting her hair. She looked around again, then sat down in the chair. Peter jumped up and began gathering the papers piled on the table.

"What is all that?" Amanda asked, grabbing a diagram before he could get to it.

"Scribblings," he mumbled. "And some drawings."

She reached out for them. "Let me see what you've been doing."

"No."

She looked at him curiously. "Why not?"

"They are private. I was keeping a personal diary. It is not for sharing—with anyone."

Amanda had never written down her thoughts. She tended to speak them, often loudly. She could not see well in this light, but Peter's voice sounded pained.

"Very well. I will not look at them. Except this one. What is it?"

"A map of—a place I used to live."

Amanda held it in a shaft of light from a roof crack.

"It looks like a manor house. Very large. Where was it?"

"Near Midhurst."

"Why were you living there?"

"I was very young, but my father was a tea trader. That made a lot of money in those days. And my mother had brought some money into the marriage from an inheritance. We lost the house when I was seven years old."

"What happened?"

"Oh, it is a long, dull story." She could hear him pacing by the wall of the shed.

"We seem to have nothing but time." The shed was getting darker in the twilight.

"Not now. I will tell you some day."

Her heart jumped that he would think there would be a future some day where they could tell each other their secrets.

"Does it have anything to do with why you became a gambler?"

She heard him stop pacing. "I suppose so. You lose things, and perhaps you make yourself feel better by pretending they have no value. If nothing has value, gambling makes sense."

They heard the shed door being unlocked, and the tall kidnapper stood there with a Tranter revolver, ready to use it. The light from the pub turned him into a silhouette. The shorter man threw a blanket and a chamber pot into the room, then placed a big bowl of hot stew and a loaf of bread inside the door, followed by a large jug of water. The door was closed again and locked.

"This hotel has excellent service," Peter said wryly.

Amanda hadn't realized how hungry she was till she smelled the stew.

"May I?" she said, holding up the bowl. There was one spoon in it.

"Go ahead. I haven't been doing enough to be hungry."

"At least have some bread." She put the loaf in his hand, sat on the floor, and ate half the stew. He sat down close beside her, handed her some bread, and took the bowl. Amanda was aware that they were alone, in the dark, with Peter using the same spoon she had just used. Sitting on the floor, his thigh alongside hers, she felt as safe as one could feel locked in a shed.

"Amanda," he said between bites. "You should not have come to find me. Now we are both trapped."

"Well, that's a fine welcome, I must say."

"For your own safety. That's what my note said. That you should just wait. What will Lady Brandon say when you do not return?"

"We will return," said Amanda with more confidence than she felt. "We will find a way out of here and leave. There are two of us now," she said, thinking of her grandfather's words. "We will do it together."

They ate in silence as the darkness surrounded them. Peter used the one cup he'd been given to dip into the jug for water, then he helped Amanda wash her face with some of it.

"Eek! That's cold." She grabbed his hand. He put it to his mouth and kissed it, then blew his warm breath on her palm.

"How is that?" he asked, his voice husky.

"Lovely," she said, and reached up to kiss him. His lips were warm, and he put his arms around her. It didn't feel cold in the shed after all. His kiss deepened and she felt her body respond, but then he pulled back.

"You're wonderful," he said, and Amanda felt warm down to her toes. "But I will not take advantage of a lady when we're locked in a shed."

Amanda sighed. She knew she wanted him, and although she could not give herself to him here, she was happy knowing that she could want him to touch her, to take her for his own.

"We should sleep," Peter said.

"How do we manage the chamber pot?" asked Amanda, embarrassed but trying to be practical. She was still off balance from kissing him.

"And I thought that kiss was intimate," he grumbled. "Let us try this. I will make use of it while you put your hands over your ears, then you do the same for me."

"That is foolish," laughed Amanda.

"If you can think of a better solution, let me know." She heard him dragging one of the chamber pots into the opposite corner of the shed.

Ablutions completed, she realized there was only one cot.

"How do we sleep? Shall I take one of the blankets and the table?" The floor was too cold to even consider.

"No, we shall both snuggle in the cot with two blankets. We will be much warmer."

Amanda felt her face flush and was very glad it was too dark for him to see.

"Very well."

Fully clothed, they squeezed into the cot. Amanda was so agitated at his nearness that she thought she would be awake all night. Within minutes she was asleep.

38 - An Inspector in London

"Wake up, Amanda," Peter said, shaking her. "I do not think that sound is our jailers."

There was a pounding on the door. Amanda jumped up to standing before she woke up properly, and almost fell down again. There was the sound of something being jammed into the lock, then a sharp crack and the door opened.

The light was so bright that both of them put their hands up to their eyes.

"Aha!" said a deep voice that could only be Inspector Hawk. "That urchin was right! Give him sixpence, Sergeant Farrow. Thank you very much for your help, Constable. I will manage things from here."

Inspector Hawk beckoned them to come out. Peter began scooping up all his papers and trying to stuff them into his coat pockets.

"What about these two?" asked Sergeant Farrow. Amanda could see the two kidnappers in handcuffs next to the constable.

"We can take them, too," said Hawk.

"I'm sorry, sir," said the constable, "but I have to take them with me. They're the Met's problem now."

Hawk frowned but nodded his assent.

"Damn," he said, then turned to Amanda. "Oh, sorry, miss—my language."

Peter made a choking sound very close to a guffaw.

"I will need to go with the constable. Those two may be the Met's problem, but they may be mine too. Farrow, take these two back to the Portsmouth police station, and send a note to Lady Brandon. We can return them to Heddington Hall this evening."

They were taken by police patrol wagon to Victoria, then the three of them caught the train to Portsmouth, with Sergeant Farrow paying the expense. The carriage was crowded, and they were forced to sit apart from each other. Amanda was well aware that she had slept in her clothes, but no one close to her smelled any better. She could just imagine what the people sitting next to Peter might think.

Herself, she hadn't noticed while she was sleeping alongside him. Well, she had noticed at first, but it was a manly smell, even if a little strong after four days. She was soothed by the fact that they had been in very close quarters but she hadn't gotten angry with him once. That was probably because she was so relieved to find him, so gratified that her guess about the shed had been right, and so enchanted with his nearness and the fact that her body accepted and delighted in that nearness. And now she was so relieved that Inspector Hawk had found them and arrested the criminals.

She was happier than she had any right to be, she thought, considering that she had not found the miniature, gotten the entail revised, or helped Peter find his papers.

In Portsmouth, they were ushered into the police station and immediately separated from each other. She was seated with a constable in a small room, and he faithfully wrote down everything she had to say about what had happened.

"And you say you had been captured before?"

"Yes, in that same yard, just a few weeks ago."

"Did your captors say why they were taking you?"

"No, they gave us no information. Just took us off the street and locked us up."

"Did you report the previous event to the police, either in London or here?"

Amanda admitted that they had not, and began to wonder why they had not. When Mr. Birch had found them, there had been all that confusion of who went where first, and she had fallen to sleep exhausted at the townhouse. Surely the next day they should have gone to the police, but she had been very concerned not to worry Lady Brandon. It seemed that Peter, or Jack as he was then known, also had no interest in contacting the constabulary.

"We have the criminals now, miss. No need to worry about them again. I am sure the magistrate will take care of them."

When she had signed her statement and gone out the front door, Peter was waiting for her.

"The police have offered us a patrol wagon to Heddington Hall," he said. "Shall we?"

"Wait," she said. "You can't go to Heddington Hall. Where do you live or stay when you are in West Sussex?"

He paused for a moment, then looked up at the sky. "That is a very good question. I think perhaps I should go to the White Hart."

Amanda thought for a moment and a picture of Flossie appeared in her mind.

"You are coming with me to Heddington Hall," she said firmly. "From there we will figure out what to do."

The wagon was slow and bumpy, and both of them were sore and cold from sleeping in the cot and bouncing along the roads, but at least the weather held. Timothy came out when he saw the wagon, and his mouth dropped open.

"Timothy, is Lady Brandon at home?"

"Yes, miss," he said, on his best behavior in front of the police driver. He kept staring at Peter, who looked like a tramp dragged in from the road.

"Good." She turned to Peter. "Please stay here with Timothy until I've talked to Lady Brandon?"

He nodded and walked off with Timothy. She looked back as she approached the house, and Timothy had produced a clay pipe and they were sitting on a hay bale, smoking. No need to worry about him, she thought.

She went quickly to her room, washed her hands and face, wet-brushed her hair, and then went to find Lady Brandon. She was in the parlor at the writing desk, composing a letter.

"Oh, thank heavens," she said as Amanda came in. "You are rescued! Inspector Hawk must have found you. I told him London, but I had only the vaguest idea where you might go. He must have known how to get information, or the Met did. Are you quite all right?"

"Yes, my lady. Thank you so much for alerting Inspector Hawk. He not only rescued us, but arrested the men who did it."

"Us? You found your Mr. Strawman?"

"I did, my lady. And I must beg yet another indulgence from your ladyship. Mr. Joshua is with me now, having been imprisoned in a shed for four days, and has nowhere to go." She did not mention the White Hart. She reflected that she was getting rather accomplished at sins of omission.

"I see," said Lady Brandon. "Well, this is highly unusual. I wonder what Mr. Burdett will have to say about it."

Amanda was curious why on earth it would matter what Mr. Burdett thought, but she held her tongue.

"Nevertheless, it is my house and I shall do as I please. Your Mr. Strawman—that is, Mr. Joshua, is welcome here. Find Mrs. Havers and tell her to make him up the room with the bath upstairs. We shall see him at dinner."

Amanda was relieved and grateful once again for Lady Brandon's grace.

"Thank you, my lady. That is exceptionally kind."

"But I must ask you, Amanda. Do you think he is trustworthy? I do have valuables in the house, though not in the guest rooms, of course. Is he still a thief, do you think?"

"No, I no longer believe so. But he is a gambler, my lady." That was the end of it, she thought. Gambling was as detestable as thievery.

Lady Brandon raised an eyebrow and thought for a moment.

"I see. Well, in that case he should use the servant's entrance."

39 - A Heddington Luncheon

For the next two days, Peter recovered his strength under the care of the housekeeper, Mrs. Havers. She wanted to fuss over him, but Peter would have none of it. Although he was a guest at Heddington Hall, he was eager to be of use, and spent much time in the stables with Timothy, helping Forsythe with decorations, and even offering to pluck the chickens for Mrs. O'Reilly.

Lady Brandon, while not quite as taken with him as the staff, seemed to enjoy his company. That Saturday she had planned a luncheon, to which a few of her local friends were invited and, of course, Mr. Burdett. The holiday decorations were complete although it was still a fortnight till Christmas, and all seemed festive. Mrs. O'Reilly's finest baked ham would be the centerpiece, and special pastries had been ordered from her favorite baker in Chichester, to be delivered that morning. Three musicians from Clanfield had been hired to play chamber music. Amanda had to wonder why such a fuss was being made.

Most of the day before had been spent wondering what Peter was doing, and hoping to catch sight of him with all the preparations going on. She had glimpses of him carrying a crate of wine, helping Forsythe move a table, and talking with Mrs. O'Reilly, but she hadn't seen him until dinner and all the conversation had been about the next day's luncheon. A pre-holiday social occasion, said Lady Brandon, something no one had done before. Beeswax candles, she decreed—no tallow.

Children would not be welcome, but Lady Vance was of course invited, as were Inspector Hawk and his wife Lavinia, Captain Rory and his wife from Chichester, Judge Septimus Trout from Portsmouth, and Mr. and Mrs. Spencer from the next manor house but one. They owned a china factory somewhere in the north. Amanda and Peter were also expected to attend.

"I do hope Lady Vance doesn't mind associating with so many people in trade, manufacturing, and service," confided Lady Brandon to Amanda. Then she gave Amanda a rather wicked grin that meant she hoped Lady Vance minded very much.

Now the table was set for ten, with pine boughs and willow wreaths decorating the room. Everyone sat down to soup, and the conversation was informal. There was news of a horrible firedamp explosion in a coal mine in Wales.

"They say there might be a hundred dead," said Judge Trout, shaking his head.

"Such dangerous work to keep us all warm and the furnaces going in the factories," said Mrs. Spencer.

"Some of those furnaces produce gas, which is safer for us but does not change the need for coal," said Peter Joshua. "I think we should find a way to harness the power of water."

"Wouldn't that be going backward?" asked Inspector Hawk. "Back to the days of waterwheels?"

"No," said Peter, warming to his theme. "I mean harness the power itself. Turn it into energy by figuring out how to store the power of falling water."

"Wouldn't help us much here, I'm afraid," said the Judge. "Not many waterfalls here."

Amanda was careful not to stare at Peter, but she was paying attention. The man was a dreamer, she thought, though harnessing the power of water sounded marvelous. Meanwhile the subject of conversation was changing.

"Looks like there will be war in the Transvaal," said Mr. Spencer. "The Boers could declare independence any day."

"I cannot say I blame them," said Peter. "They don't want British annexation."

"Then they should have paid their taxes," said Inspector Hawk.

Appalled that the discussion had turned from dead coal miners to politics, Lady Brandon smoothly changed the subject.

"Did anyone have the opportunity to see the comic opera *Pirates of Penzance*?" she asked. "I saw it in London but it was in Brighton in October. The company has been touring."

"My dear nephew Arthur took me to see it in London," said Lady Vance. "I thought it in very poor taste. All those women dancing about in nightgowns. But it was amusing, I suppose."

"I found it delightful," said Peter. "The music was wonderful; one kept humming the tunes. And the pirates wanting to marry all those girls was very funny."

"It was every bit as good as *H.M.S. Pinafore*," Lady Brandon agreed.

"Why did the pirates want to marry the girls?" Amanda asked.

"They are dazzled by their youth and beauty," Mrs. Spencer said. "But their father, the Major General, doesn't want them taken away from him."

"That sounds very sad," said Amanda.

"It is all in fun! Everyone gets married in the end, even the Pirate King."

Marriage is always the happy ending, thought Amanda. It was very annoying. But she supposed the Major General didn't have an entail on his property. She looked across at Peter, who was at this point engaged in a quiet discussion with Judge Trout. She wondered what they were talking about.

By the time the ham and vegetable course was done, and pudding was served, the party had been made livelier by the cider and the good company. Lady Vance was the only one who looked as though she were tolerating the group rather than enjoying them. Amanda reminded herself what she'd tried to do to Lady Brandon about the necklace and could find little sympathy for her. The musicians had set up in the large front parlor, and the group joined them and found places to sit on the settees and chairs.

Peter sidled up to Amanda, who was sitting near the wall.

"Why are you back here?" he asked.

"It would not be proper for me to be at the front. I am only a companion." She looked up at him with an impish smile. "Besides, I can watch everyone better from here."

"Your Lady Brandon seems very democratic in her choice of friends. It was very kind of her to take me into her home. It will be a shame to have to leave, but I am afraid I have business in Bognor Regis soon." He touched her shoulder gently and went over to talk with Mr. Spencer.

Amanda felt her spirits fall. She had enjoyed having Peter here, and would be loath to have him go. But a gambler, she supposed, must gamble. Bognor was becoming a popular seaside resort, and that would likely make it a fine town for gambling.

She had been living in a dream the last two days, in a way. The pattern of life was usual; no one was jumping out attacking anyone. But she knew that nothing had been resolved. She still had no clues to find the miniature, except to visit antique dealers and ask them to ask each other. She knew that Peter couldn't have found his papers. And she still had no answer from Mr. Comstock about the entail, despite his insistence that it would only be a day or two.

At least she had secure employment, and thus far her grandfather was not in dire need of her help. She would venture from here to learn where the miniature had been sold. But what about Peter Joshua? Amanda knew that she wanted to be with him, but she couldn't simply follow him to Bognor Regis. Perhaps he could return now and then and visit her? The thought of seeing him only occasionally was almost as sad as him having to leave.

Mr. Burdett, who had said little at luncheon but smiled at whoever was speaking, was deep in conversation with Lady Brandon. What could they still have to talk about, when they saw each other so often? Mr. Burdett's eyes were sparkling, and Amanda didn't think it was from the cider. She could not see Lady Brandon's face, but his was alive with what she took to be love.

She glanced over at Peter, who was gesturing as he explained something to Mr. Spencer. Perhaps they were talking about the war about to happen in South Africa. She felt her gaze soften as she watched him, insistent on expressing his view but always with good humor. It occurred to her that he did not get angry very often; his tendency was toward amusement instead. Even when he had been trapped in the shed for days before she got there, he had clever sarcastic remarks at the ready. A man who took life as it came, and assumed the best. So different from herself.

She was beginning to think she was in love with him. But since she had always known about the entail, she knew she would never marry. Not being inclined to isolate herself, she instead had made herself strong and self-sufficient, at least to the extent she could be. She may not need Peter, but she wanted him as part of her life. Perhaps, like Lady Brandon and Leo Burdett, they could be friends who saw each other often.

Peter, of course, could marry, and would likely wish to. She doubted his wife would want him to have a woman friend. What type of woman would marry a gambler? They were known to be quite generous when they were winning, and insufferable when they were losing, although she hadn't noticed that tendency in Peter. Maybe she simply didn't know him well enough. Gradually she found that the meal and the music, not to mention her own thoughts, were giving her a headache. The memory of the warmth of his body made her tingle, and she didn't want him to be merely a friend. Perhaps she could figure it all out tomorrow.

40 - A Position Lost

"Amanda, my dear, sit down. I am afraid we have a problem."

Lady Brandon was sitting at her desk. Amanda had noticed she hardly ever chose the settee now when she needed to write a letter, and was much more comfortable moving about.

"Yes, my lady."

Lady Brandon looked up and Amanda could see by the brooding expression on her face that this was no small problem. This was not about what Mrs. O'Reilly was making for dinner, or a passage Amanda had forgotten to read aloud, or taking time to do personal business.

"It is about your time in the shed with Mr. Joshua."

She looked so concerned that Amanda blurted out, "I assure you I am quite recovered, my lady, and so is Mr. Joshua. And Inspector Hawk has both men in jail."

"Yes, Amanda, I know."

She got up and started pacing the room, tapping her cane gently on the carpet.

"I am very glad to see you up and about so often, my lady."

"Thank you." She stopped and faced Amanda. "I am afraid I must let you go. I will pay you two weeks wages, but then you must leave Heddington Hall."

Amanda was stunned. What had she done? Lady Brandon had been so wonderful about everything, about her grandfather and Peter. She had gotten approval for every action in advance.

"My lady, if I have done anything to displease you—"

"Not to displease me, exactly. Unfortunately, Lady Vance has begun her campaign against me again, and this time the talk is a great deal more damning than stolen jewels at a party."

"What do you mean, my lady?" Amanda's hands clenched and reclenched in her lap.

"You and Mr. Joshua were trapped together in a shed for a full night."

"Yes, my lady. But we were rescued and—"

"Listen to me, Amanda. You and a man were together all night. This information has made its way to Lady Vance. She has told anyone and everyone that I am keeping a loose woman in my employ."

The shock was starting to fade, and Amanda was getting angry, but certainly not at Lady Brandon.

"I assure you, my lady—"

"That is precisely the problem, Amanda. Your assurances mean nothing in a case like this. When you combine this with your other behaviors, which are also being discussed—"

"I beg your pardon?"

"Riding out on horseback unaccompanied to Petersfield, astride the saddle. Being seen out late at night in Kensington Gardens. And now having the very man you were confined with staying at my house. As you know, I trust you and am simply amused by your Mr.

Joshua, but society does not share the same relaxed attitude."

Amanda's hands were now in fists and she was fighting back tears. "I am so sorry, my lady."

Lady Brandon sat down next to her, her hands on the top of the cane, and bowed her head.

"Not as sorry as I am. At my age, one should be able to do as one wishes without fear of social retribution. But it seems that some things cannot be tolerated, regardless of station. I do not want my wedding to be an opportunity to snub me publicly."

It took a moment for what she had said to sink it.

"Wedding, my lady?"

Lady Brandon sighed. "Yes, I have not let it be known, but I shall be marrying Mr. Burdett. And I very much wanted my wedding to be the social occasion of the season. At least out here in the country."

Amanda was so happy for Lady Brandon and so sad for herself she didn't know what to say.

"I am so glad he makes you happy, my lady, and so sorry I have brought this trouble upon you."

"Of course you are, my dear. But there is nothing for it. You must go. I wish it could be otherwise."

"Two weeks, my lady?"

"No, two weeks wages, Amanda. You need to leave in the morning. And it goes without saying that Mr. Joshua must leave today, as he was planning. The carriage can take each of you to the rail station."

Amanda wanted to say more, but she saw tears in Lady Brandon's eyes. She went upstairs and began to lay out her things, her tears turning to anger. How had this happened? It was hardly her fault that she wanted to ride a horse without falling off, or had been captured and put in a shed.

Where on earth should she go? Lady Brandon's reference would likely enable her to get a position as a companion elsewhere, but did she want to? She was rather weary of this world where wealth meant so much, but where someone as nice as Lady Brandon had to buckle under the pressure of society enforcers like Lady Vance. In a mean-spirited moment, Amanda was glad her horrid necklace had been stolen. She wished she'd done it.

She sat down to write to her grandfather, then thought better of it. She would simply return to Lufstow Farm and explain. She could help out there, and together they would find a way. Her grandfather was right: it took a team to make life right, and she and her grandfather were a team. She took out another sheet of paper and wrote to Mr. Comstock, informing him that henceforth he should write to her at Lufstow Farm with any communication about the entail as soon as possible.

She was lucky, Amanda told herself as she folded her dresses carefully on the bed. Unlike many who lose a position, she had somewhere to go.

She heard the sound of the carriage outside her window and looked down into the courtyard. Peter was shaking Timothy's hand to say goodbye. He then looked up at the window and saw her. He said something to the carriage driver and came running back into the house, his boots loud on the stairs. No gentleman would have entered her bedchamber. He entered her bedchamber and enfolded her in his arms.

"Amanda, you know I must go, and I have heard that Lady Brandon has said you must go too. I know this is because of me, and I am sorry. I am sorry I led you into these situations, and that now you have lost your position. I promise some day I will make it up to you. In the meantime," he said as he pulled back from the embrace and tipped her chin up with his finger, "know that we will meet again. I won't allow it to be any other way."

She reached up, slipped her hands behind his neck, and kissed him. He kissed her back and she wanted to melt into him, but he pulled away, tapped her chin with his finger, and ran back down the stairs. She went to the window and saw him get into the carriage. He didn't look back.

41 - Lodging in London

The chickens were settled in for the night, the barn was closed and latched, and the evening meal concluded. Amanda fell into a chair to read the letter that had arrived from Inspector Hawk.

> *Miss Goodwin,*
>
> *First, I would like to assure you that Mr. Breem and Mr. Dunn, the two criminals who imprisoned you and Mr. Joshua, will be going to trial shortly in London and will likely be convicted of kidnapping. It is requested that you attend to give evidence against them, Friday at ten in the morning, at the Old Bailey. There may also be some discussion of the recent jewel thefts.*
>
> *I will send a police trap for you to take you to the rail station in Petersfield, or you may choose other transportation. Upon your arrival I will introduce you to Jarvis King, the barrister for the prosecution.*
>
> *Since we do not know how long all the evidence may take, we can provide accommodation for you in town for both Thursday and Friday nights.*

Please reply at your earliest opportunity.

Vernon Hawk, Detective Inspector, Hampshire Constabulary

At last those two men would no longer be a hazard. Amanda was delighted to give evidence, and wrote a note back to be sent the next morning. She accepted both the trap and the accommodation for the two nights, although it would mean leaving Grandfather without her help. She would talk to Mrs. Lowry about that tomorrow.

Amanda was far more nervous about any talk regarding the jewel thefts than she was about the trial. The kidnapping had been none of her doing. But although she didn't have anything to do with jewel thefts, she knew intimately a man who . . . might. But he was in Bognor Regis, undoubtedly well-dressed, charming, and placing bets on—whatever it was that gentlemen gamblers placed bets on. Perhaps there were women there, dressed in extravagant, revealing dresses, hoping for some of the winnings. Or young ladies on holiday from London escaping from their parents for an afternoon, walking on the Esplanade hoping to meet a charming older man. Damn, it really would be best to think of something else.

Leaving her Grandfather under the watchful eye of Mrs. Lowry, Amanda did not enjoy the train ride despite the calm weather. She needed to be going the other direction, to Portsmouth to visit antique shops, or to Bognor Regis to meet a handsome gambler. It would be best, though, if she were back at Lufstow Farm. In the few days since leaving Lady Brandon's employ, she had learned how much happier she was there. Her mind had filled with ideas of what to do, how to make the farm more productive or less expensive. If they could manage another year, she might be able to bring in new crops that would sell for a higher profit. And she wanted to start that medicinal herb garden.

Arriving at Victoria Station, she was met by a constable who took her to a lodging house in Serjeants' Inn. It was run by Mrs. Slatterly, a warm and friendly woman who took care of short-term lodgers come to town on police matters.

"If you need anything, please just ask Mrs. Slatterly," the constable said. "Inspector Hawk will be here at nine to collect you."

Amanda was welcomed and shown to a small but clean room on the second floor, with a floral counterpane and a view of a courtyard. She could see the barristers walking to and from their offices.

Chilled from her journey and with no demands on her time until morning, Amanda decided she would like a hot bath. Taking the towel Mrs. Slattery had given her, she went down the hall but the bathroom was occupied. Deciding to wait and perhaps go downstairs and have some tea, she heard the bathroom door open and turned around to see Peter Joshua emerging. At first she thought she'd created him by thinking about him. Her hand flew to her throat.

"What in hell are you doing here?" she asked.

He laughed. "Miss Goodwin," he said, "is there some reason you have such a free use of language?"

"You surprised me, is all." She was very much aware that he was only wearing his dressing gown and the towel around his neck was wet.

"I am here, since you asked, because I am giving evidence in the case. You were not captured alone, you know, and I was taken twice."

Of course, she thought, he would need to testify. Why had that not occurred to her?

"Of course," she said grudgingly. "Are you also meeting with Inspector Hawk?"

He looked at her curiously, his head tilted to the side.

"Hmmm. Let me allow you to take your bath, and you allow me to get dressed. I can meet you downstairs in the parlor?"

Amanda's bath was shorter than she intended, and not only because there was not much hot water left in the boiler. She felt nervous and shaky. She had prepared herself to do without Peter Joshua for a while, and yet here he was. Both annoyed at her preparations and disturbed that they were interrupted, she went downstairs in a mood not particularly conducive to civil conversation. She plopped down in a large wing chair. Mrs. Slattery had already brought Peter a cup of tea.

"How have you been faring, Miss Goodwin?" he asked politely.

She stared at him. How should she be after being captured, run all over the county, and losing her position? It would be harrowing to confess that actually she was doing rather well.

"Tolerably well, Mr. Joshua. And you?"

"Very well, thank you."

"Have you been successful in Bognor Regis?" Those imaginary women at his side rose in her mind unbidden.

"Not as much as I would like."

"And have you found your family papers?"

He looked at her strangely. "No, but I think I have a better idea where they might be."

"Indeed? And where is that?"

There was a pause that one might describe as fairly hostile.

"Miss Goodwin, have I done something else to displease you? It seems you are perpetually angry with me."

She thought of his familiarity with Timothy and the staff at Heddington Hall, his charming nature before that at the Naval Ball, his playful manner with Flossie at the White Hart. He was personable and, even in extremity, calm and good-humored. Envy was likely at the core of her feelings, but it came out as irritability.

"You seem perpetually unfazed by what happens to you. How did you become so content?" Although she meant it as a barb, she was actually curious.

He thought for a moment. "Once I turned thirty-five, it became apparent to me that I wanted to enjoy life rather than fight troubles. But I may have always been more likely to take life as it comes. And you, Miss Goodwin?"

They were engaging in increasingly polite conversation, and Amanda was confused. How could he talk about such things after what they had been through together? Perhaps to him a kiss was just a kiss, a night in a shed was just a night in a shed. But his eyes were kind, his expression rapt as he awaited her answer. Without meaning to, she found herself sharing a confidence.

"I believe I lost that ability when I was taken advantage of in my younger years. I think perhaps it is different for a woman."

His expression was serious, and he leaned forward, speaking quietly.

"What did happen to you, my love?"

Suddenly she wanted to cry, and to tell him everything. She knew she shouldn't trust him with her feelings or, really, anything, but she couldn't help it. In quiet tones she told the story of what happened when she was nineteen, of what that man had done to her, making her feel helpless and defiled. When she looked up, his expression had changed. He looked angry, and she had not seen him look that way before.

"Are you quite all right, Mr. Joshua?"

He took at deep breath. "If I ever meet the man who did that to you, I will kill him."

She reached out to pat his hand, realizing as she did so how foolish it was that she was the one reassuring him. But it was as if a weight had been lifted off of her. She felt for a moment that he could help carry the anger she had held on her own all these years.

"Thank you," she said.

The bell rang for dinner, and they were both quiet, listening to the others in the lodging house chat with each other as they ate. The talk was, of course, about evidence and courts and barristers and procedures. Each of them answered when spoken to, but both went up to bed as soon as dinner was over.

They stood outside Amanda's door in the corridor, Peter gazing into her eyes. For a moment she thought he would take her in his arms right there, but instead he bowed over her hand and kissed it.

"Goodnight, Miss Goodwin. We shall be through one ordeal tomorrow, at least."

"Yes," she said, feeling her hand tingle. "Goodnight, Mr. Joshua."

42 - The Trial

The next morning, instead of Inspector Hawk, a constable came to collect Peter and Amanda.

"Inspector Hawk sends his regards, but is already meeting with Jarvis King, the barrister. I have been asked to take you there."

The hansom ride was short, and they were ushered into a small room inside the Criminal Courts building.

"I will take you in first, Miss Goodwin," said the constable. "It is important that you be seen separately, both here and in court."

Jarvis King was a large man, and his barrister's wig made him look even larger. He was standing talking to Inspector Hawk as Amanda entered.

"Ah, Miss Goodwin. Please be seated. This won't take a moment."

Amanda sat on the wooden chair proferred.

"Miss Goodwin," said Inspector Hawk, "please listen carefully to what Mr. King has to say. You are to follow his advice to the letter, so that we may put these men in prison."

Amanda nodded and waited for King to proceed. He was wearing half-spectacles and removed them to talk to her.

"Miss Goodwin, I assume you will be able to recognize easily both men who kidnapped you and Mr."—he looked at his notes—"Joshua, is it?"

"Yes, I will."

"And you can describe both kidnappings?"

"The part that relates to me, yes."

"Good. Good. I will be asking you questions designed to have you identify the men and make it clear that what they were doing was a crime. But Miss Goodwin, I may also need to ask questions that may be awkward, about your relationship with Mr.—um—Joshua, and your reasons for being where you were at the time the crimes were committed."

Amanda had thought about this for some time on the train to London. The barrister would have to do this, she had thought, to make her appear as a reliable witness.

"I will answer all questions as truthfully as I can," she promised.

"The barrister for the defense," King continued, "may try to trick you into sounding as though you were somehow at fault, or even that you are of low moral character. This is called discrediting the witness, and it can be uncomfortable. But if you answer truthfully and with confidence, all should go well. I do need to know one thing before we go into the courtroom."

Amanda waited, knowing what was coming.

"What precisely is your relationship with Mr. Joshua?"

"We are friends." She had decided on this answer and planned to stick to it like glue.

"Intimate friends?"

"I would say fairly close, but not intimate." Was she lying? Would any reasonable person think two kisses and a desire to be together constituted an intimate friendship? Her own feelings might qualify, but this was about facts, not feelings.

Half an hour later, Amanda aimed to be truthful and factual as she sat in the witness box, giving her evidence. The questioning had gone as Mr. King had explained thus far. She had identified the two men and detailed what they had done to her. But now the barrister for the defense, Clive Freeman, was going further about her relationship with Peter Joshua.

"Why did you become friends?"

"We had certain interests in common regarding claims to the estate of a Mr. Soffitt."

"Who is—or was—Mr. Soffitt?"

Amanda explained George Soffitt's Lesgus Scheme and how it had harmed investors, including her grandfather.

"And what was Mr. Joshua's interest?"

She had been prepared for this. "You would have to ask Mr. Joshua."

"I am given to understand," said Mr. Freeman, "that you have recently been released from the employ of Lady Constance Brandon?"

"With good references, yes," replied Amanda. Where was this going?

"Why were you dismissed from her household?"

"I was deemed unsuitable by one of her friends."

"Why was that, Miss Goodwin?"

Mr. King objected to this line of questioning as having nothing to do with the case, but the judge bade her answer.

"I have habits that the friend found objectionable."

"Would you detail some of these habits?"

"Riding a horse astride and going out unaccompanied at night."

"I see. Were there any objections centered on your activities with Mr. Joshua?"

Amanda swallowed. "There was objection to me because the kidnappers trapped us together all night in a shed. The friend assumed the worst."

"And, if I may be indelicate, did the worst happen, Miss Goodwin?"

"It did not," said Amanda. In her mind she said, it almost did, and would have if I hadn't been so tired and he hadn't been such a gentleman.

"Thank you, Miss Goodwin."

Since she had given evidence first, she was able to take a seat and watch Peter answer questions. Most were the same as hers. He also identified the two men and gave details of both kidnappings. But again, when defense barrister Freeman rose, the tenor changed.

"Mr. Joshua, have you any notion why you were kidnapped?"

"None at all." His slightly amused manner suggested that kidnapping him was a ludicrous undertaking.

"Have you not recently been suspected of illegal activities?"

"I beg your pardon?"

Freeman reached to his subordinate for a page of notes.

"According to the Portsmouth police, you were arrested in connection with the theft of jewels from a Mrs. Beekman."

"I was brought in for a conversation," Peter corrected, "and then permitted to go."

"I see. We will confirm that with Inspector Hawk in a moment. What is your connection to Mr. George Soffit, Mr.—um—Joshua?"

Peter hesitated.

"You were seen at the funeral of Mr. Soffitt. Why were you there?"

"Everyone was there," said Peter with confidence. "It seemed to be quite the social occasion."

Mr. King rose.

"I object, your lordship. It is unclear where the defense is headed with questions about Mr. Joshua's activities outside of the kidnapping."

The judge turned toward Mr. Freeman.

"Have you a direction, Mr. Freeman?"

"Your lordship, I seek to establish that Mr. Joshua is involved in activities which are highly questionable, and which may help explain his detention by my clients, Mr. Breem and Mr. Dunn."

"I will allow it," the judge said to Mr. King.

Amanda looked at Peter. He ran his finger under his collar as if it were too tight, and looked down for a moment at his shoes. His confidence, she saw, was a veneer.

"Mr. Joshua, what is your association with Miss Goodwin?"

"We are friends with common interests." She could tell he resisted looking over at her.

"What might those interests be?"

Peter seemed more confident now, as if he were pleased to be able to tell the story. "Both our families were taken advantage of by George Soffitt."

"I see," said the barrister. "And in your case, in what way had Mr. Soffitt taken advantage of your family?"

"He possessed some papers of a personal nature related to my family name." His slightly amused demeanor made evident the understatement.

"And what is your family name, Mr. Joshua?"

"I beg your pardon?" Amanda saw Peter blink, and his face turned pale, although he continued with the same tolerant expression.

"Your family name, Mr. Joshua. It is a simple question."

"My name is Peter Joshua," said Peter, bemused.

Mr. Freeman reached back for another document. "Are you not also Jack Strawman?"

Peter frowned. "Well, yes, I have used that name before."

"Are either of those names, Strawman or Joshua, your family name?"

There was a pause so long that both the judge and those viewing the trial shifted in their seats.

"Shall I repeat the question, sir? Are either Strawman or Joshua your family name?"

Amanda held her breath. Why was Peter not answering? She had seen through Jack Strawman—anyone would. But surely Peter Joshua was his name.

The judge was about to speak when Peter took a deep breath, let it out slowly, and said, "No."

"And what is your given name, sir, the one with which you were born?"

"Richard Pennington-Smythe."

43 - The End of the Trial

Amanda was aghast, and several faces turned in her direction. While she had never felt faint before, she honestly thought she might lose consciousness right there in court. Richard Pennington-Smythe? The surname was the one she'd seen on the paper she had taken from the solicitor's office. Someone named Marcus had changed their name from Soffitt to Pennington-Smythe. Was Peter also a Pennington-Smythe? Was he somehow connected to George Soffitt?

More importantly, Peter had lied to her. Absurdly, it occurred to her that she had kissed Peter Joshua twice, and had wanted him to do more than kiss her. How could she consider such a thing with a man who had three different names? She felt betrayed.

Inspector Hawk was called to the stand as Peter—was he Peter anymore?—stepped down. She expected him to come sit where she was among the spectators, but he did not appear. Perhaps he was speaking with the solicitor. He was going to need one, she thought, when she'd finished with him. She was so angry that she paid little attention to Inspector Hawk's evidence until Mr. Freeman rose to question him. Struggling to focus with her mind bent on committing various acts of violence on

Mr. So-called Pennington-Smythe, she listened as best she could.

"Inspector Hawk, how did you discover that Miss Goodwin and Mr. Joshua were locked in the shed behind the Pyrotechnist's Arms public house?"

"An informant contacted me anonymously."

"How?"

"By note to the station in Portsmouth."

"What did you do?"

"I ordered a telegraph sent to the City Police and came to London."

"And they were in the precise location indicated in the note?"

"Yes."

When Mr. Freeman rose to cross-examine, Amanda realized she was clenching her fists. She looked around. Where had Peter, or rather Richard, gone? She wanted to give him a piece of her mind.

"Inspector Hawk, when you received the note, were you already familiar with either Miss Goodwin or Mr. Joshua?"

"Yes. I had met Miss Goodwin at the house of Lady Constance Brandon in West Sussex, where she was employed as a companion."

"In what connection, Inspector?"

"In connection with the theft of a necklace from Lady Marjorie Vance. The theft had taken place in Lady Brandon's home."

"Was Miss Goodwin a suspect in the theft?" Faces turned toward her. Amanda felt like she wanted to crawl under her chair.

"We were considering all possibilities, yes."

"Did you exonerate her?"

"The investigation is technically ongoing, Mr. Freeman. No one has been exonerated."

"I see. What about Mr. Joshua? Was he also a suspect?"

"Not at first. Then Miss Goodwin informed us that he had been in Lady Brandon's house at the time of the theft."

"Did you arrest him?"

"Not at that time. He was using the name Jack Strawman, and we were unable to find him."

"And were you able to find him after the theft of Lady Beekman's jewelry?"

"We were, and questioned him. But we could not hold him because there was no evidence of any kind. No one had seen him steal anything, no jewelry had been sold by him, and there was nothing at his dwelling."

Where was his dwelling, Amanda wondered. She had never known, and now that seemed to be suspicious, just another in a web of lies Peter-Richard had woven around her, probably to get something from her. Information? About what? Were those kisses even real, or was he just trying to romance her into telling or giving him something?

"So he is a suspect in the same way as Miss Goodwin, at the present time?"

"Yes."

There were no more witnesses. With both the prosecution and defense finished with their case, the judge delivered his decision.

"I declare Mr. Breem and Mr. Dunn guilty of the kidnapping of Miss Amanda Goodwin and Mr. Peter Joshua, or rather Richard Pennington-Smythe. They are each sentenced to two years hard labor."

It only occurred to Amanda later that she did not know whom they had been working for. Surely those idiots had not conceived the plot themselves. Before she took the stand, had the criminals been questioned about this, or about what their intention was in kidnapping them? She looked around to ask Mr. King but he was gone. She decided to return to Mrs. Slatterly's lodgings as quickly as possible to confront Peter-Richard, but when she arrived she could not find him.

"He left already," said Mrs. Slatterly with a shrug. "Case is over, so he said he had no need to stay."

"Did he say where he was going, or leave a message for me?"

"No, miss, he didn't. I'm sorry. Would you like your tea brought up?"

Amanda was grateful for the consideration, and when she saw her face in the glass, she knew the reason for Mrs. Slatterly's kindness. She didn't look at all well.

But what did she expect, she thought? She'd been a deluded fool. Her grandfather had been right. He had never said anything derogatory about men in general, she remembered, only the positive aspects of being an independent woman. It looked like there was more to it than that. When you got down to it, the only person you could rely on was yourself.

After tea, she looked out the window to check the weather and decided a walk was in order. Her anger at herself was tying her stomach in knots, and she needed some fresh air before dark. Without a destination, she just began walking. Through the gardens at the Inns of Court, down to the Embankment toward Charing Cross and Whitehall. This always felt to her like the center of the giant metropolis, and at times like this it was soothing to feel part of something so much bigger than herself. The city as a living, breathing entity was fascinating, perhaps even more so since she preferred the countryside.

She walked all the way down to Westminster Bridge then turned back as twilight was falling so she could see the lights. As it got dark, she saw them come on, large lights powered by electricity, making the Victoria Embankment safer at night. There were now over fifty such lamps along the way, and she was enchanted by the way they provided such bright illumination, even if they had to be frequently replaced. She could hear them buzzing above her head.

It was a new world, she thought, with wonders in it. And yet some things didn't change. Women would fall in love with the wrong men, even women who were older and should know better. And some men, no matter how mature they become in years, would retain their lying and thieving ways. The most charming of them could lead even an intelligent woman on, enticing them into thinking they might be in love, while all the time fooling them.

As the cold night air cleared her head, Amanda tried to be more rational. Nothing had really happened other than her own feelings, nothing irreversible, no promises made. She had set off on a certain path to find the miniature. That path had bought her in contact with a charming rogue and there had been a few adventures. Her own conduct had been as much at fault for her losing her position as anything he had done.

Amanda heard the steamboats on the river, carrying people and goods to their destination. She had no idea where Peter-Richard had gone and she tried not to care. But her heart ached. Was that his betrayal? Certainly. Was it also that she might not see him again? She had to admit that was possible.

44 - Winter Preparations

Amanda had said little after her return to Lufstow Farm, and her grandfather had not pressed her. He had heard about the result of the trial, and read about it in the newspaper Mrs. Lowry brought him. Amanda had not told him that she had discovered that Richard Pennington-Smythe, previously known as Peter Joshua, was the heir to Soffitt's estate and owned the land they were living and working on. She thought at least she could spare him that.

She tried to distract herself with work, because she couldn't bear to think what Peter's new identity meant, or just how deeply he had been lying to her. She had put the paper she'd taken from the law office in the drawer of her dresser with her handkerchiefs.

The decorating for Christmas was quite different from that at Heddington Hall. Cider was pressed, ready to make into wassail punch. Amanda went for walks on the farm, bringing back pine boughs and cones for their sharp smell. Mrs. Lowry had been fattening a goose since the beginning of November, knowing she would spend Christmas with her neighbor. There was no large tree, extravagant wreaths and candles, or large gatherings.

Tasks on the farm became more urgent as winter approached. While the animals had already been housed, there was a good deal of kindling to collect from the wood, and Grandfather had hired one of Mrs. Lowry's workers to chop the trees that had been felled in August into firewood for next year, and to bring last year's wood nearer the house.

There had been little barley grown this year, just enough for the house, because the prices were still too low to sell any. But what they had grown had been processed and stored. There were hams and bacon in the pantry, and enough chickens and eggs to provide for the winter. The turnips had been pulled and were ready to feed to the animals, and if necessary themselves.

The wool from the sheep, sheared in summer, was ready. Normally it would have been sold, but the price of wool had fallen and Grandfather had kept it dry and stored for next year. Instead of doing fancy but unnecessary embroidery, Amanda planned to spend much of winter carding and spinning wool to knit into useful things.

The practical nature of tasks on the farm gradually cheered Amanda, but at night, which came quite early, she often felt lonely. Grandfather was excellent company, but he'd begun closing his eyes shortly after dinner. He didn't even bother to have a pipe anymore before bed. Still awake, Amanda would read by the light of her lamp or tallow candles, but sometimes, especially when she could hear the wind outside the house, her mind would wander, and it always wandered the same way.

Peter's voice, the way his eyes crinkled when he was amused, his unfashionably curly dark hair. The way he laughed at her cursing, and tried to interfere when she took herself too seriously.

But then she'd remember his panic on the witness stand as he realized what was about to be made public. The revelation that his name was actually Richard Pennington-Smythe. What a name! Was he aristocracy, or did the paper she had seen at the solicitor's simply mean there was a coincidence, that someone named Soffitt had renamed himself Pennington-Smythe. She was not stupid, she told herself; he must be related to George Soffitt to be his heir, whatever his name was.

She had nightmares. She would dream that Richard (she tried desperately to always think of him as Richard now—it kept the anger fresh) would appear on the farm with a piece of paper. He would explain in his most amused tone that he was taking over the farm to incorporate it with his other holdings. And then, as she started to swear at him, he would laugh and laugh, not kindly laughter as if he found something funny, but a horrible evil laugh that would echo in her head until it woke her up.

Other dreams haunted her too: Lady Brandon throwing her bodily out of Heddington Hall, with Lady Vance laughing wickedly in the background. Inspector Hawk accusing her in court of having taunted the two criminals into taking her into the shed. Mrs. O'Reilly feeding her beef and potatoes that choked her until she couldn't breathe.

She thought she might go mad, and that isolating herself at Lufstow Farms would be a very bad idea. If she spent the holidays talking farming with her grandfather and being awakened by horrible dreams, surely it would be better to try to cultivate some friendships with other farmers in the area. She could perhaps use Christmas as an excuse to trade some preserves for some mincemeat pies, and to exchange farming techniques. It would get her out of the house and into some company.

Accordingly she cleaned the cart thoroughly and gave it a fresh coat of green paint. She took the dried currants and nuts in the larder and made fruitcakes to bring as well as the preserves. The clothes she had worn at Heddington were good quality, so she wore those dresses and cloaks on her visit so that Lufstow wouldn't look like a poor and meagre farm. For the next week, she made a point of visiting all the neighbors within two miles, and a few more within three. She talked with some of the women about corn prices, and cooking techniques, and knitting. But she also talked with the men about sheep-raising and the best feed for horses and how to store the barley that had been left out in sheaves.

She began connecting with other farmers and discovered that only Lufstow was entailed. All the other local families had held on to their farms throughout the years of bad investments and poor prices. The older farmers told Amanda that the country was experiencing an agricultural depression because of all the imported foodstuffs, but that prices could stabilize soon. The entail on the farm would not prevent her and Grandfather making improvements, but she found it hard to consider loans for investing in the farm if she knew it would only be in the family until her own death.

Thus it was that even before Christmas Eve, Amanda grudgingly admitted that she must continue her quest, not for the miniature, which was lost unless she found it someday in a Portsmouth antique shop, but for a revision of the entail. While she obviously wouldn't be marrying that louse Richard Pennington-Smythe, she might someday marry someone or have a child or adopt one to continue Lufstow Farm. It would be necessary for long-term planning, she argued with herself, to get full control over the property. Her grandfather, delighted that she was bringing him a plan after so many days of silence, heartily agreed. Her letter to Mr. Comstock was posted an hour later.

45 - The Christmas Festival

In response to her inquiry as to the whereabouts of Richard Pennington-Smythe, Amanda received this curt reply from Mr. Comstock:

> *Miss Goodwin,*
>
> *We regret that we have been unable to locate Mr. Pennington-Smythe in West Sussex, Hampshire, or Surrey, and have contacted our associates in London. We have placed an advertisement in the local newspapers as well as the Times asking him to contact our office, and will request an adjustment to your entail when he replies.*
>
> *Best regards,*
>
> *Adam Comstock, Esq.*

This seemed absurd, that a man with a name like Pennington-Smythe should be so difficult to locate. She had seen him at the trial, after all. One cannot simply disappear.

The Christmas Festival in Petersfield was on Saturday. Amanda and her grandfather had only needed a few days to ready the butter, jam, and mincemeat for sale. Added to Mrs. Lowry's baked bread and brooms, they had enough for a table if not a proper stand. They traveled together in Mrs. Lowry's big farm cart, together with her worker Johan. The day was blessedly bright, although it had rained the night before.

They had a small corner next to the Corn Market, and set up everything there with the wagon behind. She could see the office of Birch and Comstock but they appeared to be closed. The morning was profitable, the jam and mincemeat selling well. Amanda was just wondering whether she should take some of the butter back to the wagon when she saw Inspector Hawk walking across The Square with a constable. They did not look like they were there to enjoy the Festival.

Hawk bowed quickly to Grandfather and Mrs. Lowry, then turned to Amanda.

"Excuse me, Miss Goodwin, but I am here in an official capacity."

She looked up at him, uncertain what that meant. Was he here to give her information on something, or to ask her questions? He looked apologetic.

"How do you mean, Inspector Hawk?"

"I regret to say that I am here to arrest you and bring you to Petersfield Jail."

He waited as the three of them absorbed this.

Grandfather spoke first. "What might the charge be, Inspector?"

The constable had taken a stance beside the table, apparently ready in case Amanda should try to make a run for it.

"Sir, I am sorry to report that the charge is theft."

"What the hell am I supposed to have stolen?" Amanda retorted.

Hawk gave her a disapproving look. "Lady Vance's necklace, stolen from Heddington Hall on the 29th of October, and Mrs. Beekman's tiara and bracelet, stolen from her home in Portsmouth the 4th of November."

"I am no thief," said Amanda, her brow creasing in anger. It occurred to her that if they thought her guilty, she should have been arrested before. "Why are you arresting me now?"

"Evidence has come to light. We now have a witness from Lady Beekman's household, and the jewels themselves. Lady Vance's necklace has also been recovered."

"Excellent. Whatever has that to do with me?" She noticed that people in The Square were now avoiding their table, having seen the police and heard loud voices.

"You have been connected to both, and are to accompany me now to Portsmouth Police Station."

Amanda looked over at Grandfather and Mrs. Lowry, who were staring at Inspector Hawk, stunned. It would not do to make them more upset than they would already be by arguing or resisting. She turned to them.

"I assure you, Grandfather, I have stolen nothing, but I have heard of these matters and am sure this is a mistake. The only way to prove it will be to go with Inspector Hawk to Portsmouth."

She took her cloak off the corner of the wagon, and grabbed her purse, which had a few shillings in it. Her Grandfather rose and came over to her.

"Must you really go with them, child?"

"I must. And I assure you everything will be quite all right. You and Mrs. Lowry finish out the day, and I shall return to Lufstow as soon as I can. But please do not worry." She glanced over at the law offices across The Square. "I know a good solicitor should I need one."

Johan had come over to see if he could help. Amanda took him aside quickly and asked him to let Mr. Comstock know what had happened if he should return to the office. Not Mr. Birch, mind—only Mr. Comstock. Then she went with Inspector Hawk and the constable to the police van, and sat herself proudly inside. She had nothing to fear, she told herself. *I have never stolen anything, except that piece of paper from the law office, and that was secured at the farm.*

As they rode the several hours to Portsmouth, she was alone in the van with the constable. Hawk must be riding outside with the driver or have remained in Petersfield. She said nothing to the constable, and after a quarter of an hour his head leaned against the side of the van and he was asleep.

She had a great deal of time to think. How could any evidence possibly point to her? Maybe it didn't. Maybe she had simply been where she shouldn't have been, in the wrong place at the wrong time somehow. Or maybe the witness had seen someone who looked like her. Did she have a thieving doppelganger in Portsmouth? Was she being considered as the actual thief or as an accessory?

But the big question was whether she knew the actual thief, and whether it was in fact Jack Strawman, also known as Peter Joshua, now apparently Richard

Pennington-Smythe. If he did the robberies, he could clear her, but would he? Or would he let her go to prison rather than admit his own wrong-doing? He obviously thought nothing of lying, and she could see no reason he would discontinue doing so for her.

So next, as she listened to the constable snoring and snorting when they went over a bump in the road, Amanda began to go through dates in her head. An accusation for Lady Vance's theft on the 29th of October made sense, since she was at Heddington Hall at the time. But the other date, the 4th of November? She had been at Heddington, but believed that was the night she had met Jack-Peter-Richard in the orangerie. If so, neither of them could have done it.

That was it, then, she thought. She could not be convicted of Mrs. Beekman's jewel robbery, because "Richard" would tell the judge they had been at Heddington, together. That could be a problem for her reputation, but better that than imprisonment for robbery. Besides, her reputation was already in tatters thanks to the overnight imprisonment.

Was the charge larceny rather than theft? She wasn't sure she knew the difference. Mr. Comstock would, of course. He would explain to her. He wasn't a barrister, only a solicitor, but perhaps he would know a barrister who could defend her in court.

46 - Two cells in Portsmouth

The police station in Portsmouth was large enough to have four holding cells for people awaiting an appearance before a judge, and Amanda was placed in one of these after her bag and clothing were checked for anything that could be used as a weapon. The cells were brick with barred windows on doors facing the corridor, so that one guard could walk down the hallway and check on everyone. Unlike in prison, the toilet was in an outbuilding in the yard, so permission had to be obtained and the prisoner accompanied each time.

Amanda sat there, no one visiting her or explaining anything, the entire day. Even the guard who took her out back for a toilet visit had said nothing. After a dinner of thin beef stew, bread, and turnips, she heard a sound of someone being brought in. The lamps glowed dimly in the cells and the corridor, but she could hear his voice joking with the constable. Peter Joshua—that is, Richard Pennington-Smythe—was clearly also being arrested and put in a holding cell, the cell next to hers. She did not think he saw her as he passed, but she assumed the police had informed him of her arrest.

Somehow she had imagined that he, that everyone else, would be outside the jail while she was in it, eager to find solutions. Mr. Comstock would do something once he heard from Johan, certainly. But now the man who called himself Richard had also been caught and thrown in here. Even though she had not written to or contacted him since the day she had lost her position as companion to Lady Brandon, she had felt aware of him. Despite the peacefulness and long, tiring days at Lufstow Farm, she had seen his face when she closed her eyes at night. Perhaps if things had been different, she would have liked the chance to know him better. His wry humor tried to hide what she was sure was a vulnerability. He had a history; she just didn't know what it was.

She wanted to write to Lady Brandon for support, but of course that was impossible. Lady Vance had threatened her reputation repeatedly, and Lady Brandon could not afford to help a former companion who was in jail for theft.

"Miss Goodwin," she heard whispered somewhere near the floor. She looked down to see a small drain in the flagstones. It must connect to the other cell on that side of the corridor, for when they washed down the cells. Richard was trying to talk to her.

Should she reply? Her heart twisted. The sound of his voice touched her somewhere inside, and she didn't want it to.

"What?"

"I want to apologize."

A flood of invectives filled Amanda's head. An apology after lying about one's name the first time might be acceptable, but the second time?

"Go away, you bastard," she hissed into the drain.

"My parents were married, Miss Goodwin, as I am sure yours were."

There was a silence. Amanda looked at the ceiling. It looked the same as three hours ago. The light was fading, and she would soon be in total darkness.

There was the sound of boots in the corridor, and the guard appeared at the bars.

"I have brought a lamp, miss. You are permitted to use it until I come round again for lights out." He unlocked the door and handed in a lamp, already lit, with a handle. She took it, he locked the door, then she heard him say something similar to Mr. Pennington-Smythe. At least she wouldn't have to sit there all evening in the dark. But it was getting rather cold. She put the lamp close to the cot and sat down.

"Miss Goodwin." Another whisper through the floor drain.

She jumped down off the cot.

"Mr. Strawman, or Joshua, or Pennington-Smythe or whoever you are, I have no interest in talking to you."

A pause.

"Then please listen. I went to the Guildhall in London and discovered who owns the shed we were trapped in."

Amanda didn't want to reply, but curiosity got the better of her.

"Who?"

"The firm of Birch and Comstock."

That was perplexing, but Amanda was suspicious. Why should he tell her this?

"So?"

"Do not trust Mr. Comstock, Miss Goodwin. He is not being truthful with you."

"Truthful? Truthful?" Amanda was trying hard not to yell, but her whisper was as full of venom as she could make it. "Who are you to warn me about truthfulness? What have you to say about truth? Nothing I want to hear, I assure you."

"Miss Goodwin, I am trying to protect you."

"Mr. Whatever-your-name-is, I do not require your protection. In fact the few times I have had it, bad things have happened to me. I have willingly accompanied you, hoping to find my grandfather's miniature, and now I am being accused of theft. A theft, I might add, that you probably committed."

"I have stolen from no one, Miss Goodwin. But you have stolen something from me."

Now this was too much.

"And what, pray tell, would that be, you reprobate?"

She could barely hear his reply.

"My heart, Amanda. My heart."

Amanda sat down hard on the floor. What fresh trick was this? She had heard of men pledging devotion just to obtain something from a woman. And certainly there had been no talk of love.

The guard came down the corridor again, this time with a blanket, a piece of bread, and a pitcher of water for each of them. When he had gone, Amanda splashed some of the water on her face. This made her even colder, but helped to calm the feelings rising within her. She crouched down by the drain.

"You lied to me, Mr. Pennington-Smythe. You have lied to me about your name and what you do. You have made a fool out of me, sir, and I do not deserve it." Tears began to form, and she swiped them away with the back of her hand. It was cold on the floor, and she took the blanket the guard had brought and wrapped it around her. They were arguing, yet she still found his voice soothing, even whispered up through a drain. Imagining being here by herself tonight made her skin crawl.

"No, Amanda, you do not deserve it. I am a cad. But believe it or not, I care very much about you."

Amanda was glad he couldn't see the tears fall. She looked around for something to put over the drain so he couldn't hear her cry, and there wasn't anything. So she sat on top of it instead.

Once the guard announced lights out, she curled up on the cot in the blanket, still cold. As she went to sleep she heard the drain whisper, "Goodnight, Amanda."

47 - A Recitation

It is never a good idea to get arrested on a Saturday. The courts typically do not operate on Sunday, which means one is in custody an additional day. Amanda was beginning to feel like she'd worn this dress for a month, but that was probably from spending so much time on the floor.

Upon waking that morning, she decided not to speak to Richard Pennington-Smythe. No amount of anger or swearing was going to fix anything. Whatever had happened between them before was just that: before. She had no need of him, nor he of her.

A breakfast of gruel and bacon was brought to them, and afterward they were each to take a walk around the yard, separately. When Amanda returned from a very unsatisfactory walk around the yard, the dark gray clouds closing in and promising rain, there was another prisoner in one of the cells. Amanda caught only a glimpse out of the corner of her eye as the guard took her past, but she could see it was a woman in brightly colored clothing. Her cell was directly across from Richard's. That should keep him entertained, she thought.

Sitting doing nothing was exceedingly dull, and on an afternoon visit to the outhouse she asked the guard if it would be possible to have something to read. He grunted, but an hour later brought her last Tuesday's *Evening News* and a battered copy of *Robinson Crusoe*. She thanked him and he grunted again.

"Ooooh we're bringing books, are we?" a brassy voice called from the third cell. "If I could read, I'd want one too, warden!" She laughed and it brought on a fit of loud coughing.

Then a few minutes later: "Say, missy! Whatcha reading?"

"Robinson Crusoe," Amanda hollered back down the corridor.

"Well, let's hear it then! Nothing else to do."

"Oh, yes, please!" said Richard loudly so he could be heard.

"See, the gennelmen wants it too. We'll be very very quiet so's we can hear you. Shhhhh."

It seemed Amanda had no choice, although she was sorry now she'd asked for something to read. She had to stand in front of the barred window in her door, and raise her voice so they could hear.

> *I was born in the year 1632, in the city of York,*
> *of a good family, though not of that country,*
> *my father being a foreigner of Bremen, who*
> *settled first at Hull. . . .*

She stopped when some bread and cheese arrived for lunch, then there were three separate walks out to the yard, after which she was prevailed upon to continue.

> *In the morning I took the Bible; and beginning*

> *at the New Testament, I began seriously to read it, and imposed upon myself to read a while every morning and every night; not tying myself to the number of chapters, but long as my thoughts should engage me. It was not long after I set seriously to this work till I found my heart more deeply and sincerely affected with the wickedness of my past life.*

It becoming dark at four o'clock, she stopped, and sat down to read the newspaper by the light of the lamp brought to her. She knew that Richard could not communicate with her without being heard by the other prisoner, so she didn't listen for him.

But she did think about Robinson Crusoe, and his gratitude to God. This had come slowly, not in his first weeks on the island. He had begun to think about his sins.

Amanda began to think about hers. She had entered George Soffitt's house in the middle of the night intending to steal the miniature. She had stolen the name-change paper from the law office, without even knowing why. She had promised herself she would find the miniature and had failed. She had wanted Richard Pennington-Smythe when he was Peter Joshua, and now she hated him. Oddly, he did not seem to hate her. On the contrary, he had tried to talk to her, and even given her a warning. It was a mistaken warning, but still, it meant he cared about her.

Some of her sins weren't sins at all, of course. She loved her grandfather, and it had been right to go back to Lufstow Farm and help manage it. Mrs. Brandon had enjoyed her company for quite some time before there had been a problem. And she had been savvy enough to avoid Mr. Birch when he made it clear what he wanted.

What he wanted from her, however, she had wanted from Richard. Self-honesty, she thought, is easier in the dark and quiet, even if it's in jail. The attraction was undeniable. That dark wavy hair, those intense eyes, that scar. She wanted to kiss it. Perhaps the dark and quiet weren't such a good idea after all.

If only he weren't so deceptive. You cannot change people, she thought. She hadn't lived twenty-seven years to learn nothing at all about human nature. She might be willing to steal when it was important to someone she loved, and lie to protect someone. But basically she was an honest and forthright person. Perhaps she swore too much and angered too easily. But her heart, she believed, was in the right place.

48 - The Honorable Judge Trout

At ten the next morning Amanda was taken to court. Her voice was hoarse from reading aloud. She was unable to say anything to Richard before she left.

She had slept fitfully, partly because she was cold but partly because her heart was heavy. While the wrongs Richard had done to her could not be repaired, the fact that she thought they should be caused her to question herself. Was she an unforgiving person?

Amanda recognized the judge the moment she entered the courtroom. It was Judge Septimus Trout, who had been to luncheon at Heddington Hall less than a fortnight ago. She looked around but there was no solicitor and no barrister, just herself to answer the charges. Mr. Comstock had not answered her call, assuming that Johan had even seen him and informed him of her plight. She realized now she should have confided that task to Mrs. Lowry.

The charges against her she already knew, but the first witness she didn't recognize. It was a maid from Mrs. Beekman's household. Amanda had heard of Mrs. Beekman, but did not recall ever meeting her, although she could have been a guest at one of Lady Brandon's affairs. The maid she didn't recognize at all, and yet this girl claimed to have seen her in front of Mrs. Beekman's house shortly after the robbery, putting something in her purse.

The judge asked her for details, and recorded them on a paper in front of him.

"How do you know it was Miss Goodwin?" he asked.

"I seen her." The maid's jaw was set stubbornly.

"The robbery took place at five o'clock," he reminded the witness. "How did you manage to see her in front of the house?"

"Beg pardon, sir?"

"It was dark before five. How did you see her?"

"Dunno. Just did."

"How big was the tiara?" asked the judge, and the maid held her hands out.

"How big was the purse you saw?"

The maid was flustered by the questions and was shaken when she left the stand.

Judge Trout then asked Amanda if she would like to answer the evidence.

"Yes, sir. I have never been near Mrs. Beekman's house to my knowledge, and was at Heddington Hall all day on the date in question."

She explained how that day had gone, and the times of day she had spent with Lady Brandon.

"What of the evening, Miss Goodwin?" the judge asked.

"That evening I was in the company of someone I knew as Jack Strawman. We met and spoke together in the orangerie."

A man in the audience, obviously a reporter of some kind, raised his eyebrows and jotted a note in his little book.

"What was the nature of this conversation, Miss Goodwin?"

"Sir, does that have any bearing on the case?"

"I do not know, Miss Goodwin, until you answer the question."

She thought how best to phrase this without lying.

"We were discussing wrongs that had been done to us, and how we might address them."

The judge looked surprised. "And what were these wrongs?"

Honest words flooded out of her. Amanda explained about the miniature, including the details of Soffitt and Lufstow Farm, and her companion's need to find a paper that would clear his family name.

"I see," said Judge Trout. "So you were not in or near Portsmouth on the 4th of November?"

"No, sir."

The next witness called was Miss Elizabeth Blythe, whom Amanda remembered had been outside the library door on the day of the Heddington Hall birthday party. They and the Morgans had been the only people who knew of the theft of Lady Vance's necklace. Amanda looked out hopefully, but did not see Lady Brandon among the visitors. Lady Vance had come into the courtroom and was now sitting in the front row, glaring at the proceedings.

"I saw the accused come out of the library in a hurry," said Miss Blythe. "We told her about the theft. Of course now we realize she already knew, since she had committed it herself."

"Did you see her steal Lady Vance's necklace?" Judge Trout asked.

"No. But I know she did."

"Did you at any time see Lady Vance's necklace in her possession?"

"No, we did not. She must have hidden it in her room."

"Did anyone ask you not to talk about the robbery?"

"Yes, Lady Brandon herself. She asked all three of us to keep quiet, which we did. But Lady Vance has since asked us to speak up."

Next was a cab driver, who had been driving past the Beekman house at the time of the theft of the tiara and bracelet. He claimed he saw someone in dark clothing leaving the area of the house, but he could not identify the person, not even as a man or woman.

The last witness was Inspector Hawk himself.

"At the Heddington Hall incident, were not all the rooms searched by the police, and all staff interviewed?"

"Yes, sir. We searched the house quietly and interviewed everyone."

"How soon after the robbery did your men arrive?"

"It was about eight in the evening, sir, that Lady Brandon's butler called to inform us of the theft."

"So the theft took place around eight?"

"No, sir. We were given to understand in the interviews that the theft occurred about two hours prior."

"Do you know the cause of the delay?"

"No, sir."

The judge dismissed the Inspector and wrote some more notes on his paper. People in the court began murmuring among themselves, and in a few minutes Judge Trout tapped his gavel.

"It is my finding that although new evidence has been presented in this case, it has not proven that Miss Amanda Goodwin is the perpetrator of these crimes. The evidence is not sufficient for full trial on either robbery, and at this point the Beekman robbery relies only on the maid's testimony, which is tenuous at best. The police will need to confirm that evidence before this case can go to trial." He turned to Amanda. "You may go, Miss Goodwin, and thank you for coming to Portsmouth for this hearing. Please stay in contact with the police."

Amanda didn't realize how frightened she had been until she left the courtroom. Inspector Hawk came up to speak to her.

"Lady Brandon sends her regards," he said quietly.

Amanda stared at him. Is that why this had gone so well? Had Lady Brandon somehow interfered? She glanced over to see Lady Vance leaving in a huff with the maid who had testified trotting behind her.

"Thank you, Inspector."

He walked her over to the police van that would take her back to Lufton Farm. Amanda looked at it.

"I have a few shillings," said Amanda. "I think I would prefer to take the train after sending a note to Johan to fetch me."

"Then I shall walk you to the rail station." She found his deep baritone reassuring.

As they walked, Amanda was not sure what to say, but she was bothered by the thought of Richard still in custody.

"Inspector Hawk, what will happen to Richard Pennington-Smythe?"

"He shall have a hearing just as you have had. His is tomorrow."

"I see."

The day was bright. Inspector Hawk was not a tall man, but his manner bespoke reliability and intelligence.

"Miss Goodwin, I do not believe that you have stolen jewels as you were accused today. But I hope you understand that the case has been building and it was necessary to have a hearing."

"Yes, Inspector, I do understand. I was in the house when Lady Vance's necklace was taken. But the Mrs. Beekman theft mystifies me."

"Indeed. It was when the maid came to us that I suspected you were not the thief, or in cooperation with the thief. Her story seemed influenced, somehow. Could you have made an enemy of Lady Vance or Mrs. Beekman in some way?"

Amanda considered. "Lady Vance is on something of a campaign against Lady Brandon at the moment, but I know nothing of Mrs. Beekman."

"She is a close friend of Lady Vance," said Inspector Hawk.

They were at the train station. Amanda went up the steps. The building was large and ornate, and looked something like a French chateau. She turned around and saw that the Inspector was turning away.

"Inspector Hawk!" she called out to him. He turned back.

"Where does Richard Pennington-Smythe live?"

At that moment a train started coming in to the station, and she could not hear his reply before he waved and turned away.

49 - At the Farm

"Thank the Lord you are here," said Mrs. Lowry. "It's Morris. I'm afraid he took a turn yesterday."

Amanda had just come back to Lufstow Farm with Johan, who had told her that although he had been fine when they returned from the Christmas Festival in Petersfield, Grandfather had struggled to get out of bed Sunday. Dr. Kirk had been called, and said he was overtired. He had given him a tonic and orders to rest.

"I think your arrest affected him more than we knew," said Mrs. Lowry. "He didn't talk about it all the way back, but we could tell."

Johan nodded in agreement.

"Then I shall go now and tell him I am quite all right, and the thievery charges have been dropped. Their evidence against me was poor."

"Thank the Lord," Mrs. Lowry said again. "I will make some tea. Do go up, child."

Grandfather lay in bed, and he was a little pale but otherwise looked all right. Amanda sat by the side of the bed, where it was obvious Mrs. Lowry had been sitting.

"Goodness, Grandfather. What has happened?"

He smiled a weak smile.

"Just tired, Amanda. I think my days of Christmas Festivals are likely few."

"Oh, don't say that, Grandfather. The doctor said you just need to rest."

Grandfather laughed softly.

"Me, rest? There are chickens and sheep to feed. Ernestina had to milk the cows for me this morning."

Amanda noticed the use of Christian names between Mrs. Lowry and Grandfather.

"Has Mrs. Lowery taken good care of you?"

"Oh, yes, except she makes me stay in bed."

"Like Doctor Kirk said."

"Yes." He smiled again. "Like Doctor Kirk said. Damn quack."

"Oh yes, he's a quack. Except that he tends to be right," she reminded him. "Where is this tonic he gave you?"

Grandfather gestured vaguely toward the washstand.

Amanda took a sniff. "Smells like nettle and chamomile, at least. A bit of laudanum too, I shouldn't wonder. This should help give you strength and deeper sleep. Are you still taking the foxglove, too?" The bottle of foxglove drops was also on the washstand.

Grandfather tried to push himself up a bit.

"What happened in Portsmouth?" he asked.

"It was a long journey, but it went well. Afterward Inspector Hawk said he had never suspected me, but the new evidence had to be considered."

"What new evidence?"

Amanda explained what had happened, about the maid and Lady Vance, then about the jail and Richard Pennington-Smythe, who had been Peter Joshua.

"That was the name you wrote me about, Pennington-Smythe, but I'd never heard of him. I did not realize this was the same man as Peter Joshua. Why does his name keep changing?" Grandfather looked confused.

"I swear I do not know. The first time I was certain that his original name, Jack Strawman, had to be false. I assumed that was because he was trying to not be known. But I found a paper at Mr. Birch and Comstock's office in Petersfield that showed someone named Soffitt changing their name to Pennington-Smythe. I am ashamed to say I took that paper with me."

"You think he's related to George Soffitt?"

"Someone in his family must be, don't you think?"

Grandfather was looking better now that they were talking. He suppressed a smile.

"You were asking about marriage before. Was this the man you were thinking about?"

Amanda hesitated. "Yes, I suppose so. But that is no longer the case."

"Because he lied about his name?"

"Oh, not just that. He has lied about so much more."

"Has he taken advantage of you, or abused your feelings?"

Amanda had to admit that he had not.

"But he makes me so angry, Grandfather. Sometimes I cannot contain my fury with him."

Grandfather smiled again and snuggled down into his bed. Amanda saw his eyes close, turned down the lamp, and left him to sleep.

After two days of rest, Amanda's nursing, and Mrs. Lowry's beef broth, Grandfather was able to sit up in bed and even read a little. He was still very weak, but Doctor Kirk visited and said he could be taken to sit downstairs in the parlor, or outside if it was warm enough. Johan was strong enough to lift him wherever he needed to go.

Amanda was relieved at his progress, and happy to take over the duties with the animals in the barn. Her mind must have been on Richard, again, because the sun was just setting when Amanda looked up from feeding the chickens and thought she saw him dismount a horse and make his way through the barn gate. She stood and watched as the figure came further up the path, her heart starting to beat faster. It was him, here at Lufton Farm. She couldn't move, so she stood and waited as he approached the house. Then he saw her at the coop.

He smiled broadly as he approached her, his red woolen cap making him look like a woodsman. He was wearing a proper farmer's coat instead of a cloak, and his face was ruddy from the cold.

"Hello!" he said cheerily. "May I put Spencer here in the barn?" The horse was pulling on the lead toward the barn, sensing where he was supposed to go.

Amanda nodded, still dumbstruck. She finished feeding the chickens and added fresh straw to keep them warm for the night. Her thoughts were in confusion. What was he doing here? At the same time, she thought how wonderful it was that he was here. She walked slowly toward the barn. Richard had removed Spencer's bridle and saddle, and was brushing him down. He had put the horse in the stall next to Annie, the old mule, who was snorting quietly. Amanda couldn't tell if she was unhappy at the invasion or happy for the company. Just like me, thought Amanda. She went over to Annie and stroked her nose.

She watched in silence as Richard brushed down the horse and covered him with a sturdy blanket. He then fetched a bucket of feed and a bucket of water from near the barn door. *Just like he's been here all the time*, thought Amanda, as she watched him move with confidence doing his tasks.

The horse cared for, he turned to Amanda.

"My dear, I bring you a treasure."

He reached into the saddlebag on the floor. Amanda's eyes opened wide as he handed her a small oval object. It was the miniature. Her grandmother's face looked out at her.

She couldn't help it. She reached out to him and took him in her arms, lifting her face to his. He kissed her softly, then with increasing urgency. She pushed her fingers up into his hair, and the red cap fell to the ground. He pulled back and looked at her face as if searching for something, then he smiled.

"Pleased to be of assistance."

Amanda shook her head to clear it. "I need to go inside. It is time for dinner with Grandfather."

"May I join you? And may I beg a bed for the night?"

Amanda swallowed, and looked up at him. If she stared at him much longer, she wouldn't want to go back inside at all. Somewhere in the back of her head a voice chided her to come to her senses.

"Yes, of course. Grandfather will be happy to meet you."

They walked together to the house. Johan was just leaving. He gave Richard a strange look.

"I am on my way, Miss Goodwin. He's settled upstairs, but he says he is hungry."

"An excellent sign, Johan. Thank you for your help today."

"I'm Richard Pennington-Smythe," Richard said with a bow. "Pleased to make your acquaintance."

"I'm sorry," said Amanda, surprised but remembering her manners. "Johan, this is Mr. Pennington-Smythe. And this is Johan. He works for Mrs. Lowry on the next farm, and has been helping me with Grandfather."

Johan bowed to Richard, then said goodnight and left.

"Is there something amiss with your grandfather?" Richard asked quietly as they took off their coats and hung them near the kitchen door.

"Yes, he has been unwell. I need to bring him his dinner upstairs." She went over to the pot on the stove, and started serving out the pea soup, putting a slice of ham and a slice of bread and butter on a plate.

"How can I help?" asked Richard.

"Pour some of that milk into a mug and bring that cloth, please? And don't say a word about the miniature just yet. He's been weak and I want him to eat first."

Amanda entered Grandfather's room first, asking Richard to wait outside for a moment. The old man was sitting up in bed, reading a book.

"I have your dinner, Grandfather," she said, setting up the tray.

"Thank you, child." He handed her the farming magazine he'd been reading.

"We have a guest tonight, Grandfather. Richard Pennington-Smythe has come, and would like to meet you." She was surprised it came out so calmly.

Grandfather looked up at her in surprise.

"I'll be damned," he said. "I would very much like to meet him!"

Richard came in with the cloth and the milk.

"I am sorry to intrude, Mr. Goodwin. I hear you are unwell."

"Have been, yes. Take a chair, my boy, take a chair. Keep me company while I eat."

Richard moved the chair closer to the bed and leaned over to put the cloth around the old man's neck. Then he looked at Amanda, who shrugged.

"I would be delighted, Mr. Goodwin."

Amanda did not want to leave them. She wanted to gaze at Richard some more, and enjoy seeing her grandfather eat heartily. But too many voices wasn't good for him, and she wanted to get the kitchen clean and prepare Richard's bed.

"I will leave you two together," she said, giving a questioning glance at Richard, who nodded agreement. "I have much to do."

Richard was busy helping Grandfather with the soup, and neither noticed her leave.

She lit a lamp and shook out the bedding in the small bedroom, then added more wool blankets from the cupboard in case Richard was cold in the night. She filled the ewer on the washstand with water, put a clean cloth next to it, and looked around the room. What else might he need? Something to read, she thought, and went to her own room to select a book. Most of them were agricultural, but she found a few recent novels and chose *Daniel Deronda* for the bedside. It occurred to her that he might not have nightclothes with him, so she folded a nightshirt over the chair. She warmed as she imagined him undressing, just on the other side of the wall from her bedchamber.

At the same time, she assumed that as soon as they started talking, they would start arguing. No, she wouldn't let that happen, she thought as she touched the miniature in her pocket. She would give it to Grandfather after his dinner. How had Richard found it, and where? How could she thank him?

Suddenly she knew how. She took the name-change paper from her dresser, and returning to the small bedroom placed it on the pillow.

50 - Unresolved Issues

Amanda and Richard had eaten together in the kitchen after Grandfather had finished his dinner, talking quietly. She had asked about the miniature.

"Wherever did you find it?"

"I discovered it before I was arrested. I had purchased a box of Soffitt miniatures in October, but this was not among them."

Amanda felt ashamed that she had assumed he had kept it a secret.

"When I left you at Heddington—is it really almost a fortnight now?—I was on the trail of the man I believed to be commanding our kidnappers. I went, as you know, to Bognor Regis, following him. It made sense that someone with stolen goods to sell would pawn them there, where so many people sell their belongings to pay gambling debts. It turned out he wasn't the top man, but just a lowly thief. He pawned not only your miniature, but at least five others. He must have stolen them, but when? and where?"

"From the solicitors' storeroom in Petersfield?" Amanda guessed.

"I don't know. We never found the miniatures there, even though they were on the manifest."

"Perhaps they were taken before we arrived?"

"We arrived so soon after the funeral. It doesn't make sense. But at least those six items are recovered."

Amanda smiled to herself as she remembered her grandfather's face when she'd given him the miniature just before preparing him for bed. He had cried, although he pretended he hadn't, and she had heard him talking to the picture as she left his room. She felt a sense of completion, of fences mended and gaps filled.

She and Richard spent the evening seated comfortably together in front of the downstairs fire.

"Your name," she ventured. "Why did you hide that you were Richard Pennington-Smythe?"

Richard exhaled slowly.

"There are several reasons. The first was that first night when we met robbing Soffitt's house. I had arrived that day, been there when he died, paid the servants and dismissed them, and was spending that night in one of the bedrooms."

"Ah, the bedroom slippers!"

"Yes, a poor choice. I hoped you wouldn't notice. You surprised me and I gave the first name I could think of: Jack Strawman."

"Another poor choice," said Amanda.

"I saw that immediately, but it was too late. I had been posing as Peter Joshua already, in the line of duty."

"What duty?" The hairs on the back of her neck stood up. Was it because she wasn't sure she wanted to hear what the duty was, or because he was so close that she could feel the heat of his body? They had curled up together in the shed on a cold night. But this night felt very different.

Richard moved a bit closer. "Well, here we have a bit of a problem. I am not supposed to tell."

As he said that, he leaned over and kissed her earlobe.

"And why is that?" She gasped as his kiss sent shivers through her.

"Because it's a secret." He turned her toward him and kissed her gently, then more intently. She pressed closer to him.

"Mmmm . . . I believe you are trying to distract me, sir." She kissed his scar gently, then wrapped her arms around his neck, moving her body closer.

"Is it working?" He lifted her onto his lap. Surely an aggressive move, but she took a breath and let it happen.

"Oh, yes," she said. He removed her spectacles and put them on the arm of the settee.

"You are beautiful," he said, his hand on her cheek. No one had ever said that to her before, and for a moment the intensity of emotion, and the feeling of the rightness of his touch, almost made her cry.

"So are you," she whispered, kissing him again.

"Miss Goodwin, I want to marry you."

She was suddenly very still. Marriage. Marriage meant so many things. It meant more than just kissing and holding him; it would mean her body would have to accept, and want, his attentions. Holding each other like this, she was overjoyed to think that would be possible, given time. Damned likely, if the feelings she felt now were any sort of guide.

But it also meant her property would be his. And as it was, he owned what she wanted. Her blissful imaginings of him when he was away, her joy at thrilling to his touch, faded to the background as she thought about her future.

"When, do you suppose, we can discuss business?"

"Business?" he said. The last thing on his mind was business, unless it was the business of getting her undressed. But she crawled off his lap and stood, somewhat unsteadily, in front of him.

"According to the entail, a Richard Pennington-Smith is the new party to the contract. To get the entail revised, I must talk to him."

"Um," Richard said, shaking his head to help him pay attention. "That's me. But I don't understand."

"You are George Soffitt's heir, are you not?"

"Yes, I believe that will soon be established. There are just a few things I must arrange first."

"Then you own this farm after my death."

"But surely I will die first." He was confused. "And if we marry, it will be ours."

"Yours by law," she said. "I want it to be mine."

He stared at her, that stubborn set jaw, those determined eyes.

"My dear Amanda, I have yet to establish myself in any legal sense. Once I do, we can revise the entail to say that you may marry and have children. But it won't be needed, because we shall be married." He looked at her serious face. "Won't we?"

A creak was heard from upstairs.

"I need to go up and check on Grandfather," Amanda said, retrieving her eye-glasses. "And then I shall go to bed." She leaned over and kissed him gently. "Goodnight, Richard."

As she went upstairs, Richard sat for a moment, his desire calmed and his mind in confusion. He had more serious business to consider than a farm. He was still being blackmailed, although he had decided not to pay anymore. That meant there might be danger from his blackmailer, "Soffitt and Son". There might still be danger from whoever had hired Breem and Dunn. He was confused why the judge had never asked about that, and he and Amanda wouldn't be safe until he knew. And he had still not found the name-change paper that would protect his family's good name.

That is, until he went upstairs and found it on his pillow.

51 - The Disappearance

It was five in the morning, and the sun had not yet risen. Neither had Grandfather, a phenomenon that Amanda assumed she would eventually become accustomed to. As he got older, the early hours were more difficult. Bundled up in her warmest woolen coat, she tiptoed past Richard's bedroom on her way downstairs. It had frosted in the night and it was hard to see out the windows.

Her heart warmed thinking of last evening, and what might have happened. Her own desire had surprised her. She had felt his firm thighs as she sat in his lap, his large hands caressing her back, and had felt no fear. While it was happening, she had not pictured that horrible man touching her all those years ago. She had often wondered whether she could ever let a man touch her again without feeling violated. Even when she was bumped into on a crowded London street, or someone reached to help her out of a carriage, she had instinctively wanted to pull away. Last night, she hadn't pulled away.

But she had stopped him, and not just because she was becoming uncomfortable.

She was not sure at what point she had decided she wanted Lufstow Farm to be in her name. It might have been last week when she was feeding the chickens, or when she had talked about the entail to Grandfather, or when she had given the old man the miniature.

It didn't matter. She had ambitions for the farm, ideas from reading about botany and agriculture. They might not have money but she now had time to study and implement discoveries. She wanted Richard with her body and her soul, but she didn't want him blindly. She needed a partner, not a master.

What if he refused? What if he continued to lie? Or what if, at forty, he was simply set in his ways and would continue to hide things from her and disappear for days at a time? Her thoughts turned darker. What if he had a wife somewhere? Maybe there was a Mrs. Joshua who didn't know he was a Pennington-Smythe. Maybe there was a Lady Pennington-Smythe? These were the questions that made her stomach knot. He would have found the name-change paper last night, and realized his family name was safe. Perhaps he would be so grateful that the farm would be a small price to pay, and they could be here together, forever. Or perhaps not. None of these musings made her inclined to want breakfast.

Out in the barn she grabbed a pail and headed over to the cows, but she noticed that the stall next to Annie's was empty. Richard's horse, Spencer, was gone. He had left, very early, without saying goodbye. The saddlebag was gone too. She ran up to his room. Sure enough, there were no clothes or personal items; everything had been tidied and the bed neatly made. Her heart sank. Her pace down the stairs was much slower, and she milked the cows and fed the chickens as if in a dream, her head down.

She had caused it, she thought. Her brash manner and her demands, her hesitation at his touch, had frightened him away. She hadn't sworn at him but she had been forceful about the farm, and she had heard that men did not like forceful women. Not that she had noticed him minding up until now. But to be so close in the evening and have him gone in the morning? It didn't take reading the stars to know that he had left her.

She tried to tell herself, as she looked around the barn, that at least during her lifetime this farm would be her grandfather's and hers. They would manage as best they could, perhaps joining forces with Mrs. Lowry. She could tell how deeply their neighbor cared for her grandfather, although he seemed somewhat oblivious to the love Amanda could see in her eyes. And he's such an astute man, she thought. But most people are astute when it comes to other people, and not so much about themselves.

She returned to the house to find Johan waiting for her, ready to help bring her grandfather downstairs before returning to Mrs. Lowry's. While he went up, Amanda made porridge and a plate with cold ham, brown bread, butter, and cheese for all of them. Johan always appreciated breakfast, and it had become routine to eat together before he went back. While it was nice to have Johan at the table, his English was limited and Amanda knew no German. She was missing Richard even though he had been at the farm for only one day. Grandfather asked where he had gone off to, and Amanda had to admit she didn't know where, or whether he would return. Grandfather nodded and said nothing, but noted her dismay.

Amanda spent much of the day doing farm chores, checking on Grandfather and making sure he took his tonic and had things to read, and making a list of items needed for Christmas dinner, including sultanas and dried currants for cake. She checked the cupboard to make sure that the supplies of cinnamon, nutmeg, and clove were enough—they were tightly sealed in containers, since a little had to go a long way. The lamb would come from Mrs. Lowry's farm in exchange for Lufstow Farm's butter.

Rain began to fall in the late afternoon, so Amanda bedded down the animals an hour early, and dinner was early too. She and Grandfather spent the evening reading quietly by lamplight, then Amanda took up her knitting. Knitting was an intermittent task, easy to take up and easy to interrupt, and she had been working on a blanket shawl. As with cooking, she did not have the patience to do it well, but she could do it quickly.

Johan came as soon as the rain stopped. He was there to help Grandfather up the stairs to perform his nightly ablutions and take another dose of tonic, but this time Grandfather insisted on making his own way up the stairs. Amanda and Johan exchanged a look; perhaps Johan's services would no longer be needed.

Once Grandfather was abed, the house seemed to ache for Richard. This was a fancy on Amanda's part, of course. The house was snug and locked up tight at night. All was right on the farm, Grandfather was improving, and in her prayers Amanda tried hard to focus on gratitude. The miniature had pride of place on Grandfather's bedside table, the animals were doing well, there was plenty of straw for winter, and tomorrow was Christmas Eve. Even Richard had what he needed with the name-change paper, which he must have taken with him.

It did enter Amanda's mind to wonder about the kidnappers, and why she and Richard had been taken to the shed not once, but twice. When she thought about it, she'd see Mr. Birch rescuing them, then Inspector Hawk. She'd feel the darkness, and Richard's body a reassuring presence near her own. Who had wanted them imprisoned, and why? She had experienced more contact with the law in recent weeks than she had endured in her entire twenty-seven years, and although she had seen justice prevail with the jewel robbery charge, she knew that this was not always the case.

And then, over and over as she went to sleep: why had Richard gone? would he ever return? It was all her fault.

52 - Christmas

Christmas morning dawned bright and clear, and Amanda was happy to find Grandfather milking the cows, having managed himself. She had told Johan the day before he wasn't needed to assist. Grandfather was so happy with his own recovery that he was taking the tonic and the foxglove without being reminded, and had even made cocoa for them both for Christmas Eve. Amanda was so relieved that she had begun talking to him about the farm, and some of the ideas she had.

"If we plant the fallow field with clover, the animals can eat that. Certain plants can help the soil recover from planting. We can do something similar with peas, and beans in late summer."

"So we will need seed," he said, tapping his finger on his lower lip.

"Yes, we will need to spend a bit now to do this, but it will help the yield if the weather is agreeable."

"Which it never is."

"And if it isn't, the clover will still grow. We also should plant more of the field in barley, because the prices are starting to come back up."

"But if everyone does that . . ."

"I know. The prices will go down. But if we do it this year only it might work."

They had talked into the night, planning for increasing the egg production of the chickens, adding value to products like butter through pat design and crocks, and collaborating with neighboring farms to share machinery and labor.

"And we should consider some form of combination with Mrs. Lowry," said Amanda.

"Combination?"

"The two farms could operate as one."

Grandfather frowned. "Mrs. Lowry is a very independent woman. She does things her own way. I doubt she would want to combine."

Amanda looked at her grandfather, still handsome despite his advanced age, with his thick gray hair and his intelligent, piercing blue eyes.

"Grandfather, you do know that Mrs. Lowry is in love with you?"

She saw several expressions of disbelief and then surprise cross his face.

"Whatever can you mean, child?"

"I could see it. She looks at you the same way Lady Brandon and Mr. Burdett look at each other."

Grandfather's eyes twinkled. "The same way you and Richard look at each other?"

She swallowed, and turned the conversation back where it belonged.

"Look, Grandfather, she's a kind neighbor to everyone I'm sure. But she nurses you when you're ill, shares her laborers with you, and looks after you. She loves you."

"Are you sure?"

"As sure as I can be."

"Well," Grandfather said, and laughed, pointing his finger, "we're not putting her into your plan there until she agrees to be my wife!"

Amanda didn't know what to say. Grandfather had never talked of remarrying; he had been too in love with Emily, and everyone knew that.

"You brought your grandmother back to me in this miniature, child," he said, taking the miniature from his pocket. "She has always been with me and she always will be. But what made life work was a partnership. I believe she would want me to have my final days be happier. And it was years ago I told her, in my prayers, that I loved Mrs. Lowry. I just haven't told Mrs. Lowry—that is, Ernestina."

Amanda smiled.

"Then that's settled," she said. "Now I must get to work on Christmas dinner, or we shan't eat till Christmas is over."

"And if you don't mind, I'll rest a bit while you do. I have been thinking a nap during the day might be a good idea, so long as everything gets done."

Mrs. Lowry and Johan arrived at two, and helped lay the table. As they enjoyed the beet salad and roast lamb, there was a knock on the door, making Amanda jump. Everyone was here.

Richard stood outside, his cloak wrapped around him and the packages he carried.

"I put the horses in the barn, and the carriage next to the shed. I hope that's all right?"

53 - An Explanation

Richard had brought gifts for everyone, and Christmas crackers for after dinner. The meal was a joyous occasion, but at first Amanda was nervous, wishing she could talk to Richard privately. Was he here for a visit? Why had he left? What were his plans? He was sitting near her, but had done nothing to indicate that anything untoward had happened.

It was Grandfather, in a jocular mood, who led the conversation.

"So, Mr. Pennington-Smythe, for what reason did you leave the hospitality of my home after staying only one night?"

"Sir, I will tell you." How novel, Amanda thought wryly, should it turn out to be the truth.

"You may know that your granddaughter was greatly inconvenienced multiple times due to the criminal actions of two men, a Mr. Breem and a Mr. Dunn. These men were put in prison, but some questions remained unanswered."

"Such as who hired them?" asked Grandfather.

"Precisely. They were both ignorant, uneducated men. It was more than likely that someone else had paid them to do these deeds. And they had to be done to keep me out of the way for a certain period of time. That had to be a period sufficient to convince a judge to shorten the time required to declare Mr. Soffitt's will irredeemable."

Amanda found her voice. "They wanted to keep you out of the way so you couldn't inherit?"

"Yes. When no heir can be found, the right of escheat means that the estate is forfeited to the crown. Normally, it would have been several years for the right of escheat to be determined, and even then if the heir showed up eventually he could reclaim the property. Our criminal couldn't afford that. What he wanted was a judge to grant the escheat immediately, with a business rather than the crown as the beneficiary."

"You would need a corrupt judge for that," commented Grandfather.

"He thought he found one, but the judge let me know what was happening. The deadline was set for the end of the year. If an heir hadn't been found by then, Soffitt's entire estate would revert to—"

"The law office of Birch and Comstock!" Amanda exclaimed.

Richard grinned at her. "Yes."

"That horrid Mr. Birch," Amanda said. "I always knew he was underhanded. Slimy, insinuating bastard." Mrs. Lowry guffawed.

"I'm sorry, Miss Goodwin. It was your trusted Mr. Comstock making all the arrangements."

Amanda was appalled. "But he seemed so kind, so helpful."

"People," said Richard, "are not always as they appear to be."

"So you have claimed the estate of Mr. Soffitt? How?" asked Grandfather.

Richard looked around the table, as if determining whom to trust. Then he looked at Amanda, and his face saddened.

"I am George Soffitt's grandson, to the great shame and degradation of my family."

There was silence around the table.

"Wait just a damn minute," said Amanda, her eyes narrowing.

A smile played around Richard's lips as he turned to her.

Amanda glared at him. "Are you saying that when I broke into Soffitt's house that night you were there as his grandson?" Her voice rose to a squeak on the last word.

"Yes, but I had arrived just before he died. He had been blackmailing me to not reveal that my family had changed their name."

Richard explained to the others. "My father left England as a young man when the Lesgus Scheme rendered so many people penniless. He never spoke to my grandfather again. He changed his name to Pennington-Smythe to make it sound aristocratic, and moved to Costa Rica. Made his fortune as an international trader in coffee and other goods. Married my mother there, and returned to England under his assumed name when I was born."

He turned to Amanda.

"The Pennington-Smythe home is in Whitby, but I had to sell it years ago. The blackmail payments were quite high."

"Wait," said Mrs. Lowry. "Are you the Pennington-Smythe who holds the entail on this farm? Morris—Mr. Goodwin, that is—mentioned the name to me."

"No, madam, I do not hold the entail on this farm."

Amanda's brows knitted in confusion. Grandfather opened his mouth and looked like he was about to say something.

"Or at least, I do not any more," said Richard. He took a piece of official-looking paper from his pocket and handed it to Amanda.

"Happy Christmas, my dear. The farm is yours, freehold."

Amanda's eyes opened wide. She looked down at the paper in her hand. There was her name, Miss Amanda Goodwin, on the freehold contract. The farm was hers in perpetuity, to be passed down to her children or disposed of as she chose. It was signed at the bottom by Judge Septimus Trout.

54 - A Wedding

The church in Witley was the choice for the wedding, with its frescoes and stained glass. It was a quiet ceremony, with only a few in attendance, which might have been because of the rain coming down in a constant drizzle all morning. But the sun came out in the afternoon, and the reception at Lufstow Farm was more lively.

The farmhouse had been scrubbed inside and whitewashed on the outside, the windows cleaned and all made fresh. The winnowing shed had been cleared by Johan and Richard, leaving only some hay bales piled in the storeroom at the back. Mr. Burdett had proudly arranged for a trio of musicians to play for dancing. A big table was pushed to the side and laden with spring ham, green onions, fresh bread, and treacle tarts. There was plenty of butter, patted with the new symbol of the combined Lufstow-Lowry Farms, a trio of barley stalks inside a circle. Planks had been laid to ensure dry walking between the house and the winnowing shed.

Amanda and Richard had just attended a much larger and grander wedding reception earlier in the month, that of Lady Constance Brandon to Mr. Leo Burdett. It had been louder too, with a brass band from Mr. Burdett's hometown of Queensbury in Yorkshire. The cakes had been white, the jewels flashy, and the ballroom full of the sound of bustled trains sweeping the floor. Even Julian Birch, returned from London, was invited and amused the single young ladies under the watchful eyes of their chaperones. Now, only a fortnight after their trip to Paris, Lady Constance Burdett and her husband were dressed more modestly to attend this wedding. It was, Amanda thought, a very considerate gesture, and she had been delighted to see her ladyship again.

Although not as grand as Lady Brandon's wedding dinner, there were almost fifty guests for this reception. These included not only local farmers but also Justice Trout, the Spencers, and the Lowry farmhands.

The bride was in her wedding gown, made by a seamstress in Godalming. It was a trim dress of ivory linen with a silk underskirt, and it was short enough to show her new dress boots. The groom wore old-style tan breeches and hose, his silk cravat so large it touched his chin. As the musicians struck up a tune, the wedding couple danced together as their friends and neighbors looked on.

"They look so beautiful," said Amanda. And it was true. Mrs. Lowry's beautiful gray waves of hair were arranged by Lady Branford's maid Evelyn and she looked like a queen. Grandfather looked elegant, his twinkling blue eyes enjoying the whole scene but always straying to his new bride. They had worked together for so long that there was no speculation whether they would make a good couple.

Richard took Amanda's hand in his own, holding it up for a moment to admire the ring. It had been his grandmother's, but it looked as good as new with its sapphire center surrounded by small South African diamonds. In another month she would be Amanda Pennington-Smythe, and he had defied convention by signing contracts with their new solicitor, Mr. Gilbreth, ensuring that despite the marriage Amanda would always own the farm in her own name. He had also reversed the dowry and become the first investing party in Lufstow-Lowry Farms.

Many of Richard and Amanda's plans had already been implemented. A seed-drill had been purchased to help with planting, and a steam plough was on order. The new livestock manager, Tom, was knowledgeable about current methods, and Amanda was in sole charge of deciding what crops to plant and planning a new herb and vegetable garden. Richard was also working with Mr. Birch and Judge Trout to determine how to return Mr. Soffitt's ill-gotten property to those families who had lost money in the Lesgus Scheme.

Amanda had fallen more in love with Richard each day. They had sat together as he listened to exactly what had happened to her when she was nineteen, controlling his own temper and focusing on helping her exorcise the demons of what she had experienced. With Grandfather going to bed earlier these days, they had evenings to kiss and touch and explore, but it was usually Amanda who wanted to experience more. Richard forestalled this, believing she had to heal first. It had taken all the willpower he had not to ravish her on the rag rug in front of the hearth.

Other than the wedding, today was special for another reason, thought Richard. He had to tell Amanda the truth, and hope she would understand. In case she needed to express herself with expletives, he asked her to return with him to the house, but they were waylaid by Judge Septimus Trout.

"What a delightful occasion," said Judge Trout, his cheeks red. He had been drinking quite a bit of the punch. "And you, Miss Goodwin," he said with a wink. "I take it you've forgiven our clever spy here?"

Richard gulped. "I was just about to talk to her, Judge Trout."

"Call me Septimus, please! Are you quite serious? He hasn't told you of his triumph?" His eyes twinkled mischievously.

"No, sir, I was—about to."

"Good heavens, my man. Being an agent of the crown is nothing to hide!" He stopped, putting his finger to his lips and looking around in exaggerated concern. "Tho' I suppose I should hide it from the general rabble, eh?"

Amanda blinked. Whatever was the judge talking about?

"Your gentleman friend," Trout said, leaning in as if in confidence, "single-handedly solved the jewel theft conspiracy of the century. Went all the way to the top! Well, almost to the top." He was swaying a bit on his feet.

"You did *what*?" she said to Richard.

"That's right," continued Trout. "Lady Vance's necklace and Mrs. Beekman's jewelry weren't the half of it. Those criminals stole from the royal family. I could hardly believe it when Inspector Hawk told me. And to find the ring-leader in Bognor Regis, no less! Viscount Newton and his reprobate son, deep in debt and taking to thievery. Who would have thought?"

Trout's drunken gaze moved back and forth between them.

"Well, you two have much to discuss, I suppose. Back to the festivities!"

Amanda stared at Richard as Judge Trout turned away.

"Why didn't you tell me?" She seemed curious rather than angry, thought Richard with relief.

"I didn't want you involved. There was so much else going on with my family name and your grandfather. Comstock had taken over blackmailing me—"

"He was the one blackmailing you?" Amanda's eyes opened even wider.

"Yes, first it was Soffitt and then since Soffitt's death it's been Comstock. And he'd hired Breem and Dunn to keep me from inheriting, which endangered you too much already. I'd been working on the jewel case for over a year—"

"As an agent of the crown?"

"Yes. That was why when they arrested me for jewel theft in Portsmouth, I was immediately let go. Inspector Hawk and Judge Trout had to know what I was doing, since I was trailing Viscount Newton."

He took a deep breath. "And now, well, it's a bit embarrassing, but I have to tell you. I hope you won't be angry." He looked around the room.

The wedding guests were getting louder, so Amanda led Richard to the smaller door at the back of the big shed, where it was quieter. She waited for some horrible revelation. He was moving to America on a mission for Her Majesty. He was secretly married to Princess Beatrice. His name wasn't Richard Pennington-Smythe, and she'd have to learn yet another name.

He sighed. "I'll be *Sir* Richard Pennington-Smythe. Her Majesty insists. I'll be a Knight Bachelor."

Amanda stood stock still. "Does that mean we cannot marry?" she finally said.

Richard looked at her in surprise. "Of course we can marry. It's an honorific title. But I'll have to be Sir Richard Pennington-Smythe and you'll have to be Lady Pennington-Smythe."

She stared at him, her mouth open.

He looked at her, abashed. "I didn't think you'd like it."

"Somehow I shall become accustomed to it." She let out the breath she'd been holding, then hit him on the arm. "You cad! I thought you were going to tell me something horrible."

"Well, there is something else."

She spoke, but only a whisper came out. "What?"

"I did not get my scar in a duel. It was—a shaving accident."

"A shaving accident?"

"Yes." He looked at the ground. "Um—I was shaving, you see, and the bathroom floor was wet, and as I fell my arm with the razor hit the edge of the basin."

Amanda couldn't help it. She started to laugh.

"It's not funny!" he said, glaring at her. "There was blood everywhere. The man next door was a barber and he had to sew me up."

"How old were you?" Amanda asked, trying to make her face serious.

"Nineteen."

"Did you even have anything to shave?"

"Some."

"You're quite a fellow, Richard Pennington-Smythe or whoever you are."

He grinned, relieved that his revelations hadn't set her running for the hills. "I told you the first night we met that I clean stables. I can be a knight and have a shaving scar and still do that too."

They looked at each other. More than one knowing neighbor exchanged glances as they passed the couple by the door.

"Did you and Johan put the hay bales back there?" She pointed to the storage room, and he could see a glint in her eye.

"We did! I'll show you." He took her hand and led her in, closing the door. They were alone.

The window let in the light from a glorious sunset, orange and red and shiny from the rain. Amanda turned to Richard and straightened his cravat, then reached up and smoothed his hair. He pulled her close.

"Amanda, I know we are to be wed soon, but the evenings with you have been intolerable."

"Thank you very much, Sir Richard. I find you intolerable too." She sounded amused.

"That is not what I meant. I want you so badly."

He held her tight against him. Even with her best dress on for the wedding, with petticoats underneath, Amanda could feel how much he wanted her.

"Do you indeed?" she teased, running her hand up his chest. "That is unfortunate, Sir Richard, as we are within a few yards of a winnowing shed full of people." She pouted, which by now she knew made him want to kiss her.

But he didn't. Instead, he lifted her by her arms and swept his right leg behind her left, sending her sprawling on top of the hay, then pounced on top of her.

About the Author

Lisa M. Lane is a historian and writer of fiction. Her other books include The Tommy Jones Mysteries *Murder at Old St. Thomas's* and *Murder at an Exhibition*, and a work of literary fiction entitled *Before the Time Machine*. She resides in southern California with her husband and her black cat Sabrina.

See https://grousablebooks.com for more and to sign up for the mailing list.

Acknowledgements

The author will like to thank her family for their unflagging encouragement and support, her editor Michele, Janet and the members of the Historical Novel Society Southern California Thursday group, and the National Novel Writing Month organization.

Typefaces: Tangerine by Toshi Omigari and Cormorant Garamond by Christian Thalmann, courtesy Google Fonts.